Love's Promises

SANDRA LEESMITH

To Donna,
Love is full of
promises.
Sandra Leesmith

AMBER PRESS

Published by Amber Press
www.AmberPressPublishing.com

Cover design: *Stone Lily Design*
Cover images: *Wavebreakmedia Ltd* (couple), *Neil Lockhart* (Emerald Bay), *Suprijono Suharjoto* (sunset/sky) | Dreamstime.com

PRAISE FOR LOVE'S REFUGE

"This heart-stirring romance in the beautiful island setting provides the perfect backdrop for healing and hope!"
—Ruth Logan Herne, RUNNING ON EMPTY (Love Inspired)

"LOVE'S REFUGE is a haunting story of a girl trapped by the trauma of her past. The refuge she's found has become a prison and when love finds her she must face her deepest fears in order to claim that love."
—Mary Connealy, bestselling author of the
TROUBLE IN TEXAS Series

"Put a hurting almost-hermit together with a compassionate city boy, and a sweet love story unfolds. Readers....will love this look at a tranquil island where there's no electricity but sparks still fly."
—Rachelle Rea of INSPIRING DARING

"Sandra Leesmith will whisk you away on a beautifully heart-pounding adventure of a love that will leave you breathless, a life full of pain waiting to be shed, and a choice that is laced with fear yet promises boundless joy and lavish dreams. Your heart will be lighter, and you'll walk away with a sharper appreciation for what you have."
—Amber of THE WONDERINGS OF ONE PERSON

PRAISE FOR LOVE'S MIRACLES

"*From heart-wrenching to heart-soaring, Sandra Leesmith's*
LOVE'S MIRACLES *will steal both your heart and your sleep.*"
—JULIE LESSMAN, award-winning author of
the DAUGHTERS OF BOSTON and WINDS OF CHANGE series

"*A real story for real people, with real love involved.
We're talking* PTSD, *family tragedies, war,
and having the guts to work toward healing.*"
—VIRGINIA CARMICHAEL, author of
the COLORS OF FAITH series

"*This book really hits home on the struggles our military face
during war, and the battle they face when they return.
This well-written novel by Leesmith delivered on a
compelling, fast-paced story.*"
—CAROLYN HUGHEY, author of
DISHING UP ROMANCE and ONE MENU AT A TIME

DEDICATION

*To my father John Wardman
and his wife Suzanne, who have
instilled in me a deep love and
concern for the environment.*

CHAPTER 1

Spring 1985

"SIX WEEKS! I can't wait that long to start building." Monica gripped the phone with one hand and raked tense fingers through her hair with the other. "This is crazy. At this rate I won't finish the house before the first snowfall."

The placating voice of Williams, the county building inspector on the other end of the line, droned on. Monica glanced at the sailboat skidding across the crystal blue water of Lake Tahoe and leaned against the railing of the redwood deck that hung over the cliff. Thirty feet below, water lapped against the granite stones, a rhythmic sound which normally would have soothed her. Not today. She tapped her foot impatiently and rolled her eyes.

"So you see, Ms. Scott, we cannot issue a permit until—"

Monica interrupted. "Of course you can. It's your job to issue permits, and I know for a fact that there is nothing faulty in my father's design."

"It's not the design." She could hear him drumming his fingers. "It's your lot. All construction has to be environmentally approved by the TRPA. Your property has a stream running through it, which means there're going to be problems."

Going to be? Since her arrival at the mountain resort, she'd run into one problem after another. In fact, snags and hang-ups seemed to be the current pattern of her life. Ever since her father had died.

"There has to be a way to handle this. I'll take the plans personally to this TP—whatever it is."

"Tahoe Regional Planning Agency," he informed her. "It won't make any difference. They evaluate proposals in the order received."

Of course Williams has to say that. But there were always ways to cut through bureaucratic red tape. She'd been doing it for years. "Where are they located? I'll go speak to them personally."

Williams let out a resigned sigh. "The TRPA office is in Zephyr Cove. You'd better make an appointment because they only meet with the public on certain days."

Monica jotted down the address and phone number on a notepad. Hanging up, she took off her glasses and twirled them in circles around her hand. Restless, she paced the deck that stretched across the front of the house. The panoramic view of Lake Tahoe went unnoticed until she reached the other end of the deck and leaned against the rail. The crystal waters of the lake were clear enough to see the gray, granite rocks several feet below the surface. Towering ponderosas reflected in the blue depths. Warm pine needles perfumed the air. The beauty made her ache.

Or was the ache from something else?

Walking over to the table, she slid her glasses on and picked up Stephen's letter. *Come to me. I need you.* The words blurred. Quickly she yanked off her bulky glasses, tossed them and the filmy airmail stationery onto the table, and rubbed her temples. Longings warred with reason. She had been right to break up with her ex-fiancé.

Monica lifted her head and glared at the lonely expanse of lake. No, she would not live under total submission. Not like her mother had.

Images of recent solitude flashed through her mind: dinners for one, lonely walks on the beaches along the Costa del Sol, the deep longings that tugged at her heart.

Monica shook away the thoughts. She grabbed her glasses and paced the deck. Work was what she needed. If only she could get on with it. Maybe the county offices had received word on the approval of the house she intended to build. When the permits came through, she could finally begin.

She pushed thoughts of Stephen aside, preoccupied with this new setback. Who would have thought building a house would be so complicated? It shouldn't be. During the thirteen years since graduation from college, she'd helped her father construct several of his famous designs. Never had they run into a barrage of red tape like this before. Of course, Armand was no longer here. No. That wasn't the problem.

Monica shook back the mass of hair blowing around her face and propped her glasses on top of her head. Her glance drifted upward, where green pine needles were silhouetted against the deep mountain sky. It wasn't Armand Scott's handling of affairs that was lacking. It was his *esprit de corps*, his vitality that sparked those around him. When Armand was creating a design, he infused those involved with his magic. Admittedly, Monica didn't have that magic.

Not wanting to think about the emptiness in her life, Monica swung around and leaned her back against the rail. Action. Finding the last design Armand had drawn before he'd died was the spark she needed to ignite the usual fire.

With a smooth motion, she picked up the notepad and the telephone before settling onto the deck chair. She stretched her legs out in front of her. Government employees endured endless piles of paperwork. If they could associate a real person with the application, it would help make hers stand out from the rest. A face-to-face meeting was always worth the effort. She'd learned that from her father.

Her nerves tightened as she punched in the TRPA number, ready for battle. She ground her teeth when a recording announced the office didn't take calls until nine.

Greg revved the engine of the white Bronco to keep it running while Carl slipped into the passenger seat.

"Thanks for the ride," Carl puffed as he slammed the door shut.

"No problem." Greg shifted into first gear. "Might as well carpool."

Carl chuckled. "Especially when it's in the agency's Bronco."

"One advantage of working for the TRPA."

"At least there's one," Carl muttered as he clicked the seat belt into place.

Greg didn't respond. Doing so would lead them into a gripe session. Usually he defended the Tahoe Regional Planning Agency, but not today. Doubts of his own had surfaced.

"Did you see yesterday's paper?" Carl pursued the discussion. "How can we make headway when we get that kind of negative publicity?"

"Everyone's for environmental restrictions until they're personally affected. Then they sure raise a stink."

"Man, that's the truth. I'm so tired of always being the bad guy." Carl pounded the dash to emphasize his point. "When I go out to a party or club, I don't dare mention where I work."

Greg nodded as he steered the Bronco around a curve. The concept of the agency held promise. The fact that they were the first of their kind meant they were pioneering new inroads into community policy. But uncharted paths had their disadvantages. People had difficulty dealing with change. Usually he was up to the challenge, but not this morning.

"Those jerks from all the environmental clubs think they're doing us a favor by staging construction blockades and protesting," Carl continued his tirade, "but they only rile public opinion against our efforts."

"What difference does it make?" Greg slowed down for the next set of curves. The view of Lake Tahoe usually brightened his day, but his thoughts focused on his work. "I wonder sometimes why we bother. We make so little progress."

From Carl's stare, Greg realized his negative attitude must have stunned the associate planner. Usually Greg was the one pulling Carl out of his doldrums.

Carl pointed toward a coffee shop. "Pull over and I'll run in and get us some java. Sounds like you need it."

Greg kept the engine running while Carl dashed inside. Impatiently, he tapped on the steering wheel while his mind spun with speculation. Maybe he should have joined his father's law firm. He'd be like his older brother, who at thirty-seven was one of the top attorneys in the San Francisco Bay Area. People treated him with respect.

Shifting uneasily, Greg drummed his fingers on the dash. He didn't want that kind of life. But what did he have to show for this one? Had his position as an environmentalist and associate planner made any difference?

He glanced at the ponderosa pines etched against the backdrop of the lake and blue sky beyond them. He loved these mountains. He loved Tahoe. But was it enough? He watched the gulls cruising over the crystal clear water. A Canada Goose strolled on the sandy shore. The crisp mountain air cooled his cheeks.

Greg pounded the steering wheel with his fist. The news article only proved that their work was important. Someone needed to fight to preserve the Tahoe Basin from population growth and overdevelopment.

Carl returned and handed Greg two steaming cups through the window. "It's strong enough to set you straight."

Greg took a sip, feeling better already. Yes. Work at the TRPA was worth the effort. He had to believe that. Ready to face the challenge, he handed Carl his cup and shifted into gear. "Let's head 'em up, partner. We have a full day ahead of us."

Once in the office, it didn't take long to become buried in paperwork. Greg glanced up from the huge pile of files littering his desk and looked out the floor-to-ceiling window that was the only wall of his triangular-shaped office. The other two walls were four-foot partitions, giving him a sense of privacy, yet not stopping the murmur of voices from the rest of the second floor.

He mentally blocked out the voices, although it was difficult to ignore Carl, with whom he shared an office. Carl evidently had another irate builder on the line. His placating explanations were a familiar sound most days.

Greg leaned back and glanced at the clear sky. Spring was definitely on its way. He could feel it. While he loved the excitement and challenge of winter sports, he was always ready for the change in seasons. Maybe that's what was bugging him today. Spring fever.

The season would bring on a heavier workload, but that rarely bothered him. Greg needed to be productive. Somehow this spring held a particular anticipation. For a month now he'd felt it—almost as if something big was going to happen. Nothing in particular loomed on his horizon, yet he couldn't shake the sixth sense that it was there waiting. Or was it an awareness that nothing was happening when it should be?

His fingers snapped in a rhythm he always used when he felt either on top of the world or troubled. He glanced at the mountain towering over Zephyr Cove. There were only a few patches of white snow visible through the trees. Soon, he'd be able to hike in the back country. He could feel the tug of his backpack and hear the crunch of gravel underfoot as he trekked to the top of the High Sierras. He could smell the aroma of pine needles and manzanita warming in the heat of the sun. The image of the last ten yards before cresting a peak filled his mind.

A loud thump snapped him out of his reverie. A quick glance in Carl's direction clued him in to the source of the noise.

Again, Carl's fist came crashing down on his desk. "No, Ms. Scott. You can't come down here today. We can make an appointment for next Monday."

Greg grinned and signaled Carl with a gesture they'd devised for conversations such as these. It was a reminder to remain calm no matter what was said or implied.

Carl moved his lips and held his hands together in an exaggerated plea for mercy before responding again to the upset woman.

"We can't give you an appointment for today. We need time to review the plans so they can be approved. You don't want further delays, do you?"

The indignant protests carried across the room as Carl held the phone away from his ear. Greg pressed his lips together to keep from expressing a wisecrack that would make Carl lose control.

Her loud voice continued with demands. "I'm leaving right this minute, and I expect to see someone when I arrive. Thank you and good day."

The click echoed, and then the dial tone hummed. Slowly,

Carl replaced the receiver. Greg released his pent-up chuckle.

"Great going there, buddy. You sure handled that one."

Carl fixed Greg with an annoyed stare. "Give me a break. There wasn't a thing I could say to the b—"

Greg immediately straightened and cast Carl a stern glare. "Don't lose it," he warned. "You know the boss has his eye on you."

Carl took a deep breath. "Because of the incident with that donkey's-rear-end Mitch Jones."

Greg nodded his approval of Carl's control of his language. His associate had been cited for profanity.

"I don't see how they expect me to treat Jones with respect when I know he's out milking bucks from innocent—"

"Forget it, pal." Greg decided to cut off the reminder of the consultant who could so easily rile Carl. "That's speculation on your part. The important thing is to get you under control before this Scott woman arrives."

A bleak expression crossed Carl's features. Then, suddenly, he brightened. "You take her on," he suggested. "She didn't specify who she wanted to talk to."

"No way." Greg held up his hands. "She's your headache." He gestured toward the pile of folders on his desk. "I've got enough of my own."

"Come on, Linsey. You always keep your cool."

"I know. I'm great. What can I say?"

"It beats me how you do it. Cocky. As if you didn't have a care in the world."

"It's not cockiness, it's self-confidence. You have to make them believe you're in charge."

"It never works. They see right through me, and that makes me mad. Come on, just this one—"

Greg interrupted. "Forget it. You're just as capable of maintaining control as I am."

"How, man?" Carl lowered his head into his hands and braced his elbows on the table. "I don't know how you do it."

"You let them get to you," Greg pointed out. "She's the one with the problem, not you. Don't let her problem become yours."

Carl straightened. "Please, Greg. Do this for me. I'm going to be in deep—" He paused and rephrased. "—big trouble if I lose it with another client. That woman was hot, man. She has murder on her mind."

Greg eyed his stack of projects. Was he actually considering bailing Carl out? The woman did sound tough, and Carl didn't need another encounter like the one with Mitch Jones.

"All right, but you'll owe me big time for this one."

Before Carl could get halfway out of his seat, Greg waved him back down. "Let me at least have peace to review her files before she arrives."

"Sure thing. Let me find them for you." Carl busied himself with his stack of folders, found the file, and handed it to Greg. "Not a sound will pass these lips. Silence is golden. Silence is yours."

Silence never happened around this place. Good thing he could mentally block out noise. He focused on the specs of the Scott proposal.

Given the traffic and the distance the Scott woman had to travel from the North Shore, Greg figured he had an hour. To his chagrin, only thirty-five minutes had passed when he got the call from reception that Ms. Monica Scott had arrived.

His opinion of her dropped another notch. The narrow mountain roads were treacherous, especially when tourists were gawking at the sights instead of the road. She must have broken every speed limit on the highway to get here this soon.

Greg didn't rush downstairs. *Let her cool off,* he thought. She'd learn that the agency was there to serve the public, not to jump at her beck and call. He stopped and chatted with Darlene

for a few minutes. What a looker. If they weren't working together, he'd ask her out.

Sun filtered through the glass wall as he sauntered down
the staircase. He opened the door and paused at the entrance. The
first thing he saw was hair. Clouds of auburn waves brushing
the backs of slender shoulders. And below that, a trim waist and
long legs.

She turned around, and he saw hesitancy flicker in her
amber-colored eyes.

For a moment in time they both remained silent, sizing
each other up. The calm before the storm. She was the most
striking and classy woman he'd been this close to in a long
time. Suddenly, his interest in this case came alive.

"Are you the man I spoke to?" Her calm words were honey-
coated, but along with her hesitancy he'd seen the fire.

Greg introduced himself. "I'll be handling your case," he
added. Carl was going to be sorry he'd given this one up. She
was his client now. Greg smiled and forced himself not to snap
his fingers.

Her returning smile could have highlighted an Ultrabrite
ad, but it didn't reach her eyes. No matter. He'd have her in a
good mood before long. That was his specialty, after all.

She didn't speak a word as she followed him back upstairs
to his office. Neither did anyone else. He could almost hear the
groans of envy as his male associates eyed Monica Scott. Carl
turned green. The women planners shook their heads at the
foolishness of men.

Feeling confident, Greg gestured for her to sit down. He
seated himself with a purposeful and relaxed demeanor. He'd
read her credentials. She was older than he was by about five
years. That didn't bother him. He had great respect for older
women.

"Now how can I help you—Miss, Mrs.?" He paused, waiting

for her to follow his cue. The paperwork hadn't mentioned marital status.

"Ms. Scott." She straightened as if to let him know a come-on wasn't going to work here. She fished a pair of horn-rimmed glasses out of her bag, but didn't put them on. Instead she waved them around while she spoke.

He watched the animated gestures and the flash of her eyes as he listened to the complaint he'd heard a thousand times from a thousand clients. When she finally ran out of steam, she halted mid-sentence and fixed him with a penetrating stare.

"Have you been listening to a word I've said? You haven't answered a single question."

He had a lot more in mind than answering questions. First things first. He needed to thaw her ice a bit.

Greg turned on his smile—the one his grandmother said could charm birds out of trees. "First off, ma'am, I sympathize with your frustration. We're in a unique setting here. There are no other agencies in the nation operating like we do. I understand you may not be aware of the procedures we must follow."

He saw her straighten and knew a protest was on its way. He held up his hand as he leaned into a laid-back pose. "I know what you're thinking. You see our short building season marching away, pulling with it wagons of red tape."

For a brief second he thought he saw her relax her guard, but she recovered too quickly to be sure.

"But you are going to have to operate under regulations set forth by the board. They were established to protect you." He always emphasized that point. Most people in her position just saw themselves up against the bureaucracy of a government agency. "Your property won't be worth a wooden nickel if the Basin gets any more polluted. We're working hard to save what we have and to reclaim what we've lost."

"Yes, I understand all of that." She shifted, and Greg tried not to notice her long legs crossed beneath her short yellow skirt. Again, he wondered if she were single or married. "I'm not out to destroy the environment," she said. "I'm all for whales and owls and that sort of thing, but..."

Whales? Owls? Greg had to smile. He was going to have to educate her on the *local* problems before she would ever realize the importance of following the codes set forth by the agency.

Reluctantly, it seemed, her expression curved into an answering smile. Its warmth captured his attention. The task of educating this woman was going to be very interesting.

Monica whipped her Jeep Cherokee into the driveway that wound through the pines to her house. Her tires squealed on the fast turns. She slammed on the brakes, ending up inches from the garage door, and stormed out of the vehicle.

She'd driven sixty miles round trip for nothing. Unless she counted a lecture on the environment of the Lake Tahoe Basin by a planner who was good-looking enough to be the answer to a woman's prayer. She admired his dedication and beliefs, but what good was that going to do her?

At the gate, she paused. If she went inside, she knew she'd continue to think about her uneventful meeting. And the handsome planner. She glanced down the beach toward the Myerses' place. Judy would no doubt be home. It would only take a few minutes to change into her slacks and a sweater and make her way to her neighbor's house.

Ten minutes later, Monica reached the steps of the Myerses' deck. Judy was stretched out on a chaise longue, reading. "I need to talk before I explode," Monica yelled from the beach.

Judy waved her on up and went inside. "Have a seat. I'll get us something to drink."

Monica climbed the redwood steps and waited by the open French doors.

"Here, this'll cool you down." Judy offered a tall glass of iced tea. "One thing about you, Monica, your temper fits the stereotype for redheads."

Monica chuckled, the action calming some of her tension. "I'll admit I have an impetuous character, but I usually have very good control of my emotions."

Judy's expression reflected obvious skepticism. Monica pleaded, "Come on. Give me a break. I have every right to be furious." She told Judy about the meeting, although she didn't mention any details about the handsome planner.

Judy clicked her tongue as she shook her head. "I told you not to bother going down there. TRPA is a powerful agency, and they always stand firm on their codes."

"I can understand his efforts to save the environment. After all, who would want to come to this beautiful resort"—Monica gestured toward the crystal clear water of one of the largest freshwater lakes in the country—"if it was polluted and over-developed?"

"Exactly. That's why California and Nevada formed the bi-state agency. The TRPA is dedicated to preserving what we have."

Monica set her glass on a table and leaned against the rail. She knew she looked composed and collected, but didn't feel it. The warm May sun beat down on her face, which was already tan after a winter along the southern coast of Spain. Unable to stay at the family estate, she had bought a condo in Málaga after her father died. Monica had enjoyed the mild winter weather, but she loved to be in the cooler mountains for the summer.

Judy stretched out on one of the chaise longues. "Sit down and enjoy yourself. There's nothing you can do."

Tempted, Monica eyed the plush cushion. "No, I've been

sitting around too long. I should be calling subcontractors for bids, and I also need to order materials."

"I wouldn't commit to anything until you get that permit. With a stream on your property, you could be denied."

Greg Linsey had mentioned the same thing. What was the big deal about a stream?

"I'll get the permit, don't worry. I'm not Armand Scott's daughter for nothing. He never let anything or anyone stand in his way." She thought about the powerful man who had raised her after her mother had died. Monica had been in her early teens, but he had raised her on his own. How would he have proceeded?

Armand Scott had never handled red tape well. He'd always relied on Monica for that. As soon as she'd graduated from Arizona State University, she'd been the one to stand firm and battle with officials, leaving her father free to create his masterpiece homes. Well, she could still do that—confront the issue head-on, which she had done. But she didn't have the upper hand. Not yet anyway.

"I'm meeting with Linsey, one of the planners, on Tuesday out at my property. He said he'd take a preliminary look."

"That's a start. And a victory, I might add. They have a tight schedule."

"I know. But I'm sure that once he sees my father's plans, he'll realize that we'll be doing very little to detract from the natural beauty."

"Look, Monica. Why don't you save yourself a lot of trouble and hire a consultant? They know the rules and regulations and can get you through the red tape."

"I'd rather work on my own. I'm better at giving orders than taking them."

"Consultants don't give orders, just advice. Let Jim recommend one. He knows the best, and it would save you time."

Judy's husband's family owned and operated one of the biggest marinas in the area as well as the popular restaurant situated on the dock, and therefore came into contact with virtually everyone.

That was a factor to consider. Perhaps Monica should dampen some of her self-sufficiency and seek help. The idea did not appeal. She preferred to use her independence while she still had it, but then again...

"Do you have any recommendations you could give me now?" Monica watched Judy's eyebrows raise and wondered about the speculation gleaming in her friend's eyes.

"I know just the man. Sean Marston."

"Why do I have the feeling there's more to this than the obvious?" Monica's suspicions grew by the second.

"Do you know him?" Judy asked, her eyes wide and innocent.

"I've never heard of him," Monica answered warily.

"I'm wondering why I hadn't thought to introduce you to him sooner," Judy mused, avoiding Monica's stare.

"Don't tell me. He's another 'you've got to meet him' bachelor." An image of Greg Linsey surfaced, causing her heart rate to flutter. Now *there* was an attractive man with penetrating eyes and a caring heart. Too bad he was her adversary.

Judy's voice cut into her thoughts. "He's absolutely divine. Rich, handsome, intelligent, a church-going man."

"I like your priorities." Monica tapped her foot. "I suppose he's the perfect age too."

"As a matter of fact, I think he's still on this side of forty."

"Great. Then I think I'll find someone else."

"Don't you dare. He's the best consultant around for handling development issues."

Monica glared at her friend, knowing what she was capable of. "I'm warning you, no interference."

"I promise."

21

In the short time they had known each other, she and Judy had become instant friends, with that rare intuitive responsiveness to each other's needs. Judy, however, did have one flaw. She was determined to find Monica someone as wonderful as she thought her Jim was. Monica thought Jim was chauvinistic, but she'd never told Judy. The matchmaking attempts were getting to be a problem, so she was going to have to have a talk. But for now, she decided to change the subject.

"All I have to figure out is how I'm going to manage to wait until Tuesday's appointment."

"You don't seem to have much patience, Monica. If you keep busy, the time will fly."

"I have my days filled, but the evenings are a drag."

"You're welcome to join us at our dinner party tonight. Jim will be talking business, so you and I can chat."

Monica hesitated, picturing an evening of restless pacing. "You're sure it won't be inconvenient?"

"Never. Besides, I can't believe any of those businessmen would object to your presence."

"Now, Judy." Monica raised a warning finger.

"They're all married." Judy laughed. "It'll be dull, but to-morrow night's another story."

"I'm almost afraid to ask."

"Don't be. You'll enjoy it. We're going to the club. There'll be dancing."

"You're right. I love dancing." Monica shimmied her shoulders and winked at Judy, trying not to think about dancing with Stephen or the fun social gatherings with her father and his associates.

She sometimes missed Stephen. But she really missed working with her father. His death a year ago had been sudden and unexpected. In spite of their overbearing personalities, there had always been excitement and challenge around the two partners.

Judy broke into her thoughts. "It would be more fun if you'd take men seriously."

"I like the challenge of meeting people. You know that. It's relationships I don't like, especially when a man starts becoming possessive."

She couldn't be the submissive wife Stephen wanted, living a restricted life in the Middle East, where women couldn't go out in public without covering themselves from head to toe. True, he would only be in Riyadh for a year or two more, but Stephen's idea of marriage and hers were worlds apart.

"Is there a bitter relationship in your past?"

"I'll tell you about it sometime." She twirled her sunglasses. "What time shall I be ready?"

"Jim'll be home early. We'll serve *hors d'oeuvres* at five-thirty."

"I'll be there." Monica propped her sunglasses on top of her head and then walked away, into the stately pines. Instead of feeling soothed by the walk, resentment and annoyance continued to build within her. This whole project was developing into one giant headache. She'd hoped it was going to be her salvation.

You know where your salvation comes from, Child—not building projects.

Monica stopped in her tracks. Her mother's voice welled up, deep and soothing. Loneliness surged. Taking a deep breath, she forced down the emotion and took a step forward. Then another. Determined, she focused on the project.

Her father's attorney had called and told her about the inheritance of land and money. The money hadn't impressed her. She had more than she could spend. She hadn't planned exactly what she would do with her life—until she flew to Lake Tahoe. One look at the parcel of land, the panoramic view of the lake surrounded by majestic mountains, prompted her to break her engagement with Stephen and build her father's house.

It had taken several months to finalize the will, but eventually all the loose ends were tied. Her friend, Rhonda Renway, had offered the use of her vacation home on the North Shore, and Monica had moved to Tahoe with hopes and plans. Now those dreams were shattered by a formidable list of restrictions presented by the TRPA.

Monica couldn't believe her ill fortune. How could she have known that her property sat in an area whose fragile ecology was threatened by the growing population? No one had told her that the environmentalists had set in motion a massive campaign to protect the Lake Tahoe Basin, which meant restricting building permits. There had to be a way to obtain one.

She let herself into the house and looked around, thankful once again for the luxurious accommodations that Rhonda had offered.

She tried to work up enthusiasm for the weekend with Jim and Judy, but her mind kept returning to Greg Linsey, sitting at his desk, the majestic mountains behind him, the sparkle in his eyes as he expounded his ideals heartily and with passion. What she'd give to feel that zeal.

Tuesday's meeting held more interest for her than the weekend's social events. She needed a strategic plan. There had to be a way to convince the planner that her father's house be approved.

"I promise you, Armand. Your house will be built."

CHAPTER 2

THE NEXT MORNING shafts of sunlight filtered through the large windows in the kitchen and reflected off the copper pots hanging from the ceiling. Monica stared absently at the patterns the light made on the honeyed gold of the hardwood flooring. On impulse she smoothed a bare foot across the surface, the boards warm from the sun.

She glanced around the spacious kitchen and once again admired Rhonda's taste in décor. She'd managed to keep the place looking like a mountain cabin, yet behind the facade were the conveniences of the modern technological age.

An oak cabinet door closed off the microwave. Another hid a pull-out work center that boasted a blender, mixer, and coffee grinder. The ceramic coffee pot was the only appliance out in the open. The dishwasher and trash compactor were concealed, and the stove was modern yet looked old-fashioned.

There were some good ideas here. Whoever had designed the layout knew what they were doing. Monica would have to ask Rhonda who'd contracted the work. Perhaps she could use them for the finish work in the house she planned to build.

Thinking of that brought her mind back to the blueprints spread across the counter. Monica frowned at the sight as she eased onto a barstool. All morning she'd been poring over the plans and couldn't come up with a single item that would disrupt any environmental ecosystems that she knew of. Provisions had been made for topsoil erosion, subsoil infiltration of contaminants, and waste water disposal.

Of course, she'd have to go through a local plumber to contract out installation of the water and sewer lines. He would be able to plan them to fit county requirements. She had also been informed that more permits would be needed for the work. Monica threw down her pencil, pulled off her glasses, and pressed her fingers against the bridge of her nose. So far she was looking at twenty thousand dollars spent for permits alone, and she hadn't even broken ground.

Frustrated and disgusted, she slid off the barstool. Her bare feet padded across the wood flooring until she reached the thick carpet in the living room. Curling her toes into the deep pile, she stopped in front of the desk and stared at the stack of papers—reports from her accountant regarding the transfer of her father's investments into her portfolio. She had to go through them soon and sign the forms. She was going to need access to the cash.

Had Armand known this area had so many restrictions? Wouldn't he be distressed right now? She glanced around. Was he peering down from heaven, pulling on his hair like he'd done so often?

Shrugging aside the absurd thought, she reached for the copy of Stephen's list of recommendations for the inheritance. Just like her ex-fiancé to have each detail planned. She'd tried his patience with her endless last-minute concerns. "Things will get done whether you worry or not," he always told her. "So why waste energy? Let me take care of it."

That was the problem. Monica tossed aside the paper. She didn't want Stephen taking care of her life. She could do it on her own. He hadn't agreed. But then, they hadn't agreed on many things—her self-sufficiency one of the causes of their dissension.

She supposed she and Stephen could learn to compromise, but their other problems never gave them a chance. Problems like her role as his wife and the prospect of children. He wanted to rule with an iron thumb, call all the shots. Was something wrong with her because she didn't want that kind of relationship? No, she'd seen how Armand had dominated her mother. He'd controlled Monica. Not that he'd ever abused her, but she liked her new freedom to pursue her own dreams.

She sighed, wondering if Greg Linsey had those same ideas about marriage. Jim Myers did. Weren't there any men who would just let her be herself?

She shook off the thoughts of Stephen and marriage and returned to the kitchen and her father's blueprints. They were the only meaningful thing of his she had left. She stretched her fingers across the paper, not quite touching it, as if doing so would be irreverent.

She missed Armand. Details like chauvinism never mattered to him. He had the gift of accepting a person just the way they were. Because of it, he always had friends. Maybe that was what she missed. Not just Armand, but the activity and vibrancy that always surrounded him.

If Armand were here, this house would be filled with men, women, and children. She could picture the crowd: builders and subcontractors mingling with members of the social elite who liked to hang around Armand Scott. He always insisted they bring their families. Children loved her father. He had a magic about him.

Monica glided her hand along the wood finish of the table. Memories were not helping to stem the ache. Her mother's words floated across her mind. *You are always so busy, Child. What you need is quiet time alone.*

No! What she needed was action. Sitting alone brought unbidden thoughts, like the realization that her life was empty.

She hurried toward her bedroom and yanked open the door to the walk-in closet. If she wanted to fill this house like Armand would, she'd have to go out and meet people. She'd made a good start into the social crowd with the help of Jim and Judy. Last night's dinner party had been interesting. Tonight she'd make more contacts.

She glanced at the clock. Good, it was only ten. She had plenty of time to go out this morning and introduce herself to more subcontractors. She found a pair of comfortable slacks—casual, but professional—and put them on. Appointments needed to be set up for estimates. She wanted to bid out the contracts, then she had to follow through on references. An Armand Scott house demanded the best.

With these decisions made, Monica moved toward the bathroom. On her way she hit the button on Rhonda's CD player. The country rock helped fill the emptiness of the house. A fast pace accompanied her quick and sure application of makeup.

She felt better already. Action and music. They both helped block out the thoughts and memories of Armand and Stephen and Greg. She didn't always like where her thoughts led her.

In fifteen minutes she'd be out the door and in her car. The heavy traffic didn't bother her. She was ready for a crowd.

Greg leaned forward to let the boom swing over the top of him as he tacked the sailboat into the wind. Time to head in to dock. He'd sailed most of the afternoon. Usually winds came up and brought on small-craft warnings. His sailboat wasn't a small craft by any means, but Greg usually heeded the Coast Guard's warnings. Lake Tahoe could get rough. When it was, he didn't want to be on it.

The boat listed slightly as he trimmed the sail. Loud screams sounded from the bow. Greg grinned. The two women

Carl had brought along were doused with icy cold water.

Carl stood and shouted. "Ease up, Linsey."

Greg waved. Served him right, bringing a crowd over on his day off. From below, he could hear the voices of two more co-workers as they argued over a cribbage game. Next he'd be hearing music. As if his thought had conjured up the fact, fast rock began to vibrate from where Carl and the women were sitting. At least it was one of his favorite groups or he might be tempted to come about again and give the trio another dousing.

Greg eased his grip on the rudder control. If he didn't stop finding fault with everything, he'd ruin his day. He glanced around at his friends, glad they were having a good time. He liked everyone here, but he preferred to be alone on the lake. To have time to daydream or meditate.

One of the women worked her way aft. Her hair blew in the breeze, the sight bringing Monica Scott to mind. The woman sat beside him. Greg pushed out the thoughts of Monica and smiled.

"Your boat is fabulous," she said, surveying the sails and rigging. "It's a lovely way to see the lake."

"Glad you like it." She was easy to smile at, long blond hair whipping about in the breeze. "Most people prefer the faster speedboats."

"I suppose they have their advantages. This has more class, and it's peaceful."

Greg wasn't sure how. Another song blared from the stereo. Laughter echoed from below deck. "Silence is peaceful, not this."

Her brow rose, reminding him to be a gracious host.

"This is my first time in the mountains. I'm glad now that Gina dragged me along on this trip."

Another tourist. That was the trouble with meeting women up here. They were only around for the weekend, making it

29

difficult to get to know them.

"You from the Bay Area?"

"Berkeley. I'm a grad student at the university."

Greg smiled his appreciation. "UC Berkeley, a good place to be. Of course, I have to say that, since it's my alma mater."

Her attention perked. "You went there? When?"

"Graduated six years ago—in Environmental Resources."

The arithmetic was clicking away. He could read it in her expression. It would be easy to just tell her he was thirty, but let her guess. It didn't really matter; he wasn't going to see her again.

She finished her figuring and must have liked the numbers. She inched closer and smiled. "Looks like we have a lot in common. Did you grow up in the Bay Area too?"

"San Francisco. And you?"

"San Jose."

"Small world." Except there were millions of people in that part of the state, which was exactly why he'd opted out of his father's law firm and headed for the Sierras.

"Do you miss the city?" she asked.

Never. "I miss my family, but I've always loved the mountains. We used to come up here all the time when I was growing up."

"Was that your family home, where we sailed from?"

He nodded. His father had sold him the place after his heart attack, since the doctor had advised the older man to stick to the lower altitudes. The house was old and needed a lot of work, but it sat on prime lakefront property with a private dock.

"You're very fortunate."

Greg agreed wholeheartedly, not caring if the acknowledgment made him appear conceited.

"But I don't know if I'd like to live here. I like all the action in the city."

"That's where you should stay then. Just come up to enjoy."

Since 1950 the population of the Tahoe Basin had gone from five hundred to over fifty-seven thousand. The population was destroying the area. People moved here for peace and beauty. But as soon as they arrived, they wanted to drag the city up with them. As far as he was concerned, let them stay away.

Sure it was more convenient to have stores and fast-foods restaurants, but if the people could only understand, they were defeating their purpose for moving here. The Basin was suffering from major traffic congestion, a threat to air quality, and a serious change in the clarity of the water. Since tourism was the main attraction, it didn't make sense to destroy the reason tourists came.

The blonde spoke again, but he missed her question.

"Pardon me. I was thinking about work," he admitted.

"On a Saturday? That's against better judgment and sound principles. You're supposed to have fun on weekends."

"You're right. Sorry I'm a bore today. Stayed up too late last night." He shrugged, knowing the late night hadn't caused the currents of discontent. It was the crisis of a thirty-year old. Questioning his purpose. Loneliness. Face it, these were the underlying causes. She deserved better than this. So did he. Determined to improve his mood, Greg flashed a grin and showed off by giving her lessons on sailing.

By the time they returned to the dock, Greg's mood turned positive, and he enjoyed the crowd. The day on the water had improved his disposition. The blonde's rapt attention hadn't hurt either. Sorry the party had to break up, but nevertheless tired, he decided not to invite them to stay for the evening.

Carl had other ideas. "Let's all go to the South Shore Club tonight. Anyone up for some dancing?"

"Sounds like a plan, but what and where is the club? I've

never heard of it." The blonde smiled.

"The 'in' place to be." Carl gave them a mock bow. "Yes, ladies. We offer you Tahoe's elite—compliments of Greg's father."

"Can it." Greg secured the boat to the dock. He hated it when Carl used Greg's family influence and club membership for his personal gain with women.

Carl ignored Greg, as usual. "It's a great place. Lots of good music. Plenty of action."

The blonde curved up to Greg and tucked her arm through his. "I'll treat for dinner since you gave us such a great day on your boat."

"You can meet us there," Carl offered. "I'll pick up the gals."

Greg snapped his fingers. Did he really want to refuse? "I'll see you at eight."

When they'd all driven out the long driveway, Greg closed the gate and locked himself in. At least he'd have some quiet time before another night out.

In his kitchen, he microwaved a cup of coffee and sat down at the old oak table. The file for Monica Scott lay in front of him. His afternoon outing and evening date—even the blonde—were suddenly forgotten. His mind filled with images of the classy woman he'd met the other day. He could visualize the flash in her eyes and the color of fire in her hair. Usually he didn't care for temper in women, but somehow Monica's sparked a challenge. Good thing he was going out tonight. If he stayed here alone, he'd spend entirely too much time wondering who she was. At least he'd found out she was single.

Monica slid into the Lincoln Continental and shut the backseat door behind her before leaning her head against the leather seat. "What a day."

Judy swiveled to look at Monica as Jim put the car in gear and headed out the drive. "No progress I take it?"

"The stream is a bigger problem than I imagined." Her head pounded from the frustration. "I'd be smart to cancel out on the dancing at the club this evening."

"So you can sit around and do nothing but think about the depressing situation?"

Monica groaned.

"You can't afford to let a defeatist attitude creep in." Judy rummaged in her purse and held out two white pills and a bottle of water. "These aspirin should help."

By the time Jim and Judy pulled up an hour later at the South Shore Club, Monica's headache was gone and she was in a mood to mix and mingle.

The place was packed, but Jim had arranged for several friends to save them a table. Monica squeezed into the crowd and immediately began talking with new people. This was her kind of action.

The band came on stage and conversation ceased. Loud and rhythmic music filled the room. Monica accepted offers to dance. The energetic exercise worked out the last traces of frustration as she completely forgot about blueprints, building permits, and the TRPA.

Ready to take a break, she slipped into a chair next to Judy and ordered a club soda with lime. "This is a great place." She twisted the lime, ducking when it squirted at her.

"What?" Judy responded, leaning closer to better hear her friend.

Jim came up from behind them and picked up their drinks. "Let's go out on the deck."

Monica nodded agreement to Jim's suggestion, and with a woman on each arm he guided them to the tiered levels of the redwood deck. Gas burners were lit along the rails, giving off a festive glow. The lapping of water against the yachts moored at the docks lent a romantic atmosphere. Lights reflected off tall masts stretching up into the starlit sky.

"Whew, this feels great. That's some crowd in there tonight," Judy remarked, fanning her face.

"The cool air is refreshing." Monica smiled and sat down across from Judy while Jim held her chair. "I was getting warm inside."

"You've been dancing every number," Judy teased.

"I'm glad for a break."

"If you relaxed in the arms of one of those good-looking men who have been after you, it'd be all right."

"They're not that bad, are they?"

"They're heavenly, Monica, and all you can say is, 'not that bad'?"

"Since when are you such an expert?" Jim scolded his wife while he winked at Monica. "Have you been busy behind my back?"

"Of course, darling," Judy teased, ignoring his frown.

"What Monica needs is for me to introduce her to some of my associates," Jim offered.

Monica interceded. "Don't start that again."

"But if you don't dance with the same man more than once, how do you expect to get asked out?" Judy's brow knit with concern.

"I don't want to go out, which is exactly why I don't dance with the same man twice." She was going to have to talk to Judy and soon.

"What a heartbreaker."

Monica ignored Jim's sarcasm and surveyed the people spilling out from the interior of the club. A familiar face drew her attention. Light brown hair, deep blue eyes, an animated smile. Someone moved, giving her a view of his broad shoulders and narrow waist accentuated by the smooth lines of the butter-colored polo shirt.

Judy nudged Monica's elbow. "What do you see?"

"Nothing." Monica dropped her gaze from the sight of Greg Linsey and toyed with her drink. "I thought I saw someone I knew."

She glanced up again and stifled a groan. Surely he wasn't coming to their table? From the assured swagger and determined look on his face, it appeared that he planned to do exactly that. Just what she needed. After all her efforts to clear up her headache, the main cause was heading right for her.

"Excuse me." To Jim and Judy's perplexity, she stood, grabbed her purse, and quickly left the table.

Skirting the crowded deck and using the outer perimeter, she entered the restaurant. She reached the lobby and headed for the entrance to the lounge.

"Hey, what's up?"

Monica turned to see one of the men she had danced with earlier.

"I'm taking a break." She smiled at him.

"What?" He looked at her with mock incredulity. "You can't do that; we need you. There are more men than women." He grinned at her with open invitation.

Monica barely paid attention.

"Come on." He grabbed her arm and pulled her to the main room. "The band's coming back. Let's dance."

About to pull away and refuse, Monica looked out again and saw that Linsey had followed her. Not wanting a scene, she returned her attention to her blond admirer.

"What are we waiting for?" She slung the strap of her purse over her shoulder and smiled. Greg Linsey wouldn't approach her while she was in the arms of this Nordic goliath.

As they moved around the dance floor, Monica prickled with the awareness of someone staring. She glanced up several times to find Greg watching her every move. *What does he want?* Surely not to talk business on a Saturday night. Maybe he was feeling guilty about causing her so many delays. Maybe she should dance with him and find out. She closed her eyes and pictured his arms around her, reluctant to admit the real reason she considered a dance.

Suddenly, he disappeared. Relieved, she concentrated on the rhythm of the music. The activity soon carried her away from her thoughts and her concerns.

When the music stopped, Monica thanked her partner and began to move off the crowded floor. Someone bumped her from the side, knocking her off balance. Before she regained her footing, strong hands on the other side gripped her arms and pulled her up.

"Thank you," she murmured, then almost lost her composure as she looked up at her rescuer.

Greg's face creased with a grin of amusement. "You act like you're avoiding me."

Monica hesitated and then drew away from him. "I have to as long as we're at odds." She paused. "Unless you have good news for me."

He shook his head slightly. "Afraid not. But this is Saturday night. We don't want to discuss business. How about dancing with me instead?"

Monica paused, wanting to but knowing she shouldn't. She moved away, but he stepped in front of her.

"I've been watching you. You're not here with a date, are you?"

"My friends are waiting." She half-heartedly tried again to move around him.

Before she realized what was happening, he grasped her

waist and pulled her onto the dance floor where a slow number was already in progress. Monica stiffened against his body, but inside her heart melted.

He glanced down at her, his smile dazzling, his expression daring. "I just wanted to extend a friendlier welcome to the Basin than we gave you the other day."

Monica took a deep breath to steady her nerves. A little friendliness would go a long way. Perhaps there was still hope for Tuesday. "Thank you. Except for my problem with the permits, it's been a pleasant move."

His expression sobered. "I really do understand the frustration you're going through."

"But you have your job to do," she added for him.

He spun her around. "Enough talk about me. How do you like the area?"

"It's beautiful country."

"Do you plan to establish yourself here and build more homes?"

"No." She didn't want to explain what her plans for the future were, nor what she had been doing since her father's death. Finding the plans had been a stroke of luck. "All of the houses I've built were for my father. They were located in various places: Hawaii, back East, and Europe. Armand passed away right after finishing the house in Spain. So this is the last one."

"Armand Scott was your father?" New respect reflected in his gaze.

He recognized her father's fame. Barriers of resistance softened in her heart. "We were a team before his death."

Greg whistled between his teeth. "No wonder you're anxious to build. But why here? Couldn't you build in another location with less restrictions?"

"I could, but my father had designed the house for this piece of land. You know his specialty was blending the building into the surrounding landscape."

The music rose in crescendo, and Greg twirled her around.

"I want the house to be a memorial. My father was respected. Many of his friends come here to vacation." She didn't add that she had made a promise. And she kept her promises.

Greg nodded as they danced around another couple. "You think the market for selling it will be enhanced by this location?"

"Exactly." Smart man. She admired a sharp mind.

Her smile must have pleased him because he tightened his hold. Monica eased away from the emotions building in her. He didn't press but continued to sweep her around, deftly avoiding the other couples crowding the floor. Monica found herself admiring his coordination and, yes, she admitted his looks weren't hard to take either. From the tanned skin and solid build she guessed he spent time outdoors. His face was open, his eyes mischievous, yet honest. Instinctively, she felt he was a man to be trusted. Good. She needed someone like that on her side. Maybe it was just as well they had run into each other tonight and in this setting.

"Is your tan from working outdoors, or do you participate in all the local sports?" she asked.

"Some of it's from work. Most is from play."

In order to hear him, she had to lean closer. He didn't seem to mind, but he did guide her outside to a less crowded area on an upper deck. The cool mountain air felt refreshing after the packed room.

"It's quieter out here." He spun her around to the beat. "We can dance and talk."

Surprised at how much she enjoyed the dance, Monica wanted to know more about this man. "What does play involve?" She smiled up at him. "Skiing for one thing, I imagine."

He smiled back, his eyes sparkling in the dim light. "Good

guess there. I ski all winter."

"Are you sorry to see winter end?"

"Not really. I'm ready for a change."

Monica understood that. Change was one of the main reasons she had left the family beach house in Spain and moved to Tahoe. Rarely did she stay in one place for more than a year, two at the most. If this building project ever got underway, she figured she'd be ready to leave the area by the time her father's house was finished.

Mitch Jones sipped his drink as he watched the couple through the crowd. It annoyed him that they'd moved to the outdoor dance floor. It was cold out here. He preferred the close quarters inside. He wasn't alone when packed between others, even if they were strangers.

Greg Linsey wasn't a stranger. Mitch watched as he swung the redhead around. A classy broad. Where had Linsey picked her up? Not that he really cared, but the information might be useful some day. Linsey was getting to be a major pain. He and that Sutton kid had really botched up his last consulting project. They were beginning to poke their noses too deep into his business. He'd have his partner, Packard, look into it.

Packard elbowed his way to Mitch's side. "What you doin' out here, man? It's colder than a—"

"Yeah, yeah." Mitch downed his drink and looked around for a waitress. "I just came out for a breather."

"Maybe you should come back inside. Our client's beginning to wonder what happened to you."

Mitch continued to stare at Linsey and the broad, wondering what their relationship was. The kid was obviously interested.

"Come on, Jones. We got this guy hooked. Let's reel him in."

Mitch tore his gaze from the couple. "Take it easy, Packard. If you appear too anxious, he'll shy off. Let him sit for a while. He's not going anywhere."

Packard shifted. "He'll need us to take him back to his hotel."

"Right." Mitch slapped the shorter man on the back. "Now go round me up a waitress. I want to check something out."

Packard hesitated for a minute, but Mitch had already turned back to the outdoor dance floor. Linsey was nowhere in sight. Mitch cursed Packard and then himself for letting his attention wander. Maybe they'd gone inside.

He shoved his way through the crowd, refocusing on the client they were entertaining. The man was from New York, an easy mark. He wanted a house now, without hassles, and he had money—tons of it. He wouldn't notice the padding Mitch would add onto fees for permits and services rendered.

Mitch glanced around, but didn't see the TRPA planner or the redhead. He shrugged aside his annoyance. The night was meant for action, and he had plenty waiting for him back at his table.

He'd get something on the puffed-up TRPA planner one of these days. After all, everyone had something to hide. He'd simply bide his time.

CHAPTER 3

THE DANCE ENDED. Greg escorted Monica back to the lower-level deck, his hand sending tingles up her spine where it rested on her lower back. Several friends had found Jim and Judy enjoying the cooler outside air. She hoped to join in relatively unnoticed.

They reached the table, and Monica turned to Greg. "Thanks for the dance."

His smile creased his cheeks, and amusement sparkled in his blue eyes. "Not trying to get rid of me, are you?"

Had her thoughts been so transparent? She invited him to join them, careful not to sound as eager as she felt.

He shook his head, regret clearly showing in his expression. "I'm with friends. Another time."

She remained standing, delaying his departure. "I'll see you Tuesday then."

He gave her hand a slight squeeze. "I'll look forward to it."

For several seconds, he held her hand in his. Unnerved, she spoke—her voice breathless, soft. "Good-bye, Mr. Linsey."

His brow quirked, but he let go of her hand and grinned. He turned and snapped his fingers as he walked away.

Monica found a seat beside Judy. She took a deep breath, determined to control her emotions.

Judy didn't give her time to contemplate long. "No wonder

you aren't interested in the men I've introduced you to. Where do you know that hunk from?"

"Don't get all excited, Judy. That's Greg Linsey from the TRPA. Remember, I told you about our meeting?"

"You're kidding. You mean you'll have to meet with him again and again?"

A sheepish grin formed as heat flushed up her cheeks. "I meet with him next week. He's going to make a preliminary check of the property."

Judy sat up straight, her interest piqued. "Let me help you decide what to wear. It's important that we get exactly the right touch."

Monica held up her hand, uncomfortable with the girlish feelings niggling inside. "Forget it. This is strictly business."

"Don't be foolish. The guy obviously has more than a business interest in you, and—"

Monica interrupted. "Hold it, Judy. Just because we danced one slow dance, doesn't mean a thing."

"I'm not talking about the dance. Didn't you notice the way he looked at you?"

Of course she'd noticed. She took a deep breath. "Come on. It's Saturday night. Everyone is flirting. It doesn't mean a thing."

"If you say so." Judy obviously didn't believe a word of it.

Jim asked Judy to dance, and that ended the conversation. Relieved, Monica remained at the table and visited with the crowd. No more dancing. She didn't dare run into Greg Linsey again.

Her rule was dance with a guy once. Greg Linsey might ask her to dance again. With Tuesday's meeting coming up, Monica didn't think that would be such a good idea. She wanted to be in control and strictly on business terms with this planner, and dancing with him ruled that out. She found his touch unsettling, his smile disturbing, and his eyes melting her steady resolve.

Putting thoughts of Greg Linsey, permits, and Tuesday aside, she concentrated on the conversation at the table.

"I love Málaga in the spring," a woman across the table stated.

Right up Monica's alley. She leaned forward. "Have you ever been to Luisa's? It's a great place near the plaza."

"Yes," another woman joined in. "They have the best *cremas* and *café*."

"That's the place," Monica said. "Colorful hibiscus, the aroma of coffee—I can smell it."

The conversation continued, but Monica drifted into memories of Spain and Stephen. Málaga had been the location for one of her father's houses. The year in Spain had been exciting and adventurous. Stephen had proposed to her there. She could almost hear his deep baritone voice. *Stephen. So much like my father—wanting total submission.*

A wave of loneliness washed over her. She couldn't be missing Stephen, could she?

Romance?

No, it was the excitement around her father she missed.

Greg left Monica and returned to the lounge to look for Carl and the two women from the Bay Area. Guilty about leaving his friends to ask Monica to dance, he shook his head. There'd be plenty of nights to get to know Monica Scott after they had finalized their business together. Her frustration was with the system, not him personally. He'd make sure she'd come to realize that. In the meantime, he'd look forward to Tuesday.

He snapped his fingers in time to the music. He pushed

through the crowd in the lounge. Fortunately, Greg was tall and could see over heads, but there was no sign of Carl and the two women.

He started toward the patio. A firm tap on his shoulder stopped him. Thinking it was Carl, he spun around and smiled.

Mitch Jones held out his hand. "How's it going, Linsey? Nice to see you guys do something besides cause grief to us locals."

Greg's defenses clicked into place. He clasped Jones in a brief handshake and pulled free, resisting the urge to wipe his hand on the leg of his pants. The consultant was shorter in stature, but formidable—not a man to underestimate. "We don't cause any grief to those who follow the rules, Jones. Keep that in mind and you won't have any trouble from us."

Jones glared. "Are you accusing me of something?"

Greg forced himself to remain calm, determined not to give the older man the pleasure of seeing him riled. "Don't give me any static. If you want to talk to me, call and make an appointment. In the meantime, steer clear."

Greg stepped around Jones and wove his way through the crowd. Most of the consultants tried to cooperate with the planners or at least make the appearance of doing so. But not this one. Greg swallowed back the annoyance. Fortunately, he spotted Carl.

"Where've you been?" Carl said, obviously glad to see Greg. "I saw Mitch Jones. I knew there was a reason I don't come here often."

"I just talked to him. Or I should say he talked to me."

Concern showed in Carl's expression. "Did he give you any trouble?"

"No way. And I don't want to discuss him." Greg turned to the women who were now rejoining them. "Would you like to go for a drive around the lake?"

The two women were delighted, but Carl looked surprised.

"Come on. They're tourists. They'll get a kick out of it.

Besides"—he gestured toward the table Jones had returned to—"this place has lost its appeal."

Mitch knew he should maintain better relations with the planners. They could make his work difficult. But he never had liked kissing up to someone, especially an arrogant kid barely out of college.

Mitch sipped on his drink as he watched the two TRPA planners leave the premises. He took careful note of the women they escorted. Linsey's date was a blonde, not the redhead he'd seen him with earlier. Interesting. Maybe he should find out who the classy redhead was.

He waited a good half-hour before seeking her out. He could see the exit, and she hadn't left. The dance floor was also visible from his table. She must be outside.

The cool air slapped him in the face. Mitch shivered and thought—as he did all winter—about moving to Hawaii or the Florida coast. Surely he could cook up some deals in those tropic locales as well. But he'd have to start from the ground floor there, and he already had a sweet gig going here. Only a fool would pass up this business for something as inconsequential as warmer weather. Besides, summer was on its way. Not only did the season bring heat, but it brought tourists. Tourists meant more customers.

Mitch refocused his attention to the dance floor of the upper deck. No sign of the redhead. The number ended, and several couples meandered to the lower deck. Mitch followed and spotted the woman he'd been looking for. Unfortunately, she was surrounded by a crowd. They were locals, though. Mitch recognized Jim Myers. Several other faces were easily known: political and social leaders of the community. People Mitch liked to keep on good terms with. The redhead seemed real chummy with the group.

What was Linsey's connection? The young punk didn't usually hang around this crowd.

The couple next to the redhead stood and headed for the dance floor. Mitch saw his chance to move. Quickly he stepped beside the woman and greeted those at the table. "Where have you been hiding this lovely lady?"

One of the men introduced her. "Monica Scott, meet Mitch Jones."

She nodded, but didn't offer her hand.

Mitch held out his. "Care to dance?"

At first he thought she was going to refuse. He called on his notable charm and flashed a winsome smile. "It would be an honor to lead the best-looking woman around that dance floor."

She stood and laughed. "I wasn't going to dance anymore, but since you put it that way, Mr. Jones."

"Call me Mitch." Mitch gave her a hand. Flattery and his good looks got them every time.

She was an inch taller, but he tried not to let that bother him. Most women were. He had spoken the truth, though. She was a striking woman, and he had no qualms about guiding her around the floor in time with the slow dance. The quieter music gave him a good opportunity to talk.

"I haven't seen you around before. Are you a tourist?"

"I just moved here."

His interest perked up. "Really? Do you have a place yet?"

"I'm house-sitting for a friend." She was careful and obviously didn't want to talk about where she lived, but Mitch wasn't interested in hustling her home. He had business on his mind.

"Do you want a place of your own? I can help you there.

I'm a development consultant."

The start she gave caught him off guard. Had Linsey said something to her about him?

"How odd that I should meet you. My friends have suggested that I seek out a consultant."

"Interesting." Mitch almost forgot to keep dancing. "And why do you need a consultant?"

"I'm trying to build a house, and I've run into nothing but snags."

Perfect. This kind of client was what he lived for. "I saw you with Linsey, from the TRPA."

She paused and stared hard into his eyes. "Do you know him?"

"I've had several occasions to work with him. Strictly business."

"Then you probably understand how frustrating that agency is with all the red tape."

"You bet I know." This was sounding better by the minute. "He giving you trouble?"

"Not exactly."

"Don't count on your feminine charms, tempting as they are, to bring Linsey around. You'll need advisory help to deal with the agency." He paused in the middle of the dance and reached in his pocket. "Here's my card. You call me and we'll set up an appointment. More than likely I can get whatever trouble you're having cleared up in no time."

She didn't exactly say she'd call, but she did hold onto his card in a tight fist. Mitch smiled. He recognized the signs. She'd get in touch.

The dance ended, and Mitch escorted her back to the Myerses and their crowd. When he returned to his own table he slapped Packard on the back. "Order a round of drinks for us. On me. We've got something to celebrate."

Not only did he have a prospective new client, he might

have found a way to stick a thorn in Linsey's side. He'd seen the way the TRPA planner looked at Monica Scott. Mitch was going to get her first and use her against that arrogant punk.

Tuesday morning finally arrived. In spite of filling Sunday and Monday with errands that took her around the lake, problems and worries plagued her.

Would Linsey approve the plans? Would the permit come through in time to build this summer? Should she call in a consultant?

The last question bothered her the most. Everybody she talked to advised her to consult with someone who knew the local codes. She had a list of recommended agents in the area, but the idea of involving one ate at her. Calling in experts meant hassles over maintaining the integrity of her father's original plans. She'd have to keep on top of every decision to be sure they didn't override her wishes.

No, do it yourself.

Besides, if she hired Mitch Jones, she wouldn't see Greg again. That thought disturbed her more than she wanted to admit.

Shifting her Jeep Cherokee into gear, Monica worked her way up the steep road skirting her property. She needed to grade an easier drive into the place. She sighed. Another set of permits.

She crested the hill and spotted a Bronco with government license plates parked at the end of the road. Her heart quickened. What was his motive for coming early?

Automatically, she set the brakes, released her seat belt, and swung out of the high vehicle. Before her legs touched ground, she searched the area. Linsey wasn't in the Bronco nor in the near vicinity. Biting her lip, Monica headed for the creek.

"Morning." His shout caught her up short.

She searched the dense brush downstream and saw movement on the other side of the gurgling water. He stepped from out of a clump of brush and crossed the stream looking like an ad from a sports magazine. Disconcerted by her reaction, Monica waited for him instead of meeting him halfway.

He approached. "I've checked out your plans and walked most of the lot."

"You must've arrived early." Heat crawled up her cheeks.

His brow furrowed and his knuckles whitened as he stared at the papers attached to his clipboard.

She took a deep breath, surprised by his anxiety. "What's the verdict? Surely you can see how the design fits right into the terrain?"

"Your father took the landscape into consideration. That's obvious from the layout of the plans."

Her spirits lifted. "There shouldn't be any problem getting the permits then."

He stepped beside her and studied the stream. It seemed that he might be picturing the house, so she didn't interrupt. Visualizing the completed structure would only be to her advantage.

"When did your father draw up these designs?"

"Several years ago."

Greg shook his head. "That explains it." He tapped the clipboard with the end of his pencil.

Monica waited, trying not to notice the woodsy scent of him or his tapered fingers gripping his clipboard.

He spoke, cutting into her musings. "He probably designed this under the Bailey System. If he'd started construction at that time, we could honor the permit. This can't be approved because of the stream."

"But Armand was always very careful to comply with local

codes."

"Do you know why he didn't complete the project at the time?"

"He was delayed for a year, and then personal circumstances came up." Her mother's death. Monica closed her eyes and mentally shook away the waves of pain.

"Do you know if he came back and tried to build? If the new IPES restrictions had gone into effect, it would explain why he didn't follow through."

Monica hadn't thought of that. Perhaps Armand had reapplied for permits. He'd never said. "Does it really matter? What concerns me now is that I obtain the permits before the summer season closes in on me. I need to get my bids in before all the subcontractors are booked."

His grip on the clipboard tightened. He shifted from one foot to another, a frown of concern marring his features. "You won't get these plans approved as they are. Revisions are going to have to be made."

Even though regret sounded in his voice, his words were a blow. "Tell me what modifications need to be made and I'll get right on it."

"The design of the house isn't a problem."

"That's encouraging," she prompted. "But…?"

His shoulders slumped as he rubbed the back of his neck. Finally he spoke. "I don't see anywhere on the property that you can place it."

"What? That's impossible. This lot is almost five acres."

"Five acres that follow the stream."

"You can't mean to tell me that there is nowhere along this stream that a house can be built."

"That's exactly what I'm telling you. This is a spawning stream for lake trout. It's protected, and no building is allowed near its banks. Setbacks must be from twenty-five to one hundred feet and more from the streams."

"But there are houses downstream from here. In fact, there are condominiums along part of it."

"Unfortunately that's true. We've had to watch carefully to keep residents out of the water so they don't disturb the spawning process."

"I assure you I have no intention of wading in the stream. The water is for aesthetics only. Look." Her heart racing, her breathing ragged, she held out her copy of the map of the property. "The deck might overhang the stream slightly, but there's no access for people to step off into the water. In fact, we can rail the deck to make sure and cover the ground with shrubbery that will discourage foot travel."

Her fingers shook as he studied the map. His breath warmed the back of her neck as he pored over the map. He sighed and covered her hands with his.

"Your plan is commendable, and I can see your father had the ecology in mind when he designed this house. Nevertheless, I can't change regulations. There can't be any construction near a stream and especially not overhanging it."

She pulled her hands from his—the map hung from tense fingers. Regret creased his brow and concern darkened his eyes.

Her voice faltered, more from the impact of his nearness than his words. "What about the other homes along the stream? How did they get their permits?" Maybe bribes were in order here; however, she would be disappointed if they'd influence this associate planner.

Greg lifted his shoulders and gestured downstream. "Those homes were built before the formation of the TRPA. Unfortunately, we've come along too late to save some parts of our environment."

He sounded depressed about the fact, but Monica focused on her plans. If only her father had not delayed construction.

But then, if he had built the house already, she wouldn't have this project to keep the loneliness from overwhelming her.

Greg watched the play of emotions on Monica's face. What was going through that attractive head of hers? He could read frustration and distress, but there seemed to be something else as well. Maybe resignation, but he suspected it was more than that. Loneliness came to mind.

"I'm sorry about this," he said, though he'd been involved in enough cases to know that she wasn't going to accept his apology.

"I can't believe this is the end of it," she exclaimed. "There must be compromises we can make. What if I build the house away from the stream? I could situate it on top of that cliff. The view of the lake would more than make up for distance from the water."

Greg hesitated, reluctant to pursue his arguments. "There are also regulations against building on steep grades. It creates too much erosion. The stream can't handle the soil that would wash into it. Nor could the fish survive the silted stream bed. They need rocky bottom to lay their eggs."

She threw up her hands in protest. Before she could speak, Greg forestalled her. "Look. There's one possible place to construct this house. In the far northeast corner. It's not as attractive, nor would the house as presently designed fit as well in that location."

"Great. You're suggesting I chuck the whole project."

"That's one option."

He ached for her. Hated the incredulous look in her eyes.

She stepped back. "You can't be serious. Do you have any idea what these plans are worth? What this piece of property is worth?"

He shrugged. What could he say? "I'd recommend you sell the property and find another more suitable location for the house."

Her shoulders slumped, but he doubted she was defeated. "The unique quality of an Armand Scott is how it blends in with its environment. Without his input there's no way we can adapt to another locale."

He appreciated what she was saying. He'd researched Armand Scott before the meeting and had seen photos of his architecture. The man rated at the top with Frank Lloyd Wright when it came to blending a structure into the environment. "I could help you look for a suitable property. There has to be some place that could accommodate these designs."

Her fingers tightened on the plans, threatening to crumple them. She straightened her shoulders. "That's your final judgment?"

He wished he could change this for her. It was doubtful, but maybe he could find something. "No, I need to review everything in more detail before I make a recommendation."

Her jaw clenched as she hastily rolled up the plans. "Is there a procedure for appeals?"

He nodded but didn't take the threat seriously. "An appeal will tie up your property and plans for over a year."

She slapped the rolled-up plans against her leg. "How long will it be before I get your final recommendation?"

If he pushed it, he could speed it up a couple of weeks. Normally he wouldn't bend the rules like that, but he felt badly about Monica's predicament. That was a first as well. Usually he maintained a professional detachment from his clients. With her, he'd already broken his code of conduct.

"The soonest would be three to five weeks." She opened her mouth in protest, but he held up his hand. "That's if I really push. Normally it takes longer, but it's early spring and we haven't built up to our peak yet."

"What am I supposed to do for three weeks?" she demanded, anger flushing her cheeks a bright red to clash with her hair.

"I'd recommend you find a good real estate agent, sell this lot, and go shopping for another property."

Before he'd finished speaking, she sent him a withering look, spun around, and stomped toward her Jeep Cherokee. She threw the plans in the back, climbed in, and slammed the door. He started to call her back, but paused. What was the use? He couldn't change the regulations. There was no way he could approve the plans as they were.

The Jeep roared to life. She backed up with a spray of gravel and sped down the treacherous driveway. She'd been gone about ten minutes before the forest settled back to a pristine state without human voices to disturb the peace. Birds flitted in the trees, their songs filling the void of silence. The scent of sun-warmed pine needles wafted up from the ground. Greg tried to absorb the tranquility of Monica's property before heading back to his office. There he'd confront more clients who were unhappy with his verdicts.

He looked skyward. Again he wondered if his efforts made any difference. Was he in the right field? Lowering his head he trudged away from the stream and to his car, wishing he could help Monica to understand.

Monica drove too fast, cornering down the steep road. Barely mindful of the heavy midday traffic, she shifted into high gear and tore down the highway. Tires squealed in protest as she swung the car into Rhonda's driveway. Slamming on the brakes, she jumped out and stomped into the house.

Frustration and anger churned inside, released by a scream. She'd actually started to like that man—she'd respected his dedication. How could he stand there and tell her she could not build Armand Scott's house? Who did he think he was? Obviously he'd never dealt with someone with Monica's determination. She'd show him! There had to be some way to deal with the situation. It was just a matter of calming herself down and finding the answers.

Taking deep breaths, she practiced some of the exercises her mother had taught her. Loneliness welled up as thoughts of her mother surfaced.

Do not worry, Child. Will worry cause anything to change?

Thinking of her brought a sudden calm. She'd been the only one who could diffuse Monica's temper. It never took an argument, nor a reproach. She'd smile and tell her to trust. It never ceased to amaze her. With a smile and a quiet word, peace would settle over the household.

Monica pulled off her glasses and brushed by the kitchen counter. Stephen's letter fluttered to the floor. Too bad Stephen wasn't here right now. He'd be able to get the permits approved. He would know what to say to the people at the TRPA and make them hand over whatever he wanted.

Monica smoothed the paper onto her lap as she sat on the sofa. No, it was better she was on her own. Stephen's help would exact a high price. *Submission.* Her breath caught in her throat. The word terrified her.

She crumpled up the letter and threw it across the room. She didn't need Stephen. She could handle this on her own.

Are you sure about that, Child? We are never alone.

Monica straightened. Her mother's voice echoed across the forgotten years. She pushed her glasses on top of her head and pressed her hands to her cheeks. Her mother's words were coming into her memory more often. Why? Monica had longed to hear her voice when she'd died so many years ago, but never had—not until Armand had died. Maybe her mother knew how lonely she was—how much she needed words of comfort.

CHAPTER 4

GREG PAUSED at the entrance to his office and peered at the mountains. Silhouetted against the blue sky, rocky spires of gray granite sparkled in the bright light. The scent of sun-warmed pine needles filled the air. He breathed deep and pushed open the door, wishing that instead of going inside, he was back on the trails skiing.

At his desk, he gave the mountains one last glance before sitting down and diving into the pile of work.

Carl looked up from the plans in front of him. "Do you have to come in here looking so pleased with yourself? It's Monday morning after all."

"Can't help it," Greg grinned and snapped his fingers. "I feel great." And he did. The weekend had been a blast. "My brother Ed came up for a visit."

"You look fried. Don't tell me you went swimming. That water's colder than a…"

"No." Greg laughed. "We were skiing." The strongest sunblock on the market hadn't kept the sun's glare off the snow from penetrating and reddening his skin.

Carl threw his pencil on his desk. His chair creaked as he leaned back. "Don't give me that."

Knowing the action meant Carl was settling down for a long visit, Greg opened a folder.

Carl ignored the hint to go back to work. "All the ski resorts are closed. Where'd you really go?"

Resigned, Greg closed the folder. Carl would bug him until he'd heard the whole story. His brother had taken one look at Greg's depressed condition, gotten the story of Monica out of him, and decided he needed to get some exercise and commune with nature. "Ed hired a chopper to fly us into the high country and drop us off. It's the last skiing until next winter, so we took advantage and skied for miles both Saturday and Sunday."

Carl shook his head. "Man. Some people have it all."

Greg shrugged. "You could've come. I tried to call you."

Carl slapped the top of his desk. "I knew I should've stayed home. I drove to Berkeley to see Michelle."

"The one you took out two weekends ago?"

"Yeah. Her friend asked about you."

Greg ignored the reminder of the blonde. He had no desire to pursue that relationship. "How'd it go?"

Carl shrugged. "Not bad, but skiing with you and Ed would've been better."

"Next time we go, come along."

Carl slapped his hands together and stood. "You're on. Let's skip this joint and go today."

Surprised, Greg eyed his colleague. "I think you're serious."

"You bet."

Greg shook his head and chuckled. "Sit down and get to work. You know we've got mountains of it."

Carl's smile faded. A frown creased his brow. "Why not, man? Who needs this?" He gestured to the stack of folders. "You don't. Your ol' man has loads of money. Why do you bother working here?"

Envy. That old enemy of Carl's. Greg couldn't tell Carl that the money didn't mean anything to him, at least not in the way it meant to Carl. Sure, it was nice to be able to afford to go skiing in the back country, but Greg didn't live for that. Until recently, he'd thought the TRPA provided purpose.

"You know how I feel about our work," he reminded Carl. "At times we don't seem to be making any headway, but the agency is making progress. We do make a difference." Did he really believe that anymore? Must have been his weekend with Ed. The family law practice carried its own frustrations and setbacks.

Carl waved aside Greg's argument. "I know that. But it would be nice to stuff it for a change and go do something."

Greg opened his file and pretended to work. This time Carl took the hint, but Greg couldn't drop the subject from his mind. The words on the page blurred as he thought about different occasions where his wealth had come between him and his friends. He liked living a simple life. He wasn't going to deny who he was, a man of principles and strong moral values.

Get real, he chided. Who did he think he was kidding? In a society where everything was judged by money, he would never find friends who weren't going to consider his family's wealth before his character traits. That especially applied to women.

He could dream all he wanted about meeting a woman who would care for him as simply Greg Linsey, associate planner for the TRPA, but would it ever happen? As he shook his head, Monica Scott came to mind.

Now there was a female who wouldn't be impressed with his family's social position. Why would she need to be? She had plenty of class of her own. Not the showy kind of the nouveau Californians, but the understated assurance of the old stock.

What had she been up to? Tempted to dig her file out from the middle of the pile, he shifted. Part of the image the agency tried to maintain was impartiality. It wouldn't do to have anyone think they were giving preferential treatment, especially to someone with a big name.

As if thoughts of her had conjured her up, Darlene knocked

at the door. "It's that Scott woman again," she announced.

Both Greg and Carl straightened, alert and curious.

"What's she up to now?" Carl asked.

"This is the third call I've had from a contractor. Evidently she's proceeding to solicit bids on these jobs."

"There's nothing wrong with that," Greg reminded her. "I'm just surprised they're taking the time to give estimates, considering she doesn't have a permit."

"That's just it." Darlene crossed her arms. "She's giving the impression that she has the permit in the bag."

Greg jumped up, sending his chair scooting across the small space. "What has she been telling them?"

Darlene shrugged. "That you'd been out to see the property, but it was still under investigation."

Greg pounded his fist into the palm of his hand. "The sly fox. That's enough to make them believe her."

Darlene fidgeted with the knob to the door. "I told them you hadn't finished with your report."

"But if they know I've been there, they might just believe her when she says I'll probably approve it."

"Did you say that?" Carl asked, surprised.

"No way." Greg shook his fist. "I'll bet a month's wages that she's telling them that I did."

Darlene started to leave, but before doing so, she turned and warned Greg. "You'd better check this out before she has the whole Basin up in arms."

Greg nodded his agreement. "I'll drive to the North Shore right now."

"So much for your good mood," Carl snarked.

Greg grinned mischievously. "Who says this is going to be a bum trip? Just remember you gave this one up. She's mine now."

He jiggled his brows and left Carl pondering what he'd

meant. He wasn't even sure himself. Part of him was annoyed that Monica had presumed his compliance, but another part of him looked forward to the confrontation. It had only been a week and a half since he'd seen her last, yet he couldn't get her out of his mind: the excitement in her eyes when she talked about her plans, the tingle that traced up his arm when he touched her, the smell of her perfume in the cloud of her hair. Even when he was charging down the steep slopes in the back country, he hadn't focused much on the thrill of the danger. His mind kept picturing Monica Scott.

He made excellent time with the light traffic and early hour. He pulled through the granite stone pillars that held the open wrought-iron gates and whistled through his teeth. Rhonda Remway's house—the famous actress. He'd been out here two years ago approving the remodeling done on the place.

He wound through the pines and swerved to avoid the pick-up. The driver recognized him and waved. Greg braked the agency's Bronco when his cab came even with the local contractor.

"Linsey! So it's true."

Greg eyed the contractor and grinned. "What's true, you son of a gun? Haven't you got better things to do than chase rainbows?"

"Not when there's a fortune like this."

"She tell you the plans are approved?"

The contractor nodded.

"Well, don't go cashing in on that pot just yet. Nothing's been approved."

"You're kidding?" The contractor looked stunned. "She's put down half for the job already."

It was Greg's turn for shock. "She's paid you?"

The contractor waved a check. "Signed for the work and supplies. If you don't approve this, she's going to be out big bucks. I'm not the only one she's hired."

Greg thanked him for the info and gunned the engine. This had to be a joke. "Monica Scott," he muttered, "you're going to have a lot of explaining to do."

Monica's sigh of relief for accomplishing that task was short-lived after she ushered the contractor out the door. She'd heard his truck travel down the drive, but now it sounded like he was returning. If he was having second thoughts about accepting the job, she didn't want to hear it.

A quick glance out the window and her interest perked up. The Bronco looked like the planner's from the TRPA. She spotted government plates. The sun reflected off the glass of the windshield, so she couldn't tell if it was Greg Linsey or not.

Must have good news. Why else would he come all the way out here? She opened the door and waved a welcome.

The Bronco pulled up. Her friendly gesture had obviously caught him off guard. He hesitated before slamming shut the cab door.

Had he forgiven her for her temper? She'd been tempted many times over the past week and a half to call and apologize. She knew he was doing the best he could about the situation and respected him for that. She shoved her glasses on top of her head and smiled. "I hope you're bringing me good news. And a week and a half early too."

Once he'd gone back to the office and studied her father's plans, he'd probably realized there was no need to delay the approval. Perhaps one of his superiors had recognized Armand Scott's name and pushed things along.

He stepped closer and she got a good look at his expression. His clenched jaw twitched. Fire burst from his eyes.

Disappointed, Monica closed her fists.

He took the steps two at a time, stood in front of her, and planted his feet apart. "We need to talk."

"You're out early and lucky to catch me at home." Might as well remind him that he hadn't followed protocol and called first. It could give her an advantage. No reaction showed except for a hardening in the glitter of his eyes.

"Come on in. I have some coffee still in the pot."

"I'll pass on the coffee." He didn't pass on the invitation, however. Following her gesture, he entered Rhonda's house.

Monica headed for the kitchen. Her heart pounded. "Suit yourself. I'm ready for another cup. So if you'll excuse me..."

"Go ahead. This won't take long." He settled onto a stool at the kitchen counter and watched her pour the aromatic liquid into a mug.

Monica scooted onto the stool next to him and waited. She wouldn't make this easy for him. She had a feeling she wasn't going to like what he had to say.

"I hear you've been taking bids and writing up contracts for that house." He didn't waste words.

Armand came unbidden to mind. Greg's demeanor reminded her of her father's self-assurance. She forced a smile. "You don't sound pleased, although I can't imagine why it concerns you."

"Maybe you misunderstood me the other day. I cannot approve those plans as they are."

Monica set down her mug with exaggerated care. "No. I think you misunderstood me. I *am* going to build that house."

He shifted. "Don't you think you should wait for your approval to contract the jobs on it?"

"By the time you government—" She almost said boys but changed her mind. "—agents get around to it, these contractors will be booked." She cast him an innocent look. "I'm not doing anything illegal, am I?"

"No." He shook his head and stared at her mouth. "You could stand to lose a lot of money. Do you think that's wise?"

Monica picked up her mug and took a sip, giving herself time to think. The hot liquid soothed her throat. She took a deep breath of the hazelnut blend. Getting upset would not help her case.

She attempted a charming smile. "It has been my experience that there's always a way around regulations. I just haven't found it yet."

"If you're talking about bypassing them, you can forget it. Every argument has already been tried in court."

"I'm not interested in litigation. That would tie me up for years."

"It's tied our hands enough in the past. When the agency first began, we were in one court battle after another."

"I can imagine." She had grounds for a case, she was certain, since the plans had been drawn up years before the agency's existence. However, she had no time nor desire for a court battle. What she needed was productive action, and she would find a way.

"You don't want that to come between us now," Greg said. "Not when we're just getting to know one another."

Monica stared in surprise at the half-cocky, half-innocent grin. Really? Was he coming on to her? Now? She grinned back. She liked men who were sure of themselves. Like Armand.

Monica shook her head. "No court battles will come between us. I promise I don't need to go that route because I know I'll get the permit without it."

It was his turn to frown in puzzlement. "Do you always get your way?" he asked.

Monica kept smiling. "Always."

He straightened. "You can't buy your way in. There isn't anyone at the agency who takes bribes."

It was Monica's turn to straighten. "I always get my way, but you hear me, Greg Linsey. I'm always fair and square, and I don't play games. I've worked hard for every accomplishment I've made."

For long seconds, they stared at each other—both holding to their convictions; neither giving in.

Suddenly Greg broke the eye contact with a snap of his fingers. "I believe I've just seen the raw edges of determination in you, Monica Scott."

Monica grinned at the compliment. "At least you didn't say stubborn."

He lifted both hands as if warding off her temper. "No way. The word would never cross my lips."

"You wouldn't be the first one to accuse me."

He dropped his hands on the counter. "I still say you're making a mistake. Hiring contractors without permits is going to cost you."

Monica didn't let him break her mood. "We'll see. At any rate it's my problem, not yours. I want to build the house and I will. It just isn't clear yet as to how."

"You'll insist even though you could be damaging the ecology?"

"I don't see how one house, especially one designed like my father's, could ruin the Tahoe Basin."

"Maybe your house alone would create minimal damage, but compiled with all that's been done…"

"I'm sure there are more critical things to watch than my house, like the casinos and new hotels."

"The casinos and the hotels are the biggest problem, it's true. The locals are always quick to point them out as the culprit. In reality, it's the local self-centered attitude that has brought this area to near destruction." He stopped snapping his fingers and waved his hands in the air. "Everyone wants to keep the area beautiful until *they're* the ones who have to sacrifice."

Heat crept up Monica's neck and into her cheeks. "Are you referring to me?"

He paused. The silence spoke volumes.

She'd heard enough. With a cool demeanor she stood and led him to the door. "It was nice of you to drive all this way to warn me."

"I don't want to see you in any kind of trouble."

Strangely enough, sincerity etched his words and his tone. She studied him. His job, after all, demanded concern for the environment. He didn't need to be concerned about her. Her respect for him deepened.

"I'll take your advice into consideration," she conceded.

He hesitated at the top of the steps as if he wanted to say more. With firm resolve, she shut the door and leaned against the hard wood until she heard his vehicle pull out.

The woods quieted. Her heart thundered with awareness in the silent house, something that happened every time she saw Greg Linsey, with his carefree assurance and cocky smile.

She marched into the kitchen and grabbed her purse. "There has to be a way to work this out. I'll make it so. Now where is that card?"

Digging through the papers in her bag, Monica found the card Mitch Jones had given her at the South Shore Club. She hated calling on a consultant, but she hated giving in and quitting the project even more.

Mitch Jones drummed his fingers on top of his desk. If he didn't get some action soon, he ran the risk of losing his investment on the old Ponderosa Inn. He had an option on the place, and the next installment was due in two weeks. Where was he going to come up with fifty grand within the next two weeks?

He took a sip of coffee and burned his lip. He jerked back, hot liquid sloshing out of the cup. He swiped a napkin across the mess on the desk and swore. If he could close out this deal, he'd have it made. The golf course was old and run down, but it sat on prime Basin property: an ideal location for a shopping mall complete with gift shops and restaurants. There was plenty of space to build a lodge or condos along the fairways, and the property came with sewage and water rights already built in.

Problem was, he'd extended himself to get in on the bidding. He needed a big cash deal. Soon.

The phone rang and his secretary answered. He glanced at the intercom, hoping it was the couple he'd shown property to last week. If they bought the Howard place, he'd have part of the cash he needed. The female voice of his secretary announced the call. "A Ms. Scott calling. Shall I punch it through?"

Scott? The redhead. His interest piqued.

"I'll talk to her." He set aside his coffee mug and picked up the phone. "What can I do for you, Ms. Scott?"

He listened to her heated conversation and made an appointment for her to meet with him in half an hour. He hung up the phone and rubbed his hands together. "Bingo," he murmured, then went out front.

"I want the red-carpet treatment," he told his secretary. She knew what that entailed without further details. "And get me the folder on the Langford property. I think I know a way we can unload that elephant."

The Langford property had been one of his first purchases after he'd arrived. He'd bought it dirt cheap, but after tangling with the TRPA he'd found out why the owner had been so happy to unload it. The land was environmentally sensitive and impossible to build on.

"Are you planning to sell the parcel to the Tahoe Conservancy and write it off as a speculative loss?"

"I was going to, but I think we have a way to make a profit instead." He rubbed his hands together.

"Good going, boss."

"If we reel this one in, there'll be cause to celebrate."

Mitch returned to his office and sat at his desk. He grabbed the coffee mug and smoothed his fingers around the hot surface.

The office suites at the top of the three-story building had an impressive view of the lake framed by majestic mountain peaks. If Jones wanted to portray an image of success, he'd done well, Monica thought as the secretary directed her to the plush couch.

"Mr. Jones will be right with you. Can I get you something to drink?"

Monica eyed the selection of beverages attractively arranged on a sideboard. "Is that juice in the crystal decanter?"

"That's wine." The secretary smiled. "But I have some chilled apple juice in the refrigerator if you'd like some."

"That would be fine, thank you."

The woman's hands shook, and she fidgeted after serving the juice, forcing the hospitality a bit. Interesting. Jones must have instructed the woman to make her welcome. That was all right. She wanted action from Jones, and she had a feeling the two of them were going to work out just fine. After glancing around the office, she also had the feeling that whatever action they worked out would cost her a pretty penny. Was she prepared to pay for it? Or should she give up on the whole deal?

The idea was tempting, but if she quit this project, there

would be nothing for her to do. No. She needed this work. Not for the money. She had plenty of that. She needed to be busy—to keep from thinking about Armand. And Stephen. Oddly, she hadn't thought much about Stephen since meeting Greg. Warmth crept up her cheeks as she conjured up the planner's image.

The secretary interrupted her thoughts with the announcement that Mitch Jones was ready to see her.

Monica walked with confidence into Jones's office. He stood and came from behind his marble-top desk, extending his hand. "I knew we'd be doing business together."

"Did you?" She quirked her brow. "First I need to know what you have to offer in the way of assistance."

"Of course. Have a seat and let's get right to it."

Monica could tell he was pleased to skip the amenities. She didn't need them either.

"Here is a copy of the design, and here's the layout and location of the property."

While he perused the papers, Monica studied him. He appeared taller than he actually was, probably due to the way he dressed. Obvious care had been taken in the selection. That was a plus as far as she was concerned. Public image counted for a lot.

When he finished with her father's designs and got to the property, a frown creased his brow. Monica forced herself to remain quiet until he was done. In an unconscious gesture he reached for an inlaid box that sat in front of him and flipped the lid. The aroma of unlit tobacco drifted toward her. He fingered the rolled cigars but didn't take one out. Monica sighed with relief.

Finally he glanced at her. "Linsey's right. I doubt they'll approve this project as is."

Monica keyed into the part she wanted to hear. "As is? Can

it be altered in any way?"

"You can relocate your building in this corner." He pointed to the same place Greg Linsey had shown her in the northeast section.

"I'm not changing the design. It's an Armand Scott original and too valuable to alter."

"Yes, I can appreciate that." He paused and took a cigar to roll back and forth in his fingers.

She heard the "but" in the pause. "There is an alternative?" she prodded.

"I believe so." He hesitated again, rolling the cigar back and forth.

She tried not to let him know that his dramatics were annoying her. They were important to a man like Jones. It was best to let him play them out.

Finally, he looked up and locked glances with her. "How badly do you want this?"

"I'm willing to pay. I'm sure there's a price."

His smile didn't reach his eyes. "I'm not asking for one. My business is here to serve."

Monica didn't believe a word of that statement. This place had to be paid for by someone, and she was sure it was his clients. However, she didn't begrudge the man his living. Obviously he was good at what he did, and she needed help.

"I've talked to Linsey," she said. "He can't be bought."

"Forget that." Jones frowned in distaste. "They won't bite."

Relieved, Monica uncrossed her legs and pushed her glasses on top of her head. A bribe would've made things easier, but she didn't want to associate Greg Linsey with shady deals. He impressed her as a man of high values.

"What do you have in mind?"

Jones settled back in his chair and twirled the cigar in his fingers. A sly grin surfaced. "There is a way we can get around the TRPA's regulations."

"I'm all ears." She slipped her glasses back on and took out a notepad and pen from her briefcase.

"There is a provision for building on environmentally sensitive sites."

"I knew there had to be." Why hadn't Greg Linsey told her about it?

"If an area is sensitive, you can find ways to up your points."

"I don't understand."

"In the new Individual Parcel Evaluation System, you're given points according to how desirable the property is for building. Because you have a stream, that will take away points."

"But there are ways we can add them back on?"

"Exactly. You can take a land-sensitive piece of property other than the one you plan to build on and propose to implement a water-quality improvement project."

Monica's frown of confusion prompted Jones to explain further.

"If, for example, you restore a piece of land, they will credit you points based on the amount of money you spend."

"That's blackmail." Monica gasped as visions formed of the cost of such a project.

Jones grinned sardonically. "There are those of us in a coalition that agree with you, Ms. Scott, and we're taking measures to discredit the plan. However, it's our only option now. You might want to reconsider."

Monica had been doing that and could come up with only one thought. She had to finish the project. The cost was not the issue at this point. "There is one problem. I don't own any other sensitive land."

Mitch Jones grinned.

CHAPTER 5

WIND WHIPPED through Monica's hair. The Myerses' boat sped across the smooth waters of Lake Tahoe, the deep blue sky a contrast to the stormy gray of the last two cloudy days. Glad to get out of the house, Monica breathed in the fresh air.

Judy leaned over and yelled above the noise of the powerful engine. "Aren't you glad we talked you into this?"

Nodding, Monica grabbed the bulk of her hair and struggled to tie a scarf at her nape to bring the strands into some semblance of control. Wisps still whipped around her face, but she didn't care. The speed and the fresh air combined to clear the stress of the last two days.

"You were right," she told Judy. "I needed to get away for a while."

"You've been working too hard. I've got to teach you that life here moves at a much slower pace."

Jim turned around from his place at the wheel. "Judy's an expert at that."

Monica ignored the gibe and so did Judy. Jim could comment all he wanted about Judy's lifestyle, but he wouldn't allow it to be any other way. Monica pitied her friend, with no outside interests other than playing social hostess for Jim's business associates.

She glanced at Judy and then at Jim. Outwardly, they appeared the ideal couple, but how happy were they? Their two children were away at private school. Judy sat around the house all day, her only outings with Jim. Like it would be if Monica married Stephen. Would Greg be a domineering husband?

Uncomfortable with the trend her thoughts had taken, she shifted position and watched the tree lined shore as they sped by. They were nearing Incline Village. She could see the huge homes sporting two-story picture windows that reflected the crystal blue waters like giant eyes piercing through the trees.

A couple of boats passed by, and Jim waved at the occupants. Judy leaned close. "Friends of his."

"You two know everyone in the Basin." Monica shook her head in amazement. "My father was like that. He collected friends like bees to honey."

"You miss him, don't you?"

She nodded. She missed the social life she'd been part of growing up as Armand Scott's daughter. If she married Stephen, she'd be part of that life again.

Jim cruised past Incline Village and headed south along the Nevada coast. Judy pointed to a spit of rocks flanked on both sides by pristine white sand beaches. "That's Sand Harbor," she explained. "We'll have to go there in August for the Shakespeare festival."

When Monica showed interest, Judy went on to explain. "A troupe comes up from the Bay Area every summer. It's a big event. The audience brings a gourmet picnic and settles down in a natural amphitheater formed in the sand dunes. The play goes on under the stars."

"Sounds fun," Monica agreed, wondering if Greg ever went to the outdoor plays.

Judy glanced at where they were heading and abruptly cut off her description. "Jim Myers, you steer clear of this beach or your name will be mud."

Jim laughed and downshifted the powerful engine to a slower speed. "It's just 'Nudie Beach.' We want to make sure Monica sees *everything*, now don't we?"

Jim practically slowed to a stop, but Monica ignored his attempt to shock her. "Hey, I've lived on the Costa del Sol. No big deal." She shrugged. "Do you know where the Langford property is located? It has a stream running through it just as my property does."

"I remember the Langfords. They tried to build on their place," Judy offered.

"They were in court for years over that piece of land," Jim spoke, although he kept his attention focused on the shore. "In fact they headed up the biggest organization that fought the TRPA. Gave the agency quite a few headaches."

"It was a full-fledged battle." Judy shook her head. "They united most of the real estate agents and property owners who wanted to build."

"I could see how their property could lose its value if they suddenly weren't allowed to build," Monica sympathized. What if she couldn't build on her property—what would she do with it? She shrugged off the question. "How did Jones end up with their land?"

"I think it was a settlement. He'd done some work for them, and they couldn't pay him. They lost everything fighting the TRPA."

How foolish. Fighting for a cause was all right as long as you were sure you were going to come out ahead. Greg's warnings came to mind, but she shrugged them off. "So what do you think of my idea to buy the place and restore the natural creek bed?"

"Isn't that going to be expensive?"

"An environmentalist from the US Forest Service showed me a similar project in Kings Beach that shouldn't be too costly. They rocked in the drainage area and then put this net stuff over the ground to keep the soil from eroding. That will be the main expense. Reseeding the ground shouldn't cost much more. I'd say the whole project will be around thirty grand."

What would Greg think of the plan? Surely he would approve of any attempt to restore the damaged property.

"Sounds feasible." Jim finally took his attention from the shore and gave it to Monica and Judy. "But I think you'd better confirm it with the agency before you dish out all that dough for what's otherwise useless property."

"A hundred thousand is a lot to pay for land you can't build on," Judy added.

"It's a couple of acres and near the lake."

"But it's worthless. It's throwing money away."

"Not really. The project will be a tax write-off. The price of the land will easily be covered by the sale of my father's house when it's finished."

"I suppose so," Judy mused as she opened the cooler and brought out small individual bottles of iced Perrier.

"Sounds like you have it all figured out," Jim said as he pushed on the throttle. The boat lurched forward as it picked up speed when Jim headed across open water toward the west shore. "When it comes down to it, the decision is yours."

Yes, it was her decision. Surprisingly the idea didn't grate on her like she thought it would. Maybe Greg's lessons on preserving the environment were having their impact after all.

Thoughts of the earnest expression on Greg's face as he explained the ecology of the Tahoe Basin brought a smile to her lips. Mitch Jones had an appointment with Greg Linsey tomorrow morning. Greg would hopefully be pleased that she sought professional help. Surely the two men could work something out.

Monica looked at the multi-storied casinos lining the shore at Stateline. They looked out of place in the mountain environment. The ski resort of Heavenly Valley cut a huge scar across the landscape where trees had been cleared for ski runs. In the winter, she supposed they looked good, with long swathes of white coming through the forest. But in the spring and summer seasons they looked like cuts where loggers had been working. No wonder Greg fought so hard for the Basin.

"Do you see the tramway?" Judy pointed to the car that carried passengers to the top of the mountain. "It runs year-round. There's a restaurant at the top. We'll go sometime. The view is worth it."

Monica nodded absently. Memories of trams in Spain distracted her: trips with Stephen that her father had encouraged. She'd been miserable.

The wind whipped past her skin. Monica closed her eyes and let the memories come. Just for a few minutes. Just until the longing turned to an aching pain. *Stephen. Why couldn't you accept me on my terms? Why was I the one that had to give in?*

Monica shook off the memories of Stephen and stared at the tram. What would it be like to ride the car and have dinner at the top with Greg? For brief seconds she could feel his arms around her. She'd tuck back into the crook of his arm and lean against his chest, feeling safe and secure, feeling valued as the woman she was.

Judy's shout cut into Monica's musings. She opened her eyes. Her heart lurched at the same time the boat did when Jim swerved suddenly to miss the bow of a sailboat. Water sprayed, blocking her view of the occupants. Surely they had been drenched.

The man at the bow swore at Jim. Monica didn't blame him. Sailboats had the right of way. Judy was yelling at Jim too until he turned and snapped at her.

"Shut up, woman. I missed him, didn't I?"

"Watch where you're going. You'll get us killed," Judy continued to scream.

Monica supposed it was nervousness on Judy's part that urged her to continue yelling. She should know better than to criticize Jim like that in front of Monica. He didn't like being ordered around by a woman, especially his wife. Hearing the two argue, Monica shuddered, again thankful she had avoided marriage to Stephen.

True love is gentle. Love is kind, Child. It does not seek its own interests.

Is it, Mother? I don't see the gentle love you talk about. I want that love, but does it truly exist? You claim you and Armand loved like that, but you always gave in. Is that what love is?

A deepening ache supplied her only answer.

Greg swung his sailboat about as the speedboat crossed his bow, making it easier to cut through its dangerous wake. Drenched to the skin, Carl screamed and cussed up front. Greg battled laughing at the sight of Carl or cursing at the cruiser's carelessness. Annoyance won out. He agreed wholeheartedly with every one of Carl's explosions.

He trimmed the sail and glanced at the motorboat. For a second he thought he saw red hair whipping about in the breeze. Monica Scott came to mind. Her hair was that same shade. Thinking of her didn't improve his mood. The disappointment in her eyes haunted him. He yearned to make things right in her world, but he couldn't.

Carl worked his way aft. "He's headed for Emerald Bay. Let's go after the—"

"Forget it, Carl. By the time we catch up to him, the incident will be history."

"Crazy fool. Probably a tourist who doesn't know what he did."

"Could be," Greg agreed, but he didn't think so. He was sure he'd seen that boat around the lake before.

"We're headed for the bay, aren't we?" Greg nodded and

Carl snarled. "I'll look for him then. If I see him—"

Greg tuned Carl's tirade out. His friend had been out on the bow and needed to vent the scare the incident had given him.

Greg's thoughts returned to Monica Scott.

Why couldn't he get her out of his mind? Her attitude represented everything he didn't like. She had no real concern for the environment. Her own interests came first and then, if it didn't interfere with her private affairs, she might consider the issues of ecology. A steady stream of clients with that same attitude trooped through the agency every week. Someday someone was going to walk in there and, instead of complaining, were going to commend the planners for their efforts. Maybe if that would happen even once, he wouldn't be tempted to consider his work futile.

Monica was just like everyone else—determined to build that blasted house. He could understand her motivation. If only there were some way he could convince her to change the location. The house could probably be accommodated to several pieces of property he knew of. Maybe he'd call and offer to take her to see them this weekend.

Greg sailed around the point that framed the entrance to Emerald Bay. Ahead he could see Vikingsholm. The main tourist season hadn't begun yet, so the beach was relatively uncrowded. Good. He didn't feel like hassling with a lot of people.

"Do you see what I see?" Carl hollered from the bow where he was trimming the jib sail.

Greg looked in the direction where Carl pointed. Docked at Fannette Island—or as the locals called it, the Tea House Island—was the boat that had almost run them down. Greg intended to sail past it until he spotted the redhead standing in the stern. His heart picked up speed. Monica Scott.

"Hang on," he shouted as he quickly came about.

"You going to land there?" Anticipation sounded in Carl's voice.

Greg nodded. "Forget revenge, buddy. I've got other motives for landing."

Carl stared at Greg and then at the shore. He whistled through his teeth.

Greg watched her hand an ice chest to the man on shore. Evidently he'd been piloting the boat. Were they involved with each other? Another woman appeared and, with relief, he recognized who they were. The couple he'd seen her with at the South Shore Club.

He tacked closer to shore. Monica noticed him then. He waved and had to chuckle at the look of surprise on the faces of all three of them. Monica grinned. Good. She recognized the humor in the situation.

As soon as they neared shore, he luffed the sails into the wind and dropped anchor. Carl jumped over the side and yelped when he hit the icy cold water. Greg laughed. The afternoon turned out to be more promising than he had earlier imagined.

"These are my neighbors," Monica explained.

The man had the grace to flush slightly and extend his hand. "Jim Myers here. Sorry about the close call. It was my fault. I wasn't looking."

Greg cast Carl a warning glance. Carl got the message and clenched his jaw shut to keep quiet. Greg returned his attention to Myers and said, "This is Carl Sutton. He also works at the TRPA."

"This is my wife, Judy, and I guess you know Monica."

Greg grinned at the inside humor of the situation.

Monica appeared to struggle with her own grin. She spoke, her voice as low and sultry as he remembered. "Won't you join us? We're going to have a picnic, and we have plenty of food."

Carl started to say no, but Greg quickly interceded. "Sure thing. We'll bring what we have."

"Good, we can share," Judy said, obviously pleased with

the arrangement even though her husband didn't appear to be.

Greg decided not to worry about it. They would all have to deal with each other because he wanted to talk to Monica.

As they hiked to the crest of the small island, Judy explained the local history to Monica. "This woman from Norway modeled her home after a ninth-century Norse fortress." Judy pointed to the huge stone structure on the shore at the end of Emerald Bay. "She built the shelter on this island and would bring her many guests out for tea."

"Which is why they call it the tea house," Jim added as he led them into the stone structure.

The walls were only a few feet high, leaving the upper portion open so that the tourists could enjoy the panoramic view.

"She wouldn't want to bring them here on a stormy day," Monica surmised.

"This lake is dangerous when there's even a hint of a storm," Greg advised. "Luckily, today's weather is perfect."

By the time they finished laying the food out, it appeared they had a feast.

"This looks like a party." Judy gestured toward the food laid out across the stone sideboard. "And look, there are the Kendalls. Call them up here, Jim."

At first Greg wasn't pleased to have the day turn into a big social gathering, but as soon as the Kendalls arrived and introduced their niece, he knew it was going to work out fine. Carl and the niece hit it off, leaving him free to focus on Monica Scott. He found a seat beside her and sat down on the cool stone.

"I'm glad we ran into each other today."

Humor flashed in her eyes. "You mean that literally, I take it."

He laughed. "No. I'm glad you missed my boat. But it's nice to see you in a social setting. Our business encounters tend to get tense."

"Then let's keep this social and not discuss business," she suggested.

"I'm all for that. Days off are especially needed during peak season."

"I can appreciate your end of it," she said, her tone a touch sarcastic. "But I'd prefer to be working today."

"Now, now." He held up his hands in mock protest. "You said no business talk today."

"Was I discussing business?" Her glance held a teasing quality that intrigued him.

Monica didn't give him a chance to pursue the subject, but started another conversation with Judy. Greg listened. He'd have his chance to talk to her later. He'd make sure of that.

As they were eating, Judy explained more of the local history, and this time Carl joined in, making sure the Kendalls' niece, Becky, heard it all.

"After the couple died, in time the State obtained the property, and it's been made into a State Park and historical monument for the public to enjoy."

Jim tossed down the cleaned chicken bone. "Monica, speaking of land, did you talk to Linsey about the Langfords'?"

Greg froze.

Monica shifted. "We aren't discussing business today, Jim. Tell me more about this lovely bay."

Jim readily expounded on his knowledge of the area to the group, and Greg heaved a sigh of relief. The Langford name stuck in his mind like a prickly thorn. What did Monica Scott have to do with Langford? Was she going to proceed with litigation after all? His fists clenched at the thought. She would be making a big mistake. The agency had become much more sophisticated since those early days. Monica wouldn't stand a chance in court.

There had to be a way to make her understand what the agency was all about. Suddenly he had an idea. He leaned close.

"How about going for a sail with me? It won't take long. I'm sure your friends won't mind if I steal you away for an hour or two."

"Now?" She raised her brow.

He thought he'd spoken low, but everyone stared in their direction.

Judy spoke right up. "Take her for the whole afternoon if you want. We'll be heading back soon. Would you be able to take her on home?"

"He can't do that," Monica protested. "He'd have to drive me clear around the lake."

"That's no problem for me," Greg assured her. "Come along. You'll enjoy the sailing."

She looked torn. "I do love to sail."

"Great. It's settled." Greg didn't want to give her time to change her mind. He stood and began gathering his gear.

"Hey, what about me?" Carl objected, not too happy about leaving his new female acquaintance.

Becky smiled at Carl. "They look like they want to talk. Why don't you come with us? We'll take you home."

"Sure," Kendall added. "And when we do, you can stay for dinner. We'll make a day and evening of it."

Carl grinned.

Perfect.

Monica breathed deep. How had Greg, the Myerses, and the Kendalls maneuvered the situation so swiftly and effectively? One minute she was enjoying a social gathering and the next she found herself alone with Greg Linsey on his sailboat. He looked entirely too pleased with himself.

"This is just a pleasant cruise," she warned. "Don't go reading anything more into it."

He sent her a look of mock chagrin. "Do I look like the lecherous type?" He handed her the tiller while he trimmed the sails.

No, he looked like Stephen, ten years ago when he'd taken them sailing in the Mediterranean off the coast of Spain. Only, Stephen would have never let her handle the tiller, or any working part of the boat for that matter. Greg didn't seem a bit concerned about her competence.

"Why did you invite me?" she finally asked. He exuded a hint of something more than male interest.

His expression sobered. "I want to show you some things about the lake."

"You couldn't just tell me about them?" She held the tiller steady and leaned back against the bench to stretch her legs out in front of her. Since she had shorts on, she might as well take advantage of the sun and get some tan.

He stared at her legs, the action causing more heat than the sun. "No. It's better if you see for yourself."

Monica had no idea what he was talking about, but it didn't really matter. She enjoyed being with Greg and learning about the area she lived in. Jim Myers had been getting on her nerves, and besides, it felt right to be here.

Only the sound of lapping water against the bow and the flapping of wind in the sails broke the quiet. Occasionally wood creaked as the movement created stress on the hull. Greg obviously enjoyed the silence, but Monica didn't. Her thoughts too often took her to places she didn't want to go.

Find a quiet place and rest, Child.

No, Mother. The silence makes me see things I don't want to see.

Monica handed Greg the tiller and shivered inside. "So

what's this great mystery about the area that you're going to show me?"

"I want to prove to you how the building going on around here is damaging the lake."

Monica straightened. "Come on. I thought we weren't going to discuss business."

"Not business—education," he said as the boat rounded the mouth of Emerald Bay and came into the main body of water. They picked up speed as the sails filled with the stronger breeze.

"And you're going to be the teacher?"

"I'm the expert." He cast her that cocky grin she was coming to like.

"Don't you think you're a biased expert?"

"Sure I'm biased. My sole interest is saving the environment."

"I'm not an environmental ogre, you know," she said. "I simply want to build a house. One that could become a historical monument."

"I'm not arguing your motivation, nor am I unaware of the importance of an Armand Scott house. But like your father's work, the Basin has rare and unique qualities that need to be preserved."

Amused by his persistence, Monica stared at Greg. "Okay. I'll listen to everything you want to say." She paused for effect. "On one condition."

He hesitated. "What's your condition?"

She chuckled. "I'm not going to bribe you if that's what you're worried about."

"I have to admit, it did cross my mind."

"But you aren't taking any?" It didn't hurt to ask.

He let go of the tiller and grasped her arms. "Maybe I should toss you overboard," he teased.

In spite of the tingles racing up and down from his touch, she didn't flinch, but held her own with a challenging stare. "I want an appointment to discuss a matter of business with you first thing Monday morning."

"That's all?" His brow quirked.

"That's it." She glanced down at his hands on her arms. "Can I stay aboard?"

He let her go and stepped back a pace. The puzzled expression remained in place. "What are we going to discuss?"

"You'll see. Remember, no business today."

He considered her words and then laughed—the confident chuckle she found appealing. "Okay. It's a deal. Who knows? What I teach you today may ultimately affect your discussion on Monday."

It wouldn't, but she didn't bother to tell him that.

The wind carried them along the west shoreline as they traveled north. Monica had to admit the scenery was beautiful.

"That's Sugar Pine Point ahead." He directed her gaze west. "It's an old turn-of-the-century estate. It was owned by a wealthy San Franciscan. When he died, his children used it for a while before turning it and all the property over to the State."

"Seems to be a popular thing to do around here."

"Originally all the lakeshore was privately owned. It's only through donations such as these that we can obtain lakefront property for public use."

His positive response gave her courage. Perhaps he would be pleased with her plan to rehabilitate the Langford property after all. "I can see the need for that. This area does have a lot of tourists."

"They're our main economy," he agreed. "However, they're also our biggest problem. Do you see that beach over there?"

He turned the craft into the wind. The sails emptied, and the boat drifted in the choppy water. "See the houses located on those slopes?"

Monica squinted her eyes against the glare and stared in the direction Greg pointed. At first all she could see were trees, and then she saw them. "They're just hanging on cliffs that are straight up and down."

"Exactly. They are built on lots we wouldn't approve now."

"Why not? They must have fantastic views."

"They do, but look at the water along the shore below them."

Monica looked but couldn't see anything out of the ordinary. "Am I supposed to see the remains of one that tumbled down the cliff?" she asked.

"They're built on bedrock, and the construction is sound. That's not what I wanted you to see."

She shrugged. "I don't see a thing except nice beaches, a few people, and turquoise water."

"That's it," he shouted excitedly.

Monica stared at him. "What's it? I don't see what you're getting at."

"The water color. See the difference?"

She studied the water. "It's clear and deep blue here, but cloudy and turquoise near the shore."

"Why do you think it's different? It's pollution. This lake is renowned for its clarity, but the buildings along the cliff cause erosion. The erosion brings silt into the water, and the silt encourages the growth of algae. Hence the opaque color."

"Do you want to run that by me again?" Monica straightened, serious now.

Greg evidently wasn't. Before she could react, he had come up beside her and lightly draped his arm across her shoulder. Along with a slight squeeze, he said, "See. You are interested."

For once, Monica couldn't think of a thing to say.

CHAPTER 6

GREG'S ARM WARMED the back of Monica's neck. She breathed in the scent of sunshine mixed with his spicy cologne. Longings surfaced with the lap of water, the breeze tugging on her hair, and Greg's nearness. Longings and a strange loneliness she didn't want to feel. She stepped away.

He didn't pursue the contact, nor did he say anything, although his blue-eyed glance held a hint of challenge.

After an endless moment, he continued with his ecology lesson. "The issue of water clarity is what started the movement to initiate the TRPA. Back in the sixties they began to notice the change and started taking readings." He explained the procedure they used, measuring how far they could see white discs that were lowered into the water.

Monica tried to focus on his words. But instead of listening, she studied the fluid movement of his hands and the way his smile crooked higher on one side than the other.

Shaking away the attraction, she moved to the other side of the boat. She shaded her eyes with one hand and forced herself to concentrate on Greg's lecture.

"When scientific proof was produced, people began to take the problem seriously. The results of the tests showed a rapid loss of clarity." He ducked under the boom and stood next to her. "Our concern is that if the algae continues to grow at this fast rate, Lake Tahoe will no longer be able to claim its fame as one of our nation's largest lakes with the clearest water."

His words blurred as she studied him. His brow creasing with concern, he placed his hand on her shoulder. Her heart skittered.

Startled, Monica blinked, aware now that he'd asked her a question. "I'm sorry. What did you say?"

"Don't tell me I'm boring you already?"

Heat flushed her cheeks. "No. I was wondering why the algae is growing. It can't be just the buildings. There has to be more to it than that."

"Exactly."

Evidently she'd said the right thing, because his grin brightened. She sighed with relief and forced herself to listen more attentively.

"Soon they realized that the problem was complex, involving sewage spills from several developments."

"And I'm sure boats provide their fair share of pollutants," she added, caught up in his passion. "Is that why you have a sailboat? To preserve the water?"

He grinned, recognizing her subtle humor. "That's part of it, but to be honest, I prefer sail to motor power."

"Let me guess. You like the silence." Her mother preferred quiet time to pray. Was that Greg's reason?

Greg ran his hand along the boom. "That's part of it. I like the control of the wind—to harness its power."

Intrigued, Monica trailed her hand along the smooth wood warmed by the sun. "Will you let me feel that when we set sail?"

He sidestepped along the boom to the stern of the boat. "Sure thing, but let me explain some more about the algae. Since the TRPA has been in effect, the water clarity has been improving."

Monica followed and sat down beside the tiller. "It's depressing." She rolled her shoulders in an attempt to shrug off the tension building across her neck. "So the problem is solved?"

"Theoretically, but runoff from construction clearing causes an increase in silt. So does local logging and storm drain runoff." He came up beside her and grinned. "Am I boring you? You look like you're in pain."

"No, no. It's my neck and shoulders. They're stiff, that's all."

His expression sobered. "Can I help?" He stretched out his hand toward her neck.

She nodded.

Gently, he reached over, and pressed the fingers of his right hand into the tightened muscles of her neck.

Tingles raced up and down her spine. She should tell him to stop. He stood a good twelve inches apart from her, but heat radiated from his body. She should pull away and move to the other side of the boat. His fingers pressed deep, causing her breath to catch.

"Blackwood Creek is a canyon along the northwest shore that was mined heavily for gravel..." His words blurred.

Relaxed and stimulated at the same time from his massage, she forced herself to carry on the conversation. "I can imagine what that did to the area."

His fingers threaded through her hair. She moaned. He paused for long seconds. Monica held her breath until he let out a sigh and continued massaging her neck. She barely heard him murmuring. "The natural vegetation couldn't restore itself..." His voice, now hoarse and breathless, wavered as he continued explaining.

She straightened her slumped shoulders. "I suppose we have a 'good news' story here as well."

"Umhmmm." His voice faded again. His fingers slowed. "It has become a haven for deer, bear, and other wildlife. Hikers and bicyclists enjoy the renewed beauty, and so do cross-country skiers in the winter."

Monica closed her eyes. "Are all your projects success stories?"

"Unfortunately, the successes are few and far between the real problems." His voice sounded far away. He pointed to the city of South Lake Tahoe. "Do you see the haze hovering at that end of the lake?"

"Air pollution. A real problem everywhere these days."

"One of the attractions of Tahoe is the clear mountain air, especially for people coming out of the smoggy city. Our struggle isn't so much to clean the air as it is to maintain the quality we have."

She turned to search his face. "And it isn't maintaining?"

His gaze didn't waver, but searched hers as well. He brushed a strand of hair from her face. Uncomfortable with the intimacy, Monica stood and moved to the center of the boat. She had never mixed business with pleasure. A policy of Armand's.

Greg looked like he wanted to follow, but must have changed his mind. Settling onto the seat she had vacated, he answered her question. "The country is beginning to look at alternative fuels. When more people realize the need for change, then we'll get action. It's a nationwide problem."

"Worldwide," she commented, thinking of Madrid where they had planted thousands of trees to combat the air pollution.

"The difference between the rest of the world and Tahoe is that we're trying to do something about it."

She tucked her feet under her. "Ideally, it sounds great. But putting it in practice infringes on a lot of people's rights."

"What we have is a compromise. It slows progress down both environmentally and economically, but over the long haul, the results will prove the effort worthwhile."

"In your lifetime?" She couldn't help the dig.

His response surprised her. He laughed. "You bet within my lifetime. I'm determined to make a difference, and I like to see results."

"Somehow I think you will." Again she couldn't help but notice the difference between Greg and Stephen. Stephen intended to make waves wherever he went. He never made showy ones, but he produced quiet undertows that would suck you in before you realized you'd given up control. Monica closed her eyes against the thought and opened them to see Greg staring.

What was she thinking? Greg wondered. She'd been listening so intently and then all of a sudden she'd drifted off. From the pained expression, he guessed it wasn't pleasant. He knew hardly anything about her. Yet, he felt close to her.

She'd been interested in all that he'd tried to explain to her. He was sure of it. He hoped she understood what he'd tried to get across.

He sighed. That was the frustrating part—getting people to understand that they needed to act now. His brief moment of enthusiasm waned. He'd told Monica he was confident he'd make a difference, but would his efforts really have an impact?

Monica grasped the rail as she stood and carefully made her way against the rocking of the boat to sit down on one of the benches near him. The action brought Greg back to the present. He looked at his watch and realized he'd been talking for quite a while.

He grinned apologetically. "How'd you like something to drink?"

"That would be nice."

"Beer, fruit juice, wine?"

"The juice sounds good."

"I'll be right back." He paused halfway down the hatch and pointed a teasing finger. "Don't go anywhere now."

She held up her hands. "You've got your captive audience."

That comment stopped him cold. He leaned against the hatch door and considered her carefully. "Have I been unfair?"

"Let's just say you're informative, but biased."

The subtle teasing in her tone eased his tension. "I didn't claim otherwise. I made that clear from the start."

"I know." She laughed. "Go get me some juice. I ought to get some reward for all that lecturing."

Greg chuckled as he lowered himself down the hatch. She was a good sport. Even though they seemed opposite in many ways, he felt attracted to her. He'd have to figure out later why that pleased him. For now he'd enjoy her company. She'd made it clear that was all she was going to allow.

He grabbed the cans of juice and a bag of nuts and tucked them in the pocket of his jammers.

"Here." He handed her the juice. "No more lecturing. I promise. From now on we'll do what the tourists do—enjoy the lake."

She held his juice while he trimmed the sails. As soon as the craft got underway, he took his drink and explained how to keep the boat on course.

Her laughter pleased him as she began to appreciate the power he'd been talking about.

"There's nothing like capturing a bit of nature," he explained.

"There should be something environmentally criminal about a statement like that," she teased in the low, sultry voice he enjoyed.

He pulled on the tiller and quirked his brows. "You aren't going to lecture me now, are you?"

"I wouldn't dream of it."

He wanted to know everything about her. Did she want a family? "What do you dream of? Besides building your father's house, of course."

She gave him a censoring glance as if she didn't like him asking something so personal.

"You know some of my dreams," he defended himself. "I've been discussing them all day."

"Are those your only dreams? Surely the environment isn't all you live for?"

She'd neatly turned the tables, but he didn't really mind. Maybe if he'd open up, she would too. "I have the basics needed for mountain living. I love the outdoors. I like good snow for skiing, good winds for sailing."

"Good music for dancing," she said, smiling.

He snapped his fingers, happy she'd remembered the time he'd held her in his arms. "You've got me there."

He liked her laugh. The wind carried a whiff of her perfume, an expensive French brand he recognized. He liked that too. At this moment, there wasn't much he didn't like about Monica Scott.

He held onto the lines as he took another sip of his juice. "So what are your leisure time activities?"

She remained silent for a moment, her attention on the sails, then she shrugged. "I don't usually have much leisure time. At least, I try not to have any."

He studied her closely, noticing the tightness in the muscles of her neck. "A workaholic, hmmm?"

"Some people call me that. I don't see it that way."

His sister-in-law was like that, and Greg was sure it drove Ed nuts. Why else would his brother come up so often to spend leisure time in the mountains with him? "How do you rationalize working all the time? I've always wondered."

She played with her drink before answering. "I guess I don't like time to think. It's easier to do than to introspect."

She might have a point. On occasion his mind went into overtime as a thought churned with the frustrations involved with his job. He liked working out solutions. It brought him peace. But what was so terrible in her life that she didn't want to think about it?

"What do you like to *do* then?"

There was no hesitancy this time.

"Build things. I grew up helping my father. I like the organizing, the productivity, the sense of accomplishment when completed."

"I can understand that." At least he could in part. "I don't have the same sense of accomplishment in my line of work. No final and finished product. So what are your plans now that your father has passed on?"

When she frowned, he immediately apologized. "I'm sorry. I shouldn't have intruded on your grief."

She shook her head. "It's been over a year. One of the reasons it's so important for me to build this house is that I haven't yet decided what to do with myself now that Armand is gone. Fulfilling his plan is like a reprieve."

"So you don't have to think about your future?"

"That's right. I suppose you have yours all mapped out."

"Not exactly, although there are definite things I can see myself doing."

"Such as?"

Once again she had maneuvered the subject of conversation to him. He grinned, letting her know he recognized her ploy. Eventually he'd swing it back around to her.

"I see myself getting married and raising children." He gestured toward the Basin. "That's why I work so hard to save this. I want my children to have what I did when I was growing up."

She nodded. "But you can't determine what the next generation is going to want or need."

He pulled on the lines to tighten the sails, enjoying the tug of the wind. "Isn't that the truth? I can see how my generation can't possibly do the things my parents' generation did."

She set her empty juice can down and shifted to face him, gesturing at the boat. "You don't look like you're having to do without." She paused and stared. "Or do you have other work you do?" Her tone implied more.

Greg stiffened. Many people in this area supplemented their income dealing drugs. He knew of at least three city officials in the Basin who were on the take. He didn't want her thinking he was into that.

"My parents have money. My father practically gave me the house when he sold it to me. Since I'm not married now, I can spend my income on toys."

She smiled. "In other words, you don't take bribes."

He had to laugh. "I do get defensive about it. You would be surprised at how much subtle resentment there is among my colleagues who are trying to make it on that lousy government income."

"I suppose."

How could she understand when she hung around others who were just as wealthy as she was? He straightened, wishing he could pace. "Most people in the world get along fine with a lot less than what Americans call 'necessities.' In fact, if they weren't so consumer-happy, you wouldn't have half the pollution there is today. That's what is happening at Tahoe. People from the city come up here to get away from the rat race. They want peace and quiet, but that isn't enough for them."

Too much energy built inside. He needed action. He gave Monica control of the tiller and sails and stood up to pace and gesture with his hands. "Instead of sitting under the trees and enjoying the silence and scenery, they want miniature golf, video games, and everything else they have in the city."

Monica adjusted the sails, causing them to luff. "Which defeats their purpose for coming." Humor sounded in her voice.

He helped her with the sails and saw that she was laughing at him. He grinned. "I do get carried away, don't I?"

She shrugged as she tried to keep the line taut. "That was the agreement we made for my joining you this afternoon."

"I don't think you realized what you were in for."

She nodded toward the tiller and lines. "True. It's been more than a bargain tour, but I enjoy hearing what you think."

He believed her. She wasn't the type to make up compliments. After helping her come about to set their course on another tack, he settled beside her.

"So tell me. What are your dreams for your children?"

"I don't plan to have children." The clenched fists in her lap were the only clue that the question had made her tense. His heart sank, and he spoke before thinking. "You can't have any?"

She cast him a challenging glare. "No. I can have children. I don't want any."

Taken aback, he stared. "Don't you like them?"

She sent him a look of disgust. "Of course I like children."

Greg didn't know what to say. He kept silent, wondering what had happened to make her so adamant and bitter.

She glared defensively. "Don't ask me why, but everyone seems to assume that the reason I don't want children is because I don't like kids or I'm selfish."

Greg had made the same assumptions about a couple of his cousins who didn't want children. "Are you saying that's not the case?"

"Of course it isn't. Having a child isn't something you do because it's expected of you. There're many things to consider."

She let out some line, then said, "I think a decision to remain childless is too recent a phenomenon for society to deal with. It's stepping out of the norm." She leaned back to get leverage on the line after a small gust of wind pulled it through her hands. "When you deviate like that, people draw conclusions based on misinformation—the definition of a stereotype, I might add."

From the way Monica eyed him, Greg knew she wasn't sure of his reaction. Neither was he for that matter. Thinking something must have hurt her terribly, he forced a calm expression. "So that I won't start forming any misconceptions here, why don't you tell me why you don't want children?"

Monica had never explained her decision to anyone, including Stephen. The judgmental attitude of others didn't invite confidences. But she sensed Greg was sincere in his request. "There are many reasons." Some were buried deep, so deep she doubted she could discuss them.

"I'm a good listener. You'll see," he encouraged.

Monica took a deep breath. "I guess I'll get on my soap box this time. Tit for tat, hmmm?"

His cocky grin and the snap of his fingers gave her confidence to go on. "It isn't that I hate children. I've been around enough of them." She explained how people had always hung around Armand. "Sure they're cute and adorable, but they're just people, only smaller. Having a child is like inviting a stranger to live with you."

"And that's not a selfish attitude?"

She thought for a minute. "I suppose when you say it like that it appears so, but there's more to it than that."

He took over the sails and adjusted them. "Now you sound like my sister-in-law. She has every statistic imaginable on why some people shouldn't be parents. She can quote figures on child abuse, molesting, abandonment, starvation."

Monica had to laugh at his sarcasm. "Don't forget overpopulation. That should concern an environmentalist like yourself."

"Now we're back to me. Let's hear more about your reasons."

She ignored his request, doubting she could really explain.

He reached over and brushed back a strand of hair blowing in her face. "Don't you see how similar our two soap boxes are?" he pointed out. "As long as someone doesn't have to make a personal sacrifice, they become all concerned about the issues. It's safe when it's vague. But as soon as you force people to consider the overall picture as it relates to them personally, they start screaming about human rights. What they don't realize is that whatever decision you make as an individual, affects everyone as a whole."

"Stop talking and take a deep breath," she teased and then started laughing. "Forgive me. But I thought you were going to turn purple before you gave yourself a chance to breathe."

He paused, obviously put out by her laughter, but then he laughed too. Monica liked the sound of his laughter—deep and rumbling—like Armand's. She noticed the breeze blowing through his hair and brushing up against his face. Did she really want to dig up her inner feelings? The issue of children had been one of the main reasons she'd left Stephen. It had caused too many disagreements.

"I'd like to say I'm altruistic and not having children because of the issue of overpopulation, but there's more to it than that."

"I'm all ears."

"When I was a child, my father always took me with him. He'd say, 'Come on darlin', leave your mum to her plants. She

98

needs the quiet time.' I always felt like I was a burden for her."

Neither condemnation nor judgment reflected in Greg's stare, just concern. His genuine interest gave her courage to continue. She took in a breath. "I guess deep down the thought of being a mother scares me. I'm not really sure how a mother should act, nor how to raise a child."

Did she see a sigh of relief? "Don't you think you'd learn as you went along?"

"You mean use a child as a guinea pig?" Monica scoffed. "Come on, dearest, let Mommy experiment now."

He laughed, but then became serious again. "I admit there are no courses on parenthood. Experience is the teacher here. But don't you think that whoever the father is could be of help?"

Would Greg be a good father? He was loving, kind, and gentle. Stephen was a perfectionist and very controlling. He'd ruin a child's self-esteem. "I don't want to take that kind of risk."

"Everything in life is a risk. There are no guarantees. Look at all the broken marriages and separated families. How are you going to know unless you try?"

"Having a child isn't something you can just try. Once you have one, you're committed. I wouldn't want to do to a child what my mother did to me, making me feel unwanted and in the way."

And there it was in a nutshell. Not hatred of children. Not selfishness. But fear. Greg must've sensed the intensity and depth of her fear because he didn't comment further. They both remained silent until he tacked again.

"We're nearing shore and my place." He pointed to a clearing along the Nevada coast. "It's the small log cabin nestled in the woods."

"How quaint. Somehow I can picture you in a log cabin."

"The outdoorsman, right?"

"That's the image," she agreed, thinking he looked the part with his rugged physique and tanned skin.

"You can see my neighbors have upgraded their places."

Surrounding his house were huge two-story homes similar in style to Rhonda's.

"I plan to rebuild someday, but I think I'll wait until I marry. I'm sure my future wife will want her say on the plans."

Monica nodded, wondering wistfully what kind of wife he would choose. "Nice of you to consider that."

"It's small, but okay for one person."

She smoothed her hand along the brass railing, cool from the wind and water. "And you can also use the money you save for your toys, like this boat."

"Guilty," he admitted, laughing.

The conversation remained light until they docked. Monica helped tie down the rigging and unload the ice chests from the boat.

Greg had been correct about the size of the rustic cabin. It suited him, she thought. Its simplicity indicated he had better things to spend his time on than domestic chores.

"How about making an evening of it?" he asked after they'd finished docking the boat. "Would you like to go out to dinner?"

Monica glanced across the lake, with its hues of gold reflecting in the late afternoon sun. She wanted to spend more time with Greg, but should she?

CHAPTER 7

IT HADN'T SURPRISED Greg when Monica refused his dinner invitation. The couple of times during their sail that he'd headed in the direction of more than friendship, he'd been cut off. There were too many differences between them. Besides, they still had business to conduct and settle.

He chuckled to himself. Good enough to sound platonic, but the smell of her hair, the sensations that raced whenever he touched her, the sound of her laughter made a lie of his good intentions.

Greg swerved his car into the parking lot as he searched for a parking place close by. A slight drizzle of rain promised to turn into a full-fledged storm by afternoon. Thankfully they'd had nice weather on Saturday.

Snapping his fingers, he dashed inside and proceeded to the second floor of the agency building. He hoped Darlene hadn't scheduled any meetings since he'd promised Monica he'd discuss her proposal today.

"Morning everyone," he announced to his colleagues as he headed for the coffee pot.

"You're in a good mood," Darlene said, intercepting him. "We'll see how long it lasts. I've got a meeting scheduled to discuss the ski resort they want to build outside the Basin."

Greg groaned. Normally he'd be challenged by the prospect, but those meetings could take hours. "I thought we were going to stay out of it since it isn't within our jurisdiction."

Darlene poured a cup of coffee and handed it to him.

"Seems the board changed their mind. Since the project will impact the Basin's traffic flow, they think we should come up with a public recommendation."

"They're right about the traffic." Greg sipped carefully on the hot liquid. "The resort will accommodate several thousand people. I think they estimated it would bring thirteen thousand more vehicles through the Basin in any given month."

Darlene shook her head. "Sometimes the odds against our success seem insurmountable."

"Cheer up. We have our good moments. And speaking of success, can you cover for me at ten? I have an important meeting." If he called Monica now, she'd have time to get here by then.

Darlene's eyes widened. "You're kidding. The board wants to meet at ten-thirty."

Greg grimaced. "That doesn't give me much time, but I'll take it. A court case is at stake."

"With whom?"

"Monica Scott. I'm almost positive she had planned to sue, but I think I managed to change her mind on Saturday."

Darlene's brows raised. "Saturday, hmmm? This wouldn't be the woman Carl's been talking about?"

Greg remained nonchalant. "The one he met?"

"No. The one *you* met." Darlene's grin teased. "And spent the day sailing with."

Greg didn't respond except to give her a look that said to be serious. "It was all in the line of duty. The woman needed some education."

Darlene laughed. "Sure, and the president is going to budget us millions of dollars."

Greg ignored her gibe and got back to his real concern. "So how about it? Can you cover for me until I finish with her?"

"No problem. I'll tell everyone you're in a meeting."

His desk had folders piled high, and he wanted to have them

cleared off before ten. Since the board was getting together at ten-thirty, he wouldn't be able to take Monica into the conference room. Greg hurried toward his office.

"Let me know how your case works out," Darlene called after him.

"Sure thing," he said before ducking inside.

Carl looked up from his work, already open in front of him. "It's going to be a bear of a day."

"That's what I like about you, Sutton. You have such a positive outlook on life." Greg reached for the phone and dialed Monica's number.

"Come off it. Two minutes in the office and you're on my case."

Greg eyed his friend closely and repented. "Bad weekend with the Kendall niece?"

Before Carl could respond, Monica's low tones captured his total attention, and he turned away from Carl.

"Greg here." He smiled even though she couldn't see it. "Can you come over now? I have a meeting at ten-thirty that's going to last all day. If I'm going to keep my promise, it'll have to be this morning at ten."

"I'll try." She hesitated. "If I can't get there, I'll call and reschedule. Will that be a problem for you?"

"No," he lied. He wanted to see her. "I'll let you go so you can make it."

She agreed and hung up. Greg held on to the receiver a moment longer, as if doing so would keep the contact. He shouldn't care, but he did. After he replaced the receiver, he swung around to face Carl.

"So what happened with Becky?"

Carl made a face. "What a phony. They were all gung-ho as long as I was associated with you or your yacht. As soon as they realized that I was just some poor sucker from a government agency, they dropped me like a hot potato."

"You're being oversensitive again."

Carl shook his head. "I'm telling you, a cold wind off a glacier couldn't have been chillier than Becky was when they took me by my apartment to get changed and pick up my car."

"You could afford something better than that beat-up old Mustang. The road salt has practically eaten it away."

"Blasphemy!" Carl slammed down his fists, sending papers flying. "That car is a classic."

Greg picked up the papers and laughed. "So you didn't score big with the Kendalls."

"Actually, the Kendalls were okay. Becky was the one who was such a snob."

"Then you're better off knowing that up-front. Besides you shouldn't waste time trying to impress on her that you're someone other than the real you."

Carl straightened the papers and frowned. "Don't tell me I'm going to get another sermon about my value as a human being. The fact is, women love money."

"When are you going to realize what a false measure that is? Find a girl who likes you for who you are."

"Don't you have any appointments?"

"Monica is coming by this morning at ten. Can I count on you to split early for the meeting?"

Obviously relieved that Greg wasn't going to continue with the lecture, Carl shrugged. "Sure thing." He sighed. "What a mistake that was, giving her case to you."

"That's the breaks, pal." Greg sat down and started to work. Monica would be there in less than an hour.

At ten, the receptionist phoned to announce his appointment had arrived. He didn't need the call, as the sudden hush in the inner office had already warned him. The only sound that could be heard was the subtle hum of the copy machine. When Carl ushered Mitch Jones into their cubicle, he understood why. What a blow. He was expecting Monica.

"We meet again, Linsey." Jones held out his hand.

Greg refused to accept it, not wanting to waste any time with the man. "What are you doing here?"

Unperturbed, Jones sat down in the chair Greg had set out for Monica. "We have an appointment."

His glance iced over as he glared at Jones. "You're mistaken. I have a scheduled appointment at ten with someone else."

Jones grinned. "I'm Monica Scott's consultant. I was advised to keep the appointment for her."

Greg sank into his chair, his heart thudding as anger surged. How could Monica do this to him?

"We have a proposal." Jones didn't waste time explaining his presence further. "There are several acres of environmentally sensitive land we'll restore for points in order to build on Ms. Scott's property."

His polite business tone sickened Greg. He couldn't believe that Monica had been taken in by this deceiver. He set the papers aside. "I can see what Ms. Scott has to gain from this transaction, but what are you getting out of it?"

"That's irrelevant to the case." Jones pointed to the map of the property. "You can see we also moved the house to the northeast corner of Ms. Scott's property, where you suggested it would be less harmful to the stream."

Greg opened the file and studied the plans and recommendations. They looked feasible, but he hated to admit it. Not to Jones. "From what I can see here, it's a possible solution. However, I'm not giving the final authority on a situation such as this until I've studied it further."

"Come off it, Linsey. You know for a fact this meets your standards."

Greg smiled, satisfied that he could see some of Jones's inner ugliness seeping through the smooth facade. He kept his tone even and calm as he responded, "I have no such knowledge. If you've been keeping up with the news, Jones, you'd know some of these proposals are being contested in court."

"This is sensitive land we're talking about here," Jones said, tapping his finger on the map where the Langford property was located. "You boys would do well to get a piece of this prime lakefront wetland."

It was true. The Tahoe Conservancy would jump at the chance to obtain that site. But something wasn't right here. Jones would never encourage philanthropy unless he stood to make a big profit.

"I'll take it under consideration." Greg made a show of looking at his watch. "I have a meeting now. You'll have to excuse me."

He stood, giving Jones no choice but to leave. Monica had thrown him a fast curve by sending this particular consultant. If they had questions, they could wait until he talked to her personally. He refused to discuss another word with Jones. He schooled his own expression so as not to reveal his distaste.

"I'll get back to you on this."

Jones stood, obviously displeased with the abrupt end to their meeting. "When, Linsey? We need an answer within the week in order to obtain the other permits."

Greg's brows raised this time. What was Jones up to? He stared directly at the consultant. "I'd like to discuss this with Ms. Scott."

"Call *me*, Linsey. I'm handling Ms. Scott's affairs now."

Jones gloated as he made his way to his Cadillac sedan. The Scott broad had made it easy by calling him first thing this morning. Linsey hadn't expected him, nor did he approve of Monica

Scott hiring him. Jones rubbed his hands together. Perfect. Not only was he unloading property at a fat profit, but he was annoying Greg Linsey.

At his car, he greeted Monica.

She stood casual and cool against the back bumper, but concern laced her words. "How'd it go?"

"Get in the car. I'll tell you all about it on our way north."

Jones opened the passenger door. She barely had tucked in her coat when he slammed it shut. On the walk around to his side, he took deep breaths to calm himself. By the time he swung into the driver's seat, a cool smile creased his face.

"Don't worry about a thing." He reached over and patted her fist clenched on the console between them. "These cases are standard."

"You don't have the approval?" she observed.

"Not yet, but there's no need to be alarmed. These matters take time."

"Did Greg sound like there would be any problem with our proposal?"

"Not at all. He wasn't pleased, mind you. They don't like anyone building on an SEZ."

Her questioning glance prompted him to explain. "Stream Environment Zone."

"Right." She nodded. "But our proposal meets their requirements."

"Definitely." *More than enough*, he added to himself.

"Then there should be no problem."

"Technically no, but Linsey is a tough dude."

"You think he might stop us? I knew I should have gone in there with you."

"No, it's better business to let me handle everything." He smiled at her. "After all, that's what you are paying me for."

She took off her glasses and twirled them in her hand. "I

suppose. I didn't figure Greg would object. In fact, I would've thought he'd prefer to work with a consultant, someone he knew."

"Maybe he was in a bad mood today. Don't worry." Let her continue to think Linsey was the ogre. "He's young. Very little experience in dealing with the public. On the other hand, I've had years of experience. Believe me, Linsey will pose no threat to you. I personally know the board chairs, and we'll work out the details. You can be assured of that."

He was lying through his teeth, but she'd never know. As far as she was concerned, he had this case in the bag. And Mitch needed the cash from the sale of the property soon. He knew Monica had it on hand. He'd found out from the bank.

But she continued to stew. "What about the court cases I've heard about? I don't want this deal tied up."

"Not to worry. The developers are initiating the litigation, not the TRPA, which has them reacting cautiously," he explained. "Our case is completely different."

Jones's fists tightened on the steering wheel as he headed north along the shore. "How about the Langford property? Shall we close the deal?"

Jones loosened his hold when Monica nodded. He eased a silent sigh of relief. "Let's stop by the title company. We can draw up the papers this morning."

Exhausted by the time Jones dropped her off at Rhonda's house, Monica was ready for a break. Worn down by the lengthy negotiations, she walked inside, threw off her raincoat, and headed for the phone. She would call Greg and thank him for considering her proposal. Maybe the personal contact would put a positive influence on his decision.

Impatiently, she waited for the series of recordings telling her which number to push in order to speak to the appropriate party. If the frustration of permits didn't have you in a bad mood, waiting for all that nonsense on the phone would put you in one by the time you got a call through.

When the receptionist finally answered, Monica snapped. "I want to speak to Greg Linsey, and please don't put me on another series of recorded messages."

The woman's tone chilled. "Mr. Linsey is unavailable at the moment. May I leave your name and number?"

Monica sighed. "When will he be available?"

The receptionist's tone grew chillier. "He's tied up in meetings all afternoon. Tomorrow he'll be in the field. I suggest you call back Wednesday."

Wednesday! Monica wanted to insist on speaking to Greg, but she knew from the woman's voice that a display of force would get her nowhere. Monica schooled her own voice to sound even and controlled. "Very well. Please tell Mr. Linsey that Monica Scott called and would like to talk to him at his earliest convenience." She'd bet her permit that it would be before Wednesday. Greg had shown too much interest in her to place her on hold.

After putting down the receiver, she glanced at the rain beating against the window. She'd go bonkers before an hour if she sat around the house, but she couldn't leave. If Greg was not in meetings, he might call. If in fact he was tied up, he might get to the phone on a break. She didn't want to take the chance of missing his call.

Snapping up the phone, she punched out Judy's number. "What're you up to?" she asked her neighbor. "I have to wait around for a phone call. How about joining me for a cup of tea?"

"I'd love to." Judy indeed sounded enthused. "Jim's off at a meeting and will be gone all afternoon."

Was the whole male population in a meeting today? With this dreary weather, they might as well be. It was too miserable out to do much else.

Judy entered through the back door, and Monica put the stainless-steel kettle on the stove. "You wouldn't believe my day."

Judy slid onto the barstool. "Give me all the details. I've been bored to tears."

Judy listened attentively as Monica related the events of the morning. The shrill whistle of the kettle interrupted. Monica turned off the stove and slid the teapot and cups across the counter. "I sure hope Greg approves this proposal."

"Your biggest problem could be Jones. I've heard about clashes he's had in the past with the agency."

The scent of raspberry filled the air as Monica opened the canister of flavored tea. "If that's the case, then it's very unprofessional for Greg to take his opinion of a consultant out on me."

"You're right, of course. I do wish that you'd gone to Sean Marston. I've heard so many rumors about Jones."

Monica finished steeping the tea and brought the teapot to the settee where she invited Judy to sit. The fire she'd lit while waiting for her friend crackled in the lava-rock fireplace. Judy held the two teacups while Monica poured.

Had she acted rashly in hiring Jones? She wouldn't admit to Judy that she had. Her hand tightened on the teapot. What had she gotten herself into?

Judy set down the full cups. "I just thought you should know in case there's any conflict." Judy sipped her tea, but kept her gaze on Monica. "How did things go Saturday? I hope there's a little romance developing between you and Greg?"

Monica swung her gaze from Judy and glanced out the window. The wind pounded the rain against the large panes, coming down so hard that she couldn't see the lake. Maybe now was a good time to explain her situation.

"Look, Judy. I know you mean well, but you've got to stop this matchmaking business."

"Why?"

"I'm not interested in forming any romantic relationships."

"How disappointing." Judy pursed her lips. "You know that thinking up liaisons brightens my dreary life."

"Then make them your own. My life is anything but dreary."

"I can't do that. I'm married."

"I'm engaged."

For the first time since Monica had known her, Judy was speechless. Monica hurried to take advantage of the lull.

"At least I was until... Well, until my father died. But it wasn't working out, so we broke it off, at least while he's living in Saudi Arabia."

"How long will that be?"

Monica sipped her tea, seeking the soothing heat and calming aroma. "Another year or two."

"From what I hear about how they treat American women, I can certainly understand not wanting to live in Saudi Arabia. Would any sane woman want to?"

"Yes, it bothers me that us Westerners have to be completely covered and escorted the few times we're allowed out of the compound," Monica said. "Although the Saudi confines aren't what bothers me. Stephen's restrictions are the ones I can't live with. He doesn't want me to pursue a career. He wants me home and waiting on him like a slave."

Judy sipped her tea. "It sounds like prison."

Monica shuddered, thinking of the horrors of pacing in a

house with nothing to do. "But to be fair and honest, it wasn't the living conditions that caused me to break up with Stephen. I've lived in enough foreign countries to know how to adapt. Other women manage fine." Monica shrugged. "I wanted out of the relationship and used the circumstances as my ticket."

Judy set down her cup. "So tell me about Stephen."

"A powerful man. Too powerful. He smothers me."

"He's domineering?"

"Not exactly. He dominates every situation he's in, but not in the usual sense of the word."

Judy sipped on her tea. "When I think domineering, I think headstrong, arrogant, lofty, proud, patronizing, overbearing."

Monica glanced at her friend and wondered if she realized she'd just described Jim. She suspected Stephen would end up like Jim. "Sounds like him."

Judy sat for a moment digesting Monica's revelation. "You mean he always wants his way?"

"Exactly." Monica agreed, thinking how opposite Greg was from Stephen. Greg admired her work, accepted her capabilities.

Judy stood and began to pace. "Chauvinistic men are a real pain. They are so prejudiced and intolerant."

Monica stared at her friend. Was she having problems with Jim? "That's not exactly Stephen. He wants his way, but his way of control is subtle. For example, he gives you everything you'll need so you feel guilty if you don't do things his way. Or he forgives you all the time so you feel guilty if you've done something he doesn't approve of." She couldn't imagine Greg acting like that, but then she didn't know him that well.

Drained from all the emotion, Monica smoothed her hand around the empty teapot.

Judy tucked her feet under her on the sofa and turned to face Monica. "From what I've just heard, I don't understand.

Sounds to me like he's out of the picture."

"He was my father's partner," Monica admitted. "Armand wanted me to marry him."

"Did you promise your father?" Judy looked incredulous.

Monica twisted away from Judy's close scrutiny. She put a pillow on the coffee table and propped her feet on it. "You have no idea what it's like living with two domineering, overbearing men."

"That's the truth," Judy muttered sarcastically. "I wouldn't know. I've only got one."

"I'm serious," Monica insisted as she crossed her legs at the ankle. "It's absolutely unbearable to try and discuss our problems or differences. He thinks because he's rich and handsome, that I should be falling at his feet." Unlike Greg, who had patiently listened to her and hadn't judged. Memories of their day on the sailboat warmed the chill caused by thoughts of Stephen.

"I know many women who would give their eyeteeth for a man like that."

Monica bristled. "Let the others have him then. I can't stand to be around someone that makes me feel so small and petty."

"No one is perfect, Monica. I don't think anyone expects that. Does Stephen really expect that from you?"

"Yes. That's the terrible part. He insists that I'm wonderful, bright, caring, but then doesn't allow me to act on my own. It's crazy."

Judy remained silent, and Monica wondered if she'd hurt her friend's feelings. After all, Judy was married to such a man.

"I'm sorry, Judy. I shouldn't go on about him. He is a good man. Hopefully he'll find someone that will make him a wonderful wife."

Like her mother had made Armand happy. She had bowed to his wishes, meek and submissive. She didn't have a life, except what Armand allowed her to have. He'd tried to treat

Monica that way, but she had rebelled. She supposed that was why Armand had always taken her with him and kept her away from her mother.

"It sounds like you tried."

Monica rubbed at her throbbing temples. "Every time I gave in to Stephen and followed his way, I felt like I was losing something of myself. It scared me, as if my identity was no longer Monica Scott."

"How could you stop being yourself?" Judy leaned forward, her forehead creased in concern. "It seems such an exaggerated fear."

Monica stared at Judy. Didn't she realize she kowtowed to Jim until she had no identity of her own? Just like her mother had done with Armand.

Monica stared blankly out the window. *Is it Stephen who frightens you, or the word 'submission,' Child?* Her mother's voice echoed in her mind. An icy finger of uneasiness trickled down Monica's spine. She would not lose her identity for anyone. She would be independent, on her own.

Judy broke the spell. "You're stronger than I am," she admitted. "I haven't the nerve to resist Jim."

Monica shook her head. It was a mistake to have tried explaining the situation to Judy. She should've said she was engaged and ended the conversation there. But no, she had to rationalize. Now all she had as a reward for her efforts was a confused friend and a throbbing headache.

She glanced at the clock on the wall. It was close to five. "Greg won't be calling now. He's probably getting ready to head out of the office."

Judy followed Monica's glance and gasped. "Good grief. Jim will be home and wanting dinner. I'd better run."

Monica escorted Judy out and gratefully shut the door behind her friend. At least she didn't have to pander to a man in this present state of agonizing pain. Judy's marriage only substantiated Monica's stand. Once you gave in to the authority of another, you lost control of your own actions. She was much better off being alone, where she could eat what and when she liked. The way she felt now, she probably wouldn't eat at all.

The pain in her head pounded. A migraine was on its way. Aspirin wasn't going to help.

Through the throbbing ache, Monica heard the doorbell ringing. Or was it her head? All she could think about was stretching out on the couch. Blindly she moved toward the door and opened it. Wind and rain rushed in with the man who entered.

"What kind of game do you think you're playing?"

The harsh voice cut through the pain, and Monica focused on Greg Linsey.

CHAPTER 8

HIS JACKET spattered with raindrops, Greg stood in the foyer glaring at Monica.

She closed the door. "This is a surprise. What brings you this far north?"

"I came to find out why you'd pull a stunt like sending Mitch Jones to my office. That was a low blow, Monica, when I thought we at least had formed a bond of respect."

His words came harsh and fast, which didn't help the pounding in her head. "I have no idea what you're talking about. I thought you would be glad to know I'd hired a consultant."

"Consultant," Greg snarled, as if it were a dirty word. "How can you give a man like Jones that much credit?"

In spite of her headache, Monica was beginning to get an inkling of the problem. Judy had been right. "It's Jones, isn't it? Have you two tangled before?" That would explain many things about Jones's attitude as well.

Rain drizzled off the porch outside. Greg shifted, obviously wanting to be invited to come in and sit down. Monica remained in the foyer. She had no intention of listening to much more.

"It appears we have a conflict of interest here. Unless you have information about my deal, maybe you'd better leave."

"You're not getting off that easy." Greg took a step nearer, bringing him closer than Monica found comfortable. "You have some explaining to do."

Monica stood her ground against his authoritarian attitude. How could she have misjudged this man and, worse, confided in him last Saturday? He'd caught her at a weak moment. She never had talked about children before. His behavior today proved she should never have done so. "It appears I've already done too much explaining. We have nothing further to discuss."

She opened the door and sidestepped, hoping he would leave before the increasing waves pounding in her head went beyond control. She could barely see as she staggered away from the door.

Suddenly strong hands had hold of her waist, steadying her. Greg's voice seemed to come from a distance, yet she knew he was right there. Concerned tones began to soothe some of the ache.

As soon as Greg saw Monica stagger, his anger disappeared. "What's the matter?" Greg steadied her with his hands.

Her facial muscles were tense as she moaned. She stumbled again, and this time he reached down and grasped behind her knees to lift her in his arms. He walked into the living room and lay her on the long couch.

As soon as he let go, she clasped her hands at the sides of her head. Her forehead lined with furrows, she moaned again.

He gently pulled her hands away and began to massage her temples and the base of her neck. "Do you get migraines often?" His mother had them occasionally.

When she didn't respond, he thought she hadn't heard his question. Pain did that. After several seconds she looked at him and said, "I don't get them often, but when I do…" Her voice trailed off. Pain reflected in her amber eyes.

"Just relax. I know how to take care of this."

Closing her eyes, she leaned back into the pillows. Greg forgot about why he'd driven up here as he concentrated on helping her through the pain. Slowly, the tension in her muscles relaxed. Satisfied his efforts were working, he smiled down at her.

"This is a new one on me," he told her. "You've scared me enough to diffuse my anger."

"I think I forgot mine too." Her lips curved into a slight smile.

"Let's take advantage of the truce." He massaged her temples again, which silenced any protest. "We had something going last Saturday, the basis of a friendship. I don't think we ought to let that go."

He wanted more than friendship, especially after sitting this close to her. The warmth from her body, the hint of her perfume, and the softness of her hair teased his senses. He could feel the stirrings of desire.

"I don't think it matters what we want." Her voice was sultry and low. "We're in a position of conflict."

"It doesn't have to be that way."

She sat up and slid down the couch past him. Swinging her feet to the floor, she leaned forward and faced him. "Doesn't it?"

"I care about you, Monica. I don't want to see you involved with a scam artist like Jones."

"He came up with solutions, Greg."

"You didn't give me much of a chance. Besides, I can't make any recommendations like you proposed before I've carefully calculated your points."

"But the proposal could give me the points?" She studied him.

Greg kept his expression open. "Probably, but it'll be expensive."

"The money is no problem. I want to build—hang the cost."

Greg frowned but didn't argue further.

"Are you hungry or would you like a drink?"

He readily accepted her change of subject. "Yes to both. Can I help?"

"Mix whatever you want to drink. Go ahead and fix some cheese and crackers."

"Sounds like a plan." He snapped his fingers. "What are you drinking?"

"Perrier and lime." She pointed to the basket of green fruit.

The soda water bubbled in their glasses. Lime juice squirted as he sliced it. He deftly sliced pieces of cheddar and arranged them on a wooden tray. When he finished, he carried the tray and drinks into the living room. Without asking, he stoked the fire. When he sat down, he surveyed the peaceful setting, not wanting to disturb it, but he knew that he must. She could do what she wanted with the proposal, but he had to warn her about dealing with Jones. If she knew the facts, she could make her own decisions about the man. From the little he'd learned about Monica, he felt her values would not condone what Jones stood for. At least he hoped he'd read her correctly.

"Without getting into an argument over this, let me tell you some things about Mitch Jones." He held up his hands to ward off the beginnings of a protest. "I'm not going to tell you what to do about him. Hear me out. That's all I ask."

She studied the contents of her glass for a moment, then leveled her gaze at him. "I'll listen, but you must realize that I consider your comments about Jones to be biased."

He held back a snide response and nodded in agreement. "I'll concede to that. It'll be enough if you keep your mind open."

She nodded before biting down on a cracker. "Believe me, I don't want my headache to return. I'll simply listen."

The reminder of her headache was a subtle hint to keep the conversation level. He wasn't sure if he could remain calm while discussing the consultant, but he would try.

"Jones has been involved in several shady deals."

"Then why hasn't he been arrested?"

"Because they've been activities that barely slide within the law."

From her expression, he could see that she found no fault in that. "Sometimes laws restrict more than they help. Sometimes they don't accomplish what they intended. I see nothing wrong with taking a law to its limit."

"Even at the expense of others?" he challenged.

"Of course not. Only if no one is hurt." She sipped her drink, remaining as cool as the chilled glass. "Proceed. I'll try not to interrupt again."

Placing a chunk of cheese on a cracker, he considered her carefully. She sat strong and immobile now. She'd certainly recovered from her headache and earlier weakness.

"First off, Jones favors clients who don't know the area. He promises to get them through all the red tape and hassles, which is advisable. However, what an outsider doesn't realize is that Jones tacks on extremely high costs to the already big expense of building in this area."

"He charged me a fee, but I didn't consider it unreasonable. After all, the man has to make a living."

"I'm not talking about the up-front fee. Let me give you an example. Say the sewage permit costs ten grand; he'll charge you twenty or thirty."

She shook her head. "He can't do that to me. I've already applied for the permits myself. I know the cost. He knows I've been handling the permits and already am aware of the actual cost. He would be foolish to try that."

Greg ate another piece of cheese on a cracker and considered that news. "Do you really want to do business with a man who pads his accounts?"

The aromatic wood chips scented the room as she considered his question. Greg didn't rush her. The snap of the fire crackling brought her attention back to him. "Is he really so bad? I mean, if people do their homework, they won't be cheated."

"How is a busy entrepreneur from New York going to know if he's charging the correct fee?"

"They can call your office and find out." She played with the cracker, apparently not really hungry. "Maybe they have the money and don't want to be bothered with the details, so they would rather pay the extra. Jones is only cashing in on what people allow."

"You have a point, but it doesn't excuse the dishonest tactics Jones uses. When someone from out of state already knows that permit fees are high in this area, they may not think to question Jones's price."

"Here we are back to research again."

Her response annoyed him. He used every ounce of his willpower to keep his irritation from showing. "And you're willing to play the fool and pay?" he asked, his voice steady and quiet.

Monica jumped up and glared down at him. "My father's success is a testimony to the integrity of my business dealings. I resent you sitting here and accepting my hospitality, all while accusing me of being a fool."

Greg stood, set his glass down, and faced her. "I know you're not a fool, but at the same time I don't want anyone else to call you one either. Jones is not to be trusted. You have to understand that."

Monica bent and picked up his empty glass. At first he thought she was dismissing him, but she went into the kitchen to refill his drink. Greg sat back down. He was not going to leave until he'd told her everything.

She returned and handed him his glass along with an icy glare.

He waited until she was seated before saying, "Jones is involved in a coalition here in the Basin which is dedicated to thwarting every move of the TRPA. They've held us up in court more times than I can count."

"Your agency wields power. Wouldn't it be wise to keep a form of checks and balances?"

He'd heard this argument many times before. "To a degree you are correct, but not when every action hinders progress."

He sipped his fresh drink. "We've been working extremely hard to keep our image clean. But Jones and his coalition use their power for money in their pockets."

"Oh, come now. Don't you think you're overreacting?"

"No." He congratulated himself on his control. "I'm talking about property owners and investors whose only interest is getting as much profit as they can squeeze out of their clients."

She was about to argue, but he held up his hands to stop her and hurried on to explain. "I'm talking about people like those who want to build in an area that has a water shortage every summer at peak season and an area that is suffering from the threat of air pollution."

He paused to take a breath, but before she could interrupt, he went on. "There are pressures by this group to bring in fast-food chains, commercial developers who want to build huge malls, and we haven't even touched on the casinos."

Monica lifted her hands in protest. "Look, I'm not out to ruin the environment, build a mall, or bring in more tourists. I sympathize with your point of view, but it doesn't have anything to do with what I'm trying to accomplish."

He waited for her to continue, but she remained silent, her brow furrowed into a frown. "Have you changed your thinking about Jones?" he asked.

"Let's just say I've been warned. I'm not going to make any rash decisions right now. There's too much at stake." She studied him. "What I really want to know is if you will approve the proposal."

He lowered his gaze and stared at the ice cubes. "I can't tell you that until the review is completed."

"But the proposal to restore the stream looks good?"

He hesitated to admit it. "Yes, it's very sensitive land. We'll probably accept the restoration project."

"Then if that's settled, I'm satisfied." She stood.

He stood too, anger flashing from his eyes.

"You're going to go ahead with this, aren't you? It doesn't matter to you what happens to the stream or the surrounding area. You could care less about the Tahoe Basin. All you want is your own way." He waved his hands in the air. "You'll build in spite of the cost. You'll sell the place and take your profit and leave. Screw the people you leave behind. Maybe Jones isn't such a poor bet for you after all. You both think alike."

Spinning around, he banged his glass on the bar and stomped out of the house, slamming the door behind him.

Monica remained frozen to the spot where Greg had left her. She didn't move until she'd heard the roar of his car's engine. His tires squealed on the highway as he tore down the road. His attack numbed her senses.

Remorse battled with common sense. He had no right to accuse her of those things. She did care about the environment. After all, it wasn't as if she were building something cheap and ugly. She had a right to construct a work of art. It would become a valuable landmark. Not every area boasted an original by Armand Scott.

But the anger and disappointment she'd seen in Greg's eyes haunted her. Could she be wrong? Was she being selfish? Was he right about Jones?

Monica entered Jones's office, but instead of being impressed by the plush décor, she eyed it with suspicion. Did the expensive furnishings testify to Greg's accusations? The doubts that Greg had planted last night reappeared. No. She shook them off. She was doing the right thing. She was sure of it. Greg was speaking for the TRPA. She respected him for that, but she had a house to build, and Jones could make that happen.

"Good morning, Ms. Scott." The secretary was her usual cordial self. "You're looking ready for business."

"I'm hoping to start building soon," Monica asserted with feeling.

The young woman ignored her comment and instead looked out the window at the view of the blue sky reflected in the lake. "It's a nice day. We need the rain, though."

"I know. To water the trees," Monica responded, wondering if Greg had been talking to this woman.

The secretary smiled. "It keeps the watershed level up also," she added before she announced Monica's presence to Jones.

Just what she needed, Monica thought, another environ-mentalist.

Jones's voice came through on the intercom. "Send her in, please. And bring us some coffee."

"Tea for me, please," Monica requested as she followed the secretary into the larger office.

Jones greeted her jovially, or was it over-eagerness? Was

Greg correct in his assessment of this man? Monica gave herself an inner shake. *Stop listening to Greg Linsey*, she scolded herself. With effort, Monica forced a smile and sat down on the chair Jones offered.

Jones sat in the chair opposite in the sitting area in front of the Swedish fireplace. If it was his way of assuring her there were no pressures here, the message didn't come across. Monica could sense tension in him. The cause of his unease was difficult to guess.

Neither said a word as they waited for the secretary to serve the coffee and tea. When she left the room, Jones sipped his. Monica left her cup on the table.

"About the Langford property," she said, studying him for a reaction. "Some interesting questions have been raised. I don't want to purchase that land without proof that it can be approved as an option."

If Jones was tense when she arrived, it didn't compare with what emanated from him now. With controlled precision, he flipped the lid of the inlaid box that matched the one on his desk and took out a fresh cigar. The smell of tobacco wafted across the small space. His smile didn't reach his eyes when he lifted his gaze from the box to her. "Your proposal will be approved. I talked to the president of the board of the TRPA earlier this morning." He rolled the cigar in his fingers, and this time his eyes gleamed when he looked at her.

That news should have pleased Monica, but the thought of Greg being bypassed didn't appeal. At this point, Monica didn't want to contemplate why.

Jones continued talking. "Linsey knows the Langford property, and I could tell from the way he was talking that they would do about anything for that piece of land."

"Why is that?" She had an idea it had to do with the battle Judy mentioned earlier. Jones confirmed her suspicion.

"The original owners brought heavy lawsuits against the TRPA. They're one of the cases that caused enough controversy to put the agency in a state of disarray for a couple of years."

Which explained Greg's anger that she'd hired Jones. It had nothing to do with her. "It also created a few changes in policy, I understand."

Jones's eyes narrowed. "So you've heard about the case?"

"The Myerses gave me some basic background on it."

She wasn't sure, but it seemed Jones's tension eased slightly. Why? she wondered.

He leaned back and said, "You know then that there was no fondness, shall we say, between the TRPA Board and the Langfords. Having the deed restriction on that property would be like a minor victory for the TRPA."

"A case of poetic justice."

"Exactly." He smiled, and this time it reached his eyes.

"The Langfords are out of the picture now. What would your role in all of this be?"

"Let's just say I enjoy poetic justice as well."

"Or a neat profit," she countered.

His expression hardened. "A good businessman always looks for gain. You should be aware of that fact, Ms. Scott."

She refused to back down. "Just so it's not at my expense. I see no need to pay an inflated price."

"Are you accusing me of something?" His voice was low and menacing.

Monica didn't like to be duped, yet she needed that piece of land in order to develop an acceptable restoration project. "Of course not, Mr. Jones. As you yourself said, good businessmen and women keep their own interests at heart. I'm after a bargain. You're after a profit. I see no problem with that." She shrugged. "Just so long as the terms remain amenable to both sides."

"If you feel the deal is imbalanced, then let us renegotiate.

I wouldn't want it said that a customer of mine wasn't happy with our dealings. Or..." He paused and twirled the cigar. "We could always call the whole thing off. If you don't feel it's to your benefit to buy the property, then don't."

Monica studied the tense muscle corded in his neck. His nonchalance was a phony show, of that she was certain. She had to hand it to him, though. His style was shrewd and to the point. He'd called her bluff.

"We both know I need the property. The question is, how badly do you want to sell it?"

His laughter filled the room, yet there was nothing humorous about it. "You do get down to brass tacks don't you, Ms. Scott? I like that in a business partner."

"We're not partners yet," she reminded him.

"But I'd like to be." He slapped his knee with his empty hand. "I'll tell you what. Since you think I'm after too much profit, let's knock off twenty grand and call it a deal."

"Fifty and you're on."

His hesitation barely registered. "It's a deal. The papers are drawn, but it'll only take a few moments to change the figures."

Jones stood and crossed his office to poke his head out the door. He could've used the intercom, but he had to release some of the tension. He'd been bested by the clever little b—

His secretary's voice cut into his fury. "Yes, Mr. Jones?"

"Bring the contract we typed up for Ms. Scott. I want to make some changes."

He spun around in time to catch the triumphant grin on Monica's face. He struggled with an urge to wipe it off. Blast the woman for getting cold feet. Or had it all been a show? It wouldn't surprise him to discover Linsey had put her up to this.

No. Linsey would have told her the restoration project wasn't necessary. He'd tell her she could buy the points for a lot less than she was paying by doing it his way. Buying points wouldn't give Mitch any profit. Selling the land would. Fifty thousand was going to cover the payment due on Friday, but it wouldn't give him the cushion he was hoping for. If Scott had gone lower he would've been in a jam. It had been a calculated risk to offer to back out of the deal. If Monica had taken him up on it, he would've been a goner. However, he had one ace up his sleeve, and she had called it. She still thought she needed his land.

His secretary walked in, bringing his tension level down.

It only took minutes to instruct his secretary to make the necessary changes. He turned his attention back to Monica.

"The sooner we close this, the faster we can present it to the TRPA. You can have your permit within a week."

Her smile reassured him. "That's the best news I've heard in ages. Mr. Jones, we have a deal."

Not quite, he thought as he accepted the handshake she offered. "There is the matter of payment. Can you write a check today?"

He thought she was going to retreat when she tried to pull her hand back, but he held it firm. "The paperwork moves faster when cash is involved."

"I see." She paused as if to reconsider. "How about half now and half at closing?"

"No way. I need to grease a few palms in the county office. Before I put my reputation on the line, I want to be certain of the sale."

"What are my guarantees?"

Jones walked over to the phone and held the receiver out to her. "Call the director of the TRPA now. He'll confirm your approval for a trade-off."

He held his breath while she considered. If she dialed the agency, the deal could be delayed if not cancelled. He made a show of glancing at his watch. "Look, if you need more time to consider this, we can wrap it up later. I have a meeting to go to and then some urgent business at the South Shore that'll tie me up for a couple of weeks. Do you want to make an appointment for…" He cast a meaningful glance at his secretary. "Go check my calendar and see if we have an opening in two or three weeks."

Monica held up her hand for the woman to stop. "I can't wait that long. I'll write you a check. Bring me the papers, and let's close this today."

A triumphant grin creased Mitch's features as he signaled to his secretary to bring the amended contract to the conference table at the other end of the room.

"Now there's a smart woman who knows how to handle business." He guided her to the conference table, forcing himself not to rush her. When she paused in front of the papers, he gripped the back of her chair to keep from forcing her to sit and sign them.

She turned to face him. "You're sure about the agency's approval?"

"Of course. You know where to find me if there's any trouble," he said, although there wouldn't be a thing she could do to him. He'd have his money and the payment made on his project. The problem would be hers.

As if she'd read his thoughts, she wrapped her arms in front of her chest and leveled a glare at him. "Don't cross me, Mr. Jones. I make a miserable enemy."

In spite of the fact that he knew she couldn't legally do a thing to him, he felt a cold chill at her words.

"Threats? At a time like this?" Forcing a smile, he avoided

Monica's eyes and waved at the secretary. "We need to celebrate. Bring the champagne and glasses along with the papers."

"I don't drink," Monica announced, pulling the chair away from the table. "Let's get on with this. You have an appointment, and I have things to do as well."

"As you wish." Jones nodded to his secretary to join them as a witness to the signing. Relieved, he finally seated Monica and sat next to her, pointing out the contents of the contract.

Jones tried to keep his cool when she stopped near the end and asked about the clause regarding the environmental agencies. "That doesn't concern you since you're not planning to build on this property."

A frown creased her brow. "This information wasn't on my father's bill of sale for my property."

"It's a recent requirement. Legally we have to inform our clients of the restrictions before they sign for property. That way they won't encounter unexpected surprises as you have done."

Her steady gaze unnerved him. She had no way of knowing that he didn't always disclose that information, especially to out-of-state clients.

"I'm glad to hear you do that. Some people might accuse you of taking advantage of clients otherwise."

"Which is exactly why I cover all the bases."

He wasn't sure what it was he'd said that eased her mind, but she relaxed and began to sign on the dotted line. He didn't give a care what it was; he was too relieved to see her name scrawled out across the pages. When she'd signed the check, a twenty-pound load lifted off his shoulders.

He didn't have to force a cheerful mood now. He smiled at Monica. "You won't regret this. Just think of how much you'll be contributing to the environment by restoring this land. You'll be a heroine in the eyes of the community."

"I don't need accolades, Mr. Jones. I need permits. When can you get them to me?"

"Call me at the end of the week. I'll have definite dates by then."

"I thought you were going to be away."

"From my desk. My secretary will know how to get in touch at all times."

"Very well." She shook his outstretched hand. "I'll call you later."

"And I won't be answering," he muttered, waving her check in the air as she exited the room. "I don't need you anymore, Monica Scott."

CHAPTER 9

WATER SLAPPED against the pilings of the pier where Monica sat having lunch with Judy. In spite of the late afternoon hour, several diners were at the other tables situated on Jim Myers's boat dock. Two speedboats, one canoe, and one sailboat were tied to the dock while their passengers ate at the famous restaurant.

It didn't matter what time of day she came to the Myerses's restaurant—a crowd always gathered, especially on the weekends. Not only was the setting on the pier unique and the food excellent, but the Myerses were very popular. Because of that, Monica would wait until they were done eating before discussing her problems with her friend. She didn't want any of the conversation overheard.

Monica barely tasted the gourmet sandwich, even though it looked inviting. Normally, the unseasonably warm breeze enticed a case of spring fever. She barely noticed. Worry and anger tumbled in her mind.

"What's the matter?" Judy asked after she'd finished her meal and sat watching Monica pick at hers. "You've barely touched your food. I know it's not the chef because that's your favorite sandwich."

"It's delicious," Monica assured her. "I have too many things on my mind."

"And you can't give them up for an hour to enjoy our famous avocado special?"

Monica eyed the nearly whole sandwich and leaned back in her canvas deck chair. "Will you forgive me if I don't finish?"

Judy reached across the table and patted her hand. "It's you I'm worried about, not the sandwich. You've barely eaten a thing for the last two days. You look pale and tense. Are you going to tell me what's wrong?"

Monica glanced at the table closest to them and indicated why she couldn't.

Judy understood immediately. "No problem. Since we're done here, let's go on over to my place."

Monica shook her head. "I don't want to sit around talking." She'd been doing enough sitting this past week. "I need to move."

"How about a drive? We could buzz down to Reno or Sacramento for some shopping."

"It's too late for that. Besides, we'd be right in the middle of the mass exodus back to the city."

Judy pretended to pout. "Sometimes you're too practical, Monica. Where's your spirit of adventure?"

"Being totally wasted by unwarranted delays and red tape."

"My point exactly. What you're really wasting is this gorgeous day." She started to gather her purse and other belongings off the table. "I'll take you somewhere I'll bet you've never been. It will be a surprise."

"The last thing I feel like doing is playing tourist," Monica protested, yet nevertheless began collecting her things.

"You'll love it. We'll see some interesting scenery and while I drive, you can tell me what's on your mind."

"Do you charge for psychology sessions?" Monica teased.

"But of course." Judy winked before bending her head to sign the check. "I charge extra for those that are combined with sightseeing. I guarantee you one thing, though. You are going to love the sights."

Monica placed her napkin on the table. "I've already been around the lake several times. You've dragged me through most of the historic museums and state parks. I know the area well enough."

"Nonsense. This is somewhere new." Judy stood and motioned for Monica to follow.

During the summer season, Judy buzzed around in her sky-blue convertible. Before they took off she lowered the roof. Monica smiled. The fresh air would clear the cobwebs spinning in her head.

Judy handed her a sporty cap to cover her hair, tucking her own into a scarf. "Get ready, because we're going to cruise."

The sights were familiar at first as they drove along the lakeshore to Tahoe City, then on to one of the few highways out of the Basin. Judy kept going straight at the "Y" and cruised along the Truckee River. The snowmelt raised the lake level, and the waters flowed fast and deep.

"Enjoy the view now." Judy pointed to the river. "Next month there'll be hundreds of people rafting to River Ranch."

Monica gave the rushing water a cursory glance and retreated into her thoughts.

Stephen had called last night, and they'd talked for over an hour. She had begun her end of the conversation with an account of the problems she'd run into. He'd finished up with an appeal for her to drop everything and meet him in Spain.

"We can rent a couple of villas by the sea." He'd lured her with her favorite resort. "We need to talk things over, rethink your plans."

Not ready to discuss things like commitment to a lifestyle she was sure she couldn't handle, she had declined.

His words echoed in her head as the breeze tugged at her hair. She wished she had her father to talk to. He would understand her frustration with the building project. But he'd side with Stephen on the issue of marriage. He wanted to see his daughter married and secure, but Monica couldn't love Stephen.

You always put your husband first, Child. Just like I do with your father. Her mother's words echoed from the past.

But did you love Armand? Weren't you just a convenience to him? I can't be the type of woman you were, Mother. I don't need Stephen.

True, Stephen promised a return for commitment: security, anything and everything she could ever want. He would provide, she knew that. So why did that seem so hard to accept?

Judy's voice cut into her thoughts. "Okay. We're out of town and away from people. What gives? Out with it, friend. I'm about to burst with curiosity."

In spite of her inner turmoil, Monica had to chuckle. "You're just what I needed, that's for sure. No messing around with small talk."

"We had enough of that at lunch, where, I might point out, I was the only one contributing to the conversation. You've been a million miles away."

No, just the other side of the globe in Saudi Arabia, she silently admitted. She wouldn't discuss Stephen with Judy. "It's the TRPA. They're holding up my permits again."

"I thought you and Mitch Jones had that all cleared up."

Monica choked. "You aren't the only one who thought that. It appears Mitch Jones lied about a few details. Like approval of the proposal." Her hands clenched into fists every time she thought about that double-dealer.

"I warned you about him. You should have listened to me and gone to see Sean Marston. At least he's honest."

Judy's reminder didn't improve Monica's mood. "I hated admitting that I needed a consultant."

"So you went to Jones. Monica, that doesn't make sense."

"At the time it seemed a logical solution. Jones promised

me what I wanted, and I was impatient," she explained, then sighed. "It doesn't matter now. The thing is, I may be stalled for another month. The TRPA Board and Conservancy have to get together and review my application for restoration before any action can be taken."

Judy glanced over at her. "That sounds perfectly logical. Surely you knew they'd do that?"

"Jones implied that the proposal was approved. He indicated that he'd spoken to someone influential on the board."

"And this person isn't one with clout?" Judy guessed.

Monica stared at the scenery as they whizzed past. "It's worse than that. Jones didn't talk to anyone at all."

The car swerved slightly when Judy turned to stare at Monica. "He lied to you?"

"Watch the road." Monica braced herself on the dash. "Not only that, he lied about the restoration project being the only alternative. It appears that I could have bought the points I need outright."

"Wouldn't that be expensive?"

"Fifty grand at the most." Monica still couldn't believe that Jones had pulled this move and, worse, that she had fallen for it.

"Isn't that what the restoration project is going to cost you?" Judy eased around the tight curve.

"I have to buy the points for the same amount, whether I pay cash for them or put the fifty thousand into a restoration project."

"So what's the big deal?"

Monica's knuckles turned white as she sat for several seconds waiting for her anger to subside. "The big deal is that I didn't need that piece of property. Jones didn't tell me about the cash option because he wanted to unload the Langford place. At a fat profit, I might add."

Sighing, Judy shook her head. "No wonder you're upset. Can you take action against Jones?"

"Not really. He didn't do anything illegal." Monica clenched her fists in her lap. Thank goodness Armand wasn't around to witness her blunder. "If only I hadn't been in such a hurry."

"Don't tell me that a woman as smart as you didn't investigate all the possibilities." Judy rounded another curve and glanced at Monica. "I don't believe it. Barracuda Scott slipped up."

Monica lowered her head, remorse mingled with her anger. "Thanks, Judy. I really needed the supportive comments." Then her defenses swung into gear. "And what's this barracuda business?"

Judy grinned. "That's what you remind me of—one of those New York dynamos. You know. Out for the kill. A shark that'll eat anything in its path."

"Lovely character description. I thought we were friends," she commented, not particularly liking the comparison to a barracuda. Hadn't Stephen made that same reference once or twice? "You may consider me all those things, but I played the fool this time."

Judy continued driving the winding mountain road. "I say that with all respect. I admire the toughness in you, Monica. I wish I had some of your backbone."

Monica silently agreed that Judy succumbed much too often to the selfish demands of her husband. "I was so anxious to show Greg Linsey that I could get my way that I became overly zealous with my dealings with Jones."

That hurt too. Monica prided herself in her meticulous care when signing contracts. It rankled that she'd been duped so easily. She should have listened to Greg.

Silence fell as they passed River Ranch, where most of the rafters disembarked. Judy pointed out the famous resort that boasted a large deck-restaurant where friends and tourists watched the adventurous rafters float through the most difficult rapids of the otherwise mellow trip. She'd been like those rafters, floating along thinking everything was going well when—boom—the rapids tumbled them out of their complacency.

Judy drove across a bridge so that the river was now on her side of the road. Monica tried to catch glimpses of it through the thick forest. The sparkle of water in the woods reminded her of Greg. "The river looks so pristine and peaceful. I suppose it has ecological controversy surrounding it also."

Judy swerved to miss a squirrel that had run out into the road. "What doesn't around here? The river supplies water to Reno. What's left of it ends up in a dead-end lake that the Paiute Indians control."

"So there's conflict between the city and the Indians," Monica guessed.

"That doesn't affect us directly. However, during a dry season, not as much water flows out of the lake. Reno can't use as much as they need. Some has to flow to keep the environment of Pyramid Lake sound."

She wondered if the TRPA was involved in this issue as well. Did Greg work to protect the ecology of the river? "So Reno gets shorted when the water is low?"

Judy nodded. "There has been some talk of pumping water from the lake. The idea is always shot down as there's no widespread public interest. Most people want to preserve Lake Tahoe. They only object when it might cost them personally."

Monica stared at Judy, amazed that she was so informed. She'd never heard her friend talk about anything other than shopping and Jim. "You sound like Greg."

Judy smiled. "Environmentalists say if Reno can't be assured of water, they shouldn't continue to build. Of course that doesn't stop the developers."

Greg's words came back to haunt her. "They want their

profit no matter at whose expense."

"That's what they say," Judy agreed and then brought the subject back to their earlier conversation. "So what are you going to do about your problem with the agency?"

"I've been asking myself the same question for the last two days. I've vacillated from wanting to chuck the whole thing to dragging Jones into court."

"Do you have a case against him?"

"No, and that's why I won't choose that route." Her father made a point of staying out of the court system. He would always find a way to work problems out. "I need to think of something. I refuse to let him get away with this."

"I know some good attorneys."

Automatically, she started to respond that she didn't need Judy's help, and then closed her mouth before uttering the protest. She should have listened to Judy before. Her friend's recommendation just might come in handy. She could swallow her pride if it meant nailing Jones.

"Why don't you talk to that good-looking planner?"

She yearned to do that. "He's not very happy with me at the moment."

He'd warned her about Jones. Wouldn't he love to gloat over the fact that she'd been taken for a ride? No. Greg was not like Stephen. He would be concerned, which was why she really wanted to talk to him about this. She simply didn't know how.

Judy slowed at an intersection. They were nearing Truckee. Monica refocused her attention on Judy. "I will get my revenge. I haven't figured out how, but there is no doubt in my mind that I will."

"I don't have any more ideas. You know me. I haven't any sense when it comes to business. That's Jim's department. When we get home you can ask him." Judy spoke as she crossed down a busy street lined with antique storefronts. "For now, we're going to forget business. Wait until you see these shops."

Monica eyed what looked like a frontier town. She wished Judy wouldn't put herself down. "This place looks like it belongs to the last century. There's no place to shop here."

Judy pulled into a parking spot. "Truckee was an old turn-of-the-century railroad town. The town council got together and planned the restoration of these historic buildings. Now they have boutiques that you are going to love."

Much to her surprise, Monica enjoyed the unique shops. The purchase of a hand-knit sweater coat made of fine wool and dyed a subtle dusty rose assuaged some of her bad mood. A carved sculpture caught her eye as well. It would be attractive in the entryway of Rhonda's house. Monica wanted to purchase something special for the use of the house, and she was delighted to find the perfect gift.

The afternoon passed quickly as Monica and Judy shopped in the quaint town. By the time they headed home, traffic to Tahoe City was building up.

"Let's go through Kings Beach. It's faster," Judy recommended.

Weekenders on their way home created heavy traffic coming in the opposite direction from the lake. The traffic lightened in their direction. Judy zipped past the airport and Martis Creek flats and drove up the mountain pass in minutes.

Since they made good time, their conversation remained light. The rush of the wind drowned out their voices at high speeds. On the steep decline into the Basin, Judy slowed down and pointed to some improved areas of Kings Beach that contrasted sharply with areas that should have been condemned long ago. "They've done a lot of restoration in this area, too. They want to make this place a tourist attraction like Truckee did. Bring in boutiques and the arts."

"I can see the advantages to that," Monica conceded. Some

of the renovated places were quite attractive.

Judy braked and swerved off to a side road. "This place might interest you," she explained. "See that old resort?"

Several large buildings sat amidst ponderosa pine trees. The architecture alone dated them to the turn of the century, as well as the faded cedar paneling still boasting the shredded bark—a structural feature that must have been popular at the time. She'd seen it on a few old homes in the area.

"The Ponderosa Inn is the oldest resort in the Basin. Quite a historical landmark."

In spite of the run-down condition of the place there were cars parked in the lot. "Is it still operating?"

Judy nodded.

"It looks like it should be a museum."

Judy laughed. "A developer bought it and plans to tear it down."

That made sense to Monica. The property had tremendous potential. It included a small golf course and fronted the lake, a large acreage to work with.

Judy drove through the resort as she continued to explain. "There's a coalition forming to prevent the change."

Monica couldn't relate to that. She preferred the challenge of creating something new.

Judy stopped and held her hands in an inclusive gesture. "Mitch Jones."

Monica tensed. "Where? Do you see him?"

Judy shook her head. "I thought that name would interest you. He's the one who plans to develop this place."

"How revolting. Suddenly the place loses its appeal."

Judy laughed. "Okay, I get the hint. We're out of here." She easily swung the sports car around and headed back toward the highway.

"I hate to see him succeed with the project, especially after hearing how he's conducted business with you," Judy commented. "Unfortunately, we have our fair share of corrupt entrepreneurs in the area. Jim and our friends try hard to maintain a clean community. One rotten apple affects the reputation of all of us." Judy picked up speed as they left the lakeshore community.

Monica hardly heard any more of Judy's dissertation on the Tahoe Basin. Her mind spun with ideas concerning Mitch Jones's reputation. She'd warned him not to cross her. Maybe she had found a way to put a thorn in his side.

Monica interrupted Judy. "Do you know much about the historical group that wants to save that resort?"

Judy hesitated before speaking. "I might. Why?"

"I want to join it."

Judy almost swerved off the road when she turned with a look of surprise. "I'm afraid to ask."

Monica shrugged. "This coalition interests me. Especially when it opposes Mitch Jones."

It was Monica's turn to be surprised when Judy turned off the road and parked in a small pullout.

With an earnest expression, she studied Monica carefully. "You're serious about getting involved?"

"Yes," Monica assured her.

"I can take you to a meeting. It's Tuesday night at seven, but you've got to promise me one thing."

"What's that?" Monica was intrigued more by Judy's behavior than by her request.

"Don't tell Jim. He'd kill me if he knew I was involved."

Greg slipped into his jacket. It'd been a sunny spring day, but the night air was chilly, letting Tahoe residents know summer hadn't quite arrived. He closed his eyes for a moment. Did he really want to go into the building and attend the meeting of the coalition? Tired, he rolled his shoulders. He had promised.

A car pulled up beside him and he saw a friend from his end of the lake. So he wasn't the only one who'd traveled to the North Shore. Many people were unhappy about the future of the Ponderosa Inn. He should go in, but he doubted his presence would do much good. He couldn't act as a representative of the TRPA. He could only advise from his personal viewpoint. He sighed. Was he accomplishing anything these days?

Greg set the parking brake and locked the passenger door. The thought of Mitch Jones upset him, and the thought of Monica dealing with the man had kept him awake these past few nights.

Why had the woman continued to torment him? They had nothing in common, yet visions of her constantly clouded his mind. How could he dream about someone who was associated with Jones?

He slammed the car door and hurried toward the building before he changed his mind. He shoved through the swinging doors of the public building and found the room where they told him the meeting had been held these past weeks. He'd been invited to this one because the group hoped his expertise of the area would give them an angle of approach to block Jones's project. He wasn't sure there was a solution, but he'd make every effort to find one if it existed.

Heads turned when he stepped inside. He started to greet the group, but froze when he saw the swathe of red hair. Monica Scott looked as surprised to see him as he was to see her. Not taking her gaze from his, she leaned over to whisper something to the woman next to her. Judy Myers shook her head. It didn't take much guesswork to figure out that Monica was uncomfortable with his presence.

No longer tired, he walked toward a seat, snapping his fingers.

"Our guest has arrived. We appreciate you coming all the way from the South Shore," the president of the group announced. "We can begin our meeting with questions directed at Mr. Linsey so that he can move on."

The group of about twenty men and women clapped for Greg. For thirty minutes he answered questions. Monica remained silent in spite of the challenging glares he sent her way.

An activist he'd met on other occasions stood. "Are you telling us that there's nothing the agency can do to stop the development?"

"I've made that clear. I can't speak for the agency. Each case is reviewed separately, and the outcome depends on what the developer submits."

Several protests and mutters followed his statement.

Greg braced himself when Monica stood. "If no other solution is available, we can at least count on the agency to delay matters for months at a time, can't we, Mr. Linsey?"

Several chuckles filled the room. Greg didn't crack a smile as he focused his attention on Monica.

"Our board strives to remain unbiased. We cannot let our personal views interfere with policy."

"Commendable, I'm sure." Her words complimented, but humor glinted in her eyes.

Fortunately, she remained silent through the rest of the meeting. When the chairman thanked him, Greg glanced at his watch and grimaced at the late hour. He should go home, but he knew he wouldn't rest. Not until he'd talked to Monica. Stepping to the back of the room, he sat in the empty chair next to her.

Electric currents charged the air between them. His senses filled with Monica Scott: the sound of her breathing, the faint scent of her perfume, the sight of her fist clenched around the purse in her lap.

The meeting finally adjourned and Judy leaned over Monica's lap to greet him. "It's nice to see you again. It was my suggestion to invite you. After we met the other day, I thought you might be able to give us some ideas."

"I'm sorry I couldn't be more specific. Jones is clever. It won't be easy to stop him."

Before Greg finished speaking, Monica reached up and grasped Judy's arm. "You knew he was going to be here?"

Judy smiled innocently. "You were the one who insisted on coming, Monica. You never asked me about who was going to be here."

"My mistake."

"What are you doing here?" Greg asked. "Spying for Jones?"

Monica bristled. Someone called to Judy from across the room. Obviously relieved to get away from the cross fire, Judy left and headed for her friend. Monica started to join her, but Greg grasped her hand and guided her back down.

"Don't leave. We have to talk."

Monica glanced around the room. "Do we? Here?"

"You're right. Not here. Come with me for coffee."

She surprised him by agreeing. "I came with Judy. Let me tell her you'll be taking me out."

As he waited for her, he called himself all kinds of a fool. He didn't need a woman like Monica Scott in his life. Her approach turned that thought into a lie. Something about her appealed to him. Was it the touch of loneliness he sensed in her?

She slung her purse over her shoulder. Her smile trembled.

"Don't look so glum. What can happen over a cup of coffee?" He tried to cheer them both up.

She didn't speak until they were both in the car. "You'll be pleased to know you were right about Jones."

Surprised, he studied her penitent features. Concern crept in. "In what way?"

"He pulled the wool over my eyes, as the old saying goes. Something I thought would never happen to me."

"It can happen to the best of us. What did he do?"

She explained the consultant's promises, ending with, "When I called your offices, they explained that the process would take weeks. They also explained about the cash option to buy points. I'm surprised you didn't bring it up."

Remorse coursed through him. "Restoration projects are rarely proposed. I figured if you knew the option Jones proposed, you surely must be aware of the cash purchase of points. I'm sorry I didn't make it clear."

"It's not your fault. I went into the deal too quickly."

Her apology brought hope. Greg pulled into the parking lot of the first coffee shop he found open. It wasn't much to look at, but once inside, the atmosphere improved. He guided Monica to a table by the window. Moonlight reflected on the waters of the lake. A clear night. There could be frost this late in the spring.

After ordering coffee for himself and herb tea for Monica, Greg said, "I'm surprised you didn't call me and verify the information on the point system."

"We weren't exactly on terms to consult with."

"Personally, maybe. But that shouldn't have stopped you in regards to business." Monica was a sharp woman. He must've rattled her.

"It has been a bitter pill to swallow. I had plenty of good advice given to me, yet I ignored it. I was so determined to do this on my own that..." Her voice trailed off.

Greg gripped the bench he was sitting on to keep from reaching out to her. She looked vulnerable and uncomfortable admitting failure. "It surprised me, that's all. I won't mention another word about it." He reached for a card displayed between the napkin holder and the sugar jar. "Would you like to order some pie?"

She smiled and nodded.

He smiled back. Relief poured through him. The fire had returned to her eyes. "My favorite is chocolate cream."

"I shouldn't really. The last thing I need at ten o'clock at night is pie. But I'll have the blueberry."

"So what are your plans now?"

CHAPTER 10

MONICA STUDIED the lines of concern in Greg's face, the caring in his eyes. So unlike Stephen or her father, who would have gloated over her mistakes. The waiter arrived with the tea and coffee. She waited until he left before continuing the conversation.

"My hands are tied. Unless by some miracle the permits come through by the end of this month, I won't have time to finish the house this season."

"You have all the paperwork completed, the jobs lined up, and production set to go. Are you going to cancel out and wait until next year?"

Monica dunked the tea bag a few times before setting it aside. "I'll need to do some clearing in the new location," she said. "A road to the site needs to be established." She took a sip of tea. "I'd also like to get the foundation poured since I've already paid for the work. If I get those things done this summer, it'll give me a good head start for next year."

"I'm glad to hear you've resigned yourself to making this a two-year project. It'll make things a lot easier on you." Greg played with his cup.

"You mean by next spring, I'll know the ropes."

He grinned, the cocky one that she hadn't seen in a while and suddenly realized she'd missed. "A main rule of thumb for this area is that every project takes twice as long here as anywhere else."

Monica chuckled. "Now *that* advice of yours isn't difficult to believe."

His expression grew serious. "And my advice about Jones? Why was that so hard to take?"

The reference to Jones sobered Monica's mood. When she saw the sincere concern in his expression, she confessed, "I hate to be proven wrong. It never sits well with me."

Greg shook his head. "I don't think anyone enjoys mistakes, but we can learn from most of them."

Monica gripped the handle of her cup. "Jones will be the one to learn from this one. He's going to pay for what he has done to me."

"Revenge usually backfires. Stay away from the man."

Heat crept up Monica's neck to flush her cheeks. She set her cup down with care. "He not only steered me wrong with his advice, he unloaded a worthless piece of property for a pretty penny. I tell you, he'll be sorry he ever laid eyes on me."

Greg shifted in his seat. "You're going to use the coalition committee for your revenge, aren't you?"

"From what I heard tonight, I won't be at cross-purposes. There are plenty of people in that group who feel like I do. And I'm capable of rounding up more," she said. "What about you? How can you criticize my involvement when you belong too?"

"I don't participate or belong. I only came tonight in a consultant capacity."

"But you support their cause?" she insisted.

Greg reached across the table and laid his hand over hers. "Monica. Call it a lesson and let it go. Jones can only bring you more grief."

The contact unnerved her. She closed her eyes against the attraction calling her to forget Jones and focus all of her attention on this man. The strength of the pull frightened her. She shook off his hand and lifted her cup for another sip of tea. Her fingers trembled, and she wondered if he noticed.

He left his hand resting in the middle of the table and smiled. "Want to go sailing this weekend?"

His question surprised her. "Why? So you can convince me to forget about Jones?"

"Partly." He smiled. "Although I had your company more in mind."

A day spent alone with Greg. The idea appealed more than she cared to admit or contemplate at this point. "Sounds like a plan. I'll order us a lunch from the Myerses' restaurant."

He looked slightly taken aback by her ready acceptance. "You were serious about the invitation, weren't you?" she asked, wondering what she would say if he wasn't.

That sly grin of his returned. "You bet I'm serious. I'll sail up here and pick you up at your dock." He paused for a minute. "Or do you want me to pick you up at the restaurant?"

Heart-thumping relief flooded Monica, causing her to take a moment to think. "Actually, the restaurant would be easier. I can order our lunch and then be ready to sail."

"Is nine too early?"

Monica shook her head. "Not for me, but call me before Saturday. I'm not sure the restaurant is open at that hour."

"No problem." He glanced at his watch. "Speaking of early hours, I probably should head south. I have to be at work at seven-thirty."

He drove her home and walked her to the door.

Monica turned to face him. "I'm sorry it's so late. I'd invite you in, but I don't want you to be too tired tomorrow." His presence soothed her loneliness.

"I'm tempted. But you're tired too." He caught her hand before she went in. Monica paused. He let go and brushed a tendril of hair back from her face. "I am really sorry about Jones. I hate to see you hurt."

She smiled at his concern. "I'm a long way from hurt. You might save your pity for Jones."

"Don't do it, Monica. You were wronged, so pray for Jones. That's the best way."

Suddenly annoyed, Monica stepped inside, said goodnight, and shut the door. He sounded like her mother. Why did everyone think God would take care of their problems?

God provides for all your needs, Child.

She threw her coat on the couch. "I'll take care of myself, Mother."

The next couple of weeks flew by quickly. With her permits on hold, Monica found herself working with the coalition more and more. The involvement with the PIC—Ponderosa Inn Concern, as they were now called—demanded time and energy. Most days engaged her in committee projects and research, which suited her fine. It left her little time to worry about the permits or miss Greg while he was at work.

She tried to convince herself that her main focus was on defeating Mitch Jones, but during the rare moments she stopped to contemplate, she would have to admit she enjoyed the project because it included time with Greg. Most evenings she went with Greg to meetings or volunteered for work crews.

Since she had become involved in PIC, Greg made a point of joining also. She accused him of doing so to propagandize her to his point of view, but truthfully, he didn't need to. The more she worked in the Basin, the more convinced she was that Greg's position was for the best.

Tonight, she and Judy were bundling fliers. For the tenth time, she glanced at the outer door. Greg should be here any minute to help her deliver them.

Judy tossed Monica several bundles of fliers to put into the back of her Jeep Cherokee parked inside the warehouse. Monica laughed. "When you get involved in something you don't mess around, do you?"

Judy closed the back door of the Jeep and took a deep breath. "I think *you* need to go take a vacation so *I* can get some rest."

Monica glanced at the lines of strain on Judy's face. Pangs of remorse slowed her pace. They'd been folding fliers since mid-morning. "Greg will be here soon. Why don't you head for home?"

Judy's tense features softened. "I can hang in there. Honest. We just have to take these around the west side and drop them off at the businesses who will distribute them."

"Which is why Greg and I can do this on our own."

Judy hesitated and then chuckled. "You want time alone with Greg."

Monica shrugged, unable to deny Judy's claim.

"I guess Jim would be easier to live with if I was home when he arrived."

That rationale reminded Monica that Judy's recent political involvements had created havoc in the Myerses' household. In Monica's opinion, it was time Jim learned that his wife had a brain and some backbone. But since that wasn't any of her business, she said, "I'm still full of energy. Go on ahead. This will give me something to do."

"And you'll be with Greg."

Monica chuckled as she glanced again at the outer doorway.

"I'll see you tomorrow then." Judy smiled happily as she waved goodbye.

"Don't forget that we have a meeting in the morning too. There's also the meeting tomorrow night at the South Shore

Club. Rhonda's going to call tonight. She may have good news for the publicity committee."

Judy paused. "Do you think she'll come do a benefit show?"

"I'm sure of it. With the summer tourist season just around the corner, we ought to make a killing."

"That would be great. We could buy more television time."

"Don't forget lobbying the legislators."

"Nothing gets left out with you in charge." Judy started off toward the open sliding doors of the warehouse. "I'm out of here before you think of something else for me to do."

Monica stared after her friend. Her comment sounded like one her father would receive. She shook her head, her hair slipping from the band. Could it be possible that she did have the backbone for political action?

She stared at the inside of the warehouse, crammed with workers and activity. Her Jeep and a van were parked in the loading bays. The inside walls were lined with Post-its, the tables filled with fliers, the far table filled with phones where volunteers called for support. Stunned, she stepped back, realizing for the first time that activity surrounded her as it once had surrounded Armand.

You are so like your father, Child.

Monica shivered, hoping this was a good thing.

One of the workers looked up and waved. "See you tomorrow, Monica."

She waved back and eyed the load of fliers in her Jeep Cherokee. The ones she had in back were destined for the small communities between here and Sugar Pine. It would take most of the evening to deliver them, and that suited Monica fine. She looked again at the parking lot door, wishing Greg would hurry up and arrive.

She loaded more bundles of fliers, thinking about how Greg usually accompanied her or invited her to his place on the rare occasions she didn't have a project or meeting. His companionship kept her loneliness at bay, as well as warmed places in her heart she didn't know were there. Was she being fair? She couldn't offer a permanent commitment, but he wasn't pressing for one either. She grabbed another bundle and shrugged. He seemed content to enjoy her company.

So why do I feel like there could be more? His laugh, his positive outlook on life, his calm and peaceful manner filled a need in her. Monica sighed, brushing back loose strands of hair.

The outer door slammed, and a shout brought her out of her reverie. "Hey, beautiful. Looks like you're ready to go."

Her heart racing like a schoolgirl's, she swung around and greeted him. "Just a few more bundles left. I'm hoping you'll go with me to deliver these."

He snapped his fingers as he approached. When he reached her, he lifted her into his arms, giving her a big bear hug. "Hmmm, what are you going to bribe me with?"

She braced her arms on his shoulders. "Dinner? Some of our stops are restaurants."

He set her down, but didn't let go of her. "I had a kiss in mind."

She could feel his chest pounding against hers. "Is that all? I'm getting off easy."

He laughed and bent down, brushing her lips with his. His day-old beard was rough against her cheek. She nuzzled into his neck, taking in the masculine scent and enjoying the strength of corded muscles as she wrapped her arms around his chest.

"Hmmm. That will get you to the moon and back."

She chuckled. "I only need to get around the lake."

He leaned back, studying her features as he pulled the band out of her hair and let the strands fall free. Monica returned his stare and smiled. "We'd better get going."

He let her go, hefting a couple of bundles and throwing them in the back of her Jeep. "I'm ready now, but I warn you, I might need more of those kisses to keep me going. It's been a tough day."

She studied him, seeing the lines of strain down his cheek and across his brow. Concern washed away the desire that had surfaced so readily. "I can do these on my own. You should go home early and get some rest."

He paused, an armload of fliers against his chest. "Oh no, you don't. You promised me dinner." He hefted the fliers inside and headed for the passenger seat.

She climbed into the driver's seat, happy that he was beside her. "I thought I'd already paid up with that kiss."

He leaned toward her and, with his finger, turned her cheek toward him. Dropping a kiss on her trembling lips, he smiled. "Doesn't hurt to have another."

Hands gripping the steering wheel, she remained staring as he let go of her cheek and fastened his seat belt.

"Better get moving, or we'll be here all night."

Shaking her head at how easily he distracted her, she switched on the ignition and backed out of the warehouse. Once on the highway, she floored the pedal and cruised along the wooded road.

Greg turned off the radio and leaned back, resting his head against the doorframe. "I need a quick power nap. Wake me when we get to our first stop."

The engine hummed, creating the only sound in the silence. Monica wanted to turn the radio back on, but didn't. She glanced at him, admiring the strong jawline, the hair she'd ruffled during their kiss. How she'd changed these past weeks. When Stephen wanted silence, she'd insisted on the radio. She used to hate the silence. She was discovering it wasn't so bad.

Pray in silence, Child. Listen to the voice of God.

What voice? She only heard the hum of the engine, the sound of Greg's even breathing. A strange peace settled over her. She glanced again at Greg. His presence did that to her.

At Sunnyside, she stopped and put the Jeep in gear. She hated to awaken Greg, but the change in motion did that for her. He sat up and stretched.

She pulled the keys out of the ignition and smiled. "Feel better?"

He yawned and combed his fingers through his hair. "Much better. How many bundles do we leave here?"

"There's the restaurant and lodge over there and several shops in this building."

Greg pulled a couple of bundles out and headed for the shops. Monica grabbed a bundle and followed.

"More 'Save the Inn' propaganda?" the proprietor teased. "How many people do you have in that organization now?"

Monica handed him her bundle. "Several hundred, and we're growing all the time."

He gestured to the pile of fliers. "I can see why. Too bad you aren't running a popularity contest. The coalition against your movement doesn't stand much of a chance with all of your literature out there."

"If only the issue were political, we'd have a fighting chance. As it is, Jones has the right to do what he wants with his property. What we're trying to do is pressure him with public opinion to change his plans."

"Jones wouldn't give a—" He quickly backtracked. "Excuse me, missy. I mean, a man like Jones doesn't care about public opinion. All he or any of the coalition want is to make big bucks. They don't care about the damage they do along the way."

Monica cringed and glanced at Greg. He had flung the same

156

accusation at her about her house. "Jones is an unscrupulous cheat, which is why he must be stopped."

Greg stacked his bundles on the counter. "Don't worry. We're still searching the law books. There has to be something somewhere that we can use to stop him."

"I hope you're right. I hate to see that old place torn down. Why, I remember when President Eisenhower came to stay there."

"Quite a few other celebrities too," Monica concurred.

The man shook his head. "The whole area has changed. These here mountains used to be that—plain old mountains. Not torn up with fancy, highfaluting places like yonder." He pointed to the sophisticated inn along the shores of the lake.

Monica preferred the modern resort to the Ponderosa if the truth were told. She liked hot and cold running water and sunken tubs, not the cranky pipes that fed antique tubs on claw legs like those at the Ponderosa. In fact, her idea would be to renovate the historic inn. Leave the rustic appeal, but gut the innards and give the place modern conveniences.

Jones had the right idea. He just had the wrong plan. He wanted to tear the place down completely. From a businessman's point of view, that would be less costly.

"We'd better head off." She and Greg said goodbye and continued on their way. In two hours they delivered the last bundle.

Monica braced herself against the Jeep and rolled her shoulders, trying to ease some of the aches caused by lifting the heavy bundles. Greg approached, and placed his hands beside her neck and gently massaged. "Tired?"

She nodded. "You must be."

He leaned forward and placed a light kiss on her forehead. "I'm proud of you, you know."

She looked at him, trying to read his expression in the dim

moonlight. "What for?"

"When I first met you, all you could think about was your building project. You didn't much care about what was going on here at the lake." He placed another kiss on her cheek this time. "You care about the Basin now. I like the change in you."

Monica reached around him and rested her arms on his hips. "It's all because of you."

He chuckled. "True, I had some part in it. But no one can change another person's mind. You did that on your own."

How like Greg to not take credit. She leaned against his chest. "I'm starving."

He laughed, the action shaking her head. "We'll feel better when we get some food in us. How about that little place we just passed?"

Reluctant to leave his embrace, she pulled away and climbed into the car. "As long as they have a full menu."

Greg slid into his seat and slammed the door. "I've eaten there before. It's clean, fast, and delicious."

Monica started the Jeep. "Good. We should get home soon as tomorrow's Friday and we have that big meeting at the club."

Greg mingled among the sophisticated guests packed into the South Shore Club. Not his usual crowd, but having been raised as one of the elite in San Francisco, he didn't feel uncomfortable. In fact, he enjoyed some of the people he'd talked with in a business capacity.

Steve Schuster, a local contractor, had been to the agency many times with applications for permits. He always researched before designing his plans and knew exactly what would be approved on his piece of land. His permits always went through. When asked about that, he'd always reply, "It's just as easy to stay within the law as buck it. I don't see any percentage in trying to work outside the system."

Greg admired the man. If only more contractors held the same value system. The preservation of the lake—not to mention his work at the agency—would be much easier.

"Howdy, Schuster." Greg shook hands. "I can see you've been hooked into the 'Save Ponderosa Inn' campaign."

"My normal inclination is to stay out of this kind of involvement," he admitted with a wry grin.

"So what brings you out?"

"I don't care that much about the inn itself, but it wouldn't hurt to clean up the place."

"So what makes it worth your effort on a Friday night?"

Schuster frowned. "The truth is, I can't stand Mitch Jones. He makes the whole contracting business look bad. I'd give my support to anything that'd get him the heck out of the Basin."

"I can't disagree with you there." Greg signaled to a waitress for a couple of beers. "Let's drink to that."

When the waitress returned, Schuster grabbed the two glasses off the tray and handed one to Greg. "Here's to keeping the Basin clean."

"And honest."

Their pilsners clinked as they made the toast. Carl joined them to say, "Monica's looking for you, Greg."

"You know Monica Scott?" Schuster asked. "I hear she's the one responsible for this affair."

"She's been in charge of everything," Greg said with open admiration. "I've never met a woman who could get this much action in so short a time."

"So I've heard." Schuster grinned. "She sounds like someone I should meet."

"I'll introduce you," Carl offered.

Greg tensed, remembering Schuster was single. Suddenly his feelings toward the man were not so amiable. He'd find her first and make sure the man understood Monica was not available. He found Monica talking to the other leaders of PIC. He slipped behind her and came up, wrapping his arm around her waist. He felt the small start of surprise in her, but she didn't step away. That pleased him.

"We should gather the group and get our meeting started." Monica said, using his arrival as an excuse to break up her conversation. "If we wait too long, everybody will be too far in their cups to make any decisions."

Several chuckled at her comment. Greg gave her an unnoticeable squeeze. It pleased him that everyone liked and respected Monica. She'd smile and they'd be like putty in her hands, as the old adage went.

Since Schuster didn't make it to her in time to be introduced, Greg relaxed and moved with the others, filing into the meeting room. Half the club emptied as the room filled. Good. The turnout was even more than Monica had predicted. He stayed near the rear when she moved up front to conduct the meeting.

Carl and Schuster came to stand beside him. "I'm surprised you were able to have this meeting here," Schuster commented. "Many of the members belong to the Coalition of Property Owners, not to mention Jones."

"PIC offered the club a fee they couldn't refuse," Greg confided the information. "Besides, anything Monica Scott sets her mind to, she accomplishes."

"Look around," Carl added. "Most of the people in here also belong to the club."

"It isn't my bag," Schuster said.

"Nor ours. We're here because of Monica," Carl glanced over at Greg. "You aren't taking her out afterwards, are you? I'd hoped you'd want to go party after this was over."

Greg couldn't have asked for a better lead in. He gave his friend a masculine grin. "You bet I am," he said, making sure Schuster was aware of how things stood.

"Might as well stay here," Schuster said. "Looks like plenty of action on the floor."

Carl's expression brightened.

Greg turned to watch Monica pound a book on the table. When the room quieted down, she said, "Let's begin so we can get on with our evening. It's Friday night, and I'm sure most of you have plans. I appreciate your attendance, and, for a reward, I have good news."

Murmurs echoed around the room as the audience reacted to Monica's commanding presence.

"As most of you know, Rhonda Remway is a friend of mine, and it's her house I'm living in. I talked to her last night, and the good news is she's willing to perform for a benefit concert."

Cheers resounded. When the clapping subsided, Monica continued. "More good news. Rhonda knows most of the celebrities who have places around Tahoe. She's going to contact them and see how many others will support our cause."

Another volley of cheers went up. Monica held up her hands to quiet the group. "The next item we need to discuss is what kind of a function to have, and where. Rhonda will agree to any place but the casinos."

Hands shot up and ideas were debated. Greg tuned most of it out and focused his attention on Monica. A mass of auburn hair flowed around her face and shoulders. She waved delicate-looking hands that, in fact, were as strong as most men's. Her vivacious smile melted his heart.

His reaction to Schuster's interest in Monica had caught him off guard. It was time he admitted that his feelings for Monica were deepening. True, she'd never given him any inclination that their relationship was more than casual dating. Yet he felt a deeper attraction and was certain she did too. At least, he'd made that assumption. Maybe it was time to test the ice and see how far out he could go.

A wave of uneasiness coursed through him. With Monica he'd have to venture out with extreme caution. He didn't want to risk overstepping the situation and ending up outside with a closed door.

He had no chance of getting her to himself tonight. The main meeting was over, but he and the committee chairmen were meeting at her house after dinner.

"What time is everyone arriving?" he asked Monica when she joined him.

"Not until eight-thirty. Everyone has families to feed."

"Speaking of food, do you want to stay here and have dinner with me?"

"You aren't coming up, then?"

"I'd drive there to see you." He smoothed a finger down her cheek. "But I'd be a fifth wheel most of the evening."

She frowned slightly. "I guess it would be unfair of me to ask you to drive all that way."

He took her hand and pulled her toward the dance floor. A slow piece played. He enfolded her in his arms. The soft feel of her body and the feminine scent of her skin teased his senses.

"I want to be alone with you," he murmured in her ear.

Her body tensed slightly. She leaned back and cast him a considering look. "You know the meeting will be late."

He nodded. "How about tomorrow? You kept the day open, didn't you?"

"You asked me to." She smiled, swaying to the soft music. "Are we going sailing again?"

He shook his head and grinned. "It's going to be too windy and rough. How would you like to hike into the back country? The trails are clear. What little snow is left will be easy to cross over."

"A hike?" She quirked her brow. "It's been a while since I've been on one."

"We'll go easy." He laughed. "Do you have hiking boots?"

"Yes, although I can't figure for the life of me why. They seemed to go with my concept of mountain living, I guess."

"You were right, there." He swung her around. "Wear comfortable clothes. I'll see to the rest."

"Lunch, you mean."

He nodded.

"Just so long as it isn't hardtack and beans."

He laughed again. "Where do you get your ideas?"

"From the movies, of course."

"Your education is sorely lacking. We'll see to it that you get firsthand experience."

She sighed, but the light in her eyes let him know she was game. Greg chuckled.

The song ended. Reluctant to let her out of his arms, Greg waited for another dance. After several pieces played, he gave up his hold and guided her to the table. At least he'd have tomorrow.

Mitch Jones watched Greg Linsey guide Monica Scott off the dance floor. There was a sense of *déjà vu*, except this time he watched the couple with more than mere curiosity. A dark cloud of hatred curled within him. What he'd give to be able to walk down there and strangle both of them, especially Monica Scott.

"I sure would like to know what went on in that meeting of theirs," Jones muttered more to himself than to his companion.

"Me too," Packard said, stepping close. "There's Schuster, the contractor from the North Shore. I met him a couple of months ago. We were both held up in the county planner's office. Got real chummy with him, in fact."

Jones stared at Packard, then grinned. "Chummy, you say? Does he know you work for me?"

"Couldn't say that he does." Packard grinned slyly. "Shall I go have myself a chat? Man to man."

Jones peeled off some bills from a roll he took out of his pocket. "Buy him a few drinks." He slapped Packard on the back. "And then come back and join me."

Jones watched Packard and Schuster sit at a table and order drinks. Jones ordered his own, but barely touched it. He hadn't liked the sound of those cheers sounding through the thick walls of the club. PIC was up to something, and he wanted to be prepared to counter whatever plot they'd hatched.

Schuster finally left the club, and Packard joined Jones and relayed what had happened at the meeting. "Do you know how many Hollywood celebrities have places here? Think of the attention they'll get if they all show up. They could even interest national news media with those names."

Jones held up his hand. "Don't get all panicked. This could be to our advantage."

"How do you mean?"

"Think of it. The media will want to hear both sides They'll want to focus on the big names." Jones sipped on his drink. "So we get a few big names of our own and make sure we do get the media's attention."

"You could have something there," Packard said.

Jones leaned forward. "I have a friend who handles the bookings at the casinos. They'll know how to contact some big names. We'll make Monica Scott sorry she ever heard of the Ponderosa Inn."

In more ways than one, he silently vowed. She was going to be sorry she ever decided to mess with him. Revenge was something Mitch Jones dished out—not received.

Packard ordered another drink. "So, boss, what else are you planning?"

Jones raised his brow and drummed his fingers on the table. "Rhonda Remway is coming to town. Let's plan a welcoming party. While they're out celebrating and putting on this shindig, you'll pay their place a visit."

Packard grinned. "I knew I was going to like this."

CHAPTER 11

GREG HAD SUGGESTED they use her Jeep Cherokee, and after traversing the rough road, Monica could see why. The engine hummed as she pulled up a steep incline. The narrow road wound around sheer cliffs. Thankfully she'd taken Greg up on his offer to drive so she could enjoy the scenery. The view of the canyon below was spectacular. In the distance, she caught glimpses of Lake Tahoe.

"Where are we headed?" she asked.

Greg shifted down another gear. "That's a secret. We locals never disclose our favorite haunts."

"I see. I don't qualify as a local yet?"

He smiled, the cocky grin he always had when he was in a teasing mood. "You have to live here at least two winters to obtain that lofty status."

"You mean most people don't last out a season?"

"That's right. We get a lot of city folk that think it's romantic to live in the woods. A cold, stormy winter brings harsh reality in a hurry."

"I don't see where snow has to be such a big deal. Most of the country has snow in the winter—back East and in the Midwest."

"It isn't the snow itself. Most of the older houses up here were built as summer cabins. They aren't winterized and have poor insulation."

Monica chuckled. "That would be a deterrent to enjoying a stormy night. It seems strange that they wouldn't build insulated homes in a mountain resort where they know it snows."

"It's only been recently that the whole Basin has been a year-round resort. The West Shore highway was not maintained in the winter, nor were many of the areas that are now populated." Greg shifted up a gear as they came to a level valley. "Because our summers are so temperate and warm, there was no need to insulate the houses. The owners boarded them up in the winter."

"But Tahoe has always been a big ski area. The Winter Olympics were held in Squaw Valley quite a while ago," Monica pointed out.

"The major ski resorts were open all year round, that's true. Many of our resorts like Northstar and Diamond Peak are fairly new."

"I guess when you think about it, most of the condos around those areas are modern."

"As more people settled in California in the fifties, sixties, and seventies, it began to put a heavier load on our resort trade. Those people wanted to come to the mountains."

The road ended, and Greg brought the Jeep Cherokee to a halt. Monica eyed the steep granite cliffs with some misgivings.

She stepped out of the vehicle. "We're going to climb those?"

Greg snapped his fingers. "No problem. There's a pass between them."

"Good thing. I didn't bring my mountain-climbing gear."

He paused at the tailgate and stared at her. "Do you have some?"

"No." She glanced around. "I've done a lot of hiking in the Rockies, the mountains in Spain, and the Alps, so don't worry about me."

"I doubt I'd ever *worry* about you, Monica. You're too self-sufficient to get stuck somewhere without knowing what to do."

"You sound like you might resent that."

He shrugged. "Men like to feel they're needed. You know, for protection and all that."

"The ol' chauvinism bit." She eyed him as she helped him unload their gear.

He hefted the backpack onto his shoulders. "I don't understand why women knock it. It has served mankind in most civilizations since recorded history. There must be something to it."

Monica grabbed the camera and the canteen and slung them over her shoulder. A slight chill still cooled the air, so she left her sweatshirt on. "Considering the social and economic structure, the system worked in primitive cultures. But times have changed, in case you haven't noticed."

"Technology has changed, but sexual roles haven't really. Women still reproduce and therefore need security. Men still provide. Or at least they should."

Her mother had made similar statements. Monica didn't want to discuss commitment today. Instead of responding, she fell in step beside Greg. The path was wide at first, and the hard-packed gravel easy to traverse. It didn't take long, however, for Monica to feel the altitude. After a few yards, she huffed and puffed.

Greg wrapped an arm around her waist and pulled her close. "What? No argument? I've been waiting for the words to fly after the statement I just made."

Monica stepped away from him. "I'm saving my breath for hiking."

He grabbed her hand, the warm pressure a simple gesture of friendship. Except when she looked into his eyes, she knew it could be more.

"I'm an old-fashioned guy when it comes to relationships. I

want the traditional role of a husband, and I want a wife who wants the same."

"Love, honor, and obey."

"Is that so much to ask? Would it be difficult to love?"

"It's the *obey* I have trouble with. I don't like someone telling me what to do."

"If a man really loved you, Monica, he would never ask you to do anything you wouldn't want to."

Monica stopped walking and turned to stare at Greg. "How would you or any man know what I want? One person cannot possibly be aware of what is in another's heart."

Love is gentle, love is kind, Child.

"A deep sincere love gives you that insight, Monica. When two people submit to each other, they truly do become as one. The man's wants and needs become the woman's, and vice versa."

"That sounds like idealistic nonsense. I seriously doubt that such a love can even exist."

I love your father, Child.

You have no life of your own, Mama. You do everything for Armand and nothing for yourself.

That is love, Child.

Greg let go of her hand when the trail narrowed, forcing them to walk single file. "I've seen that kind of love," he said. "I admit it's rare, but it does happen."

"Are you sure you're not just seeing a facade? There are many couples who put on a good show and then end up in divorce court."

Greg paused and turned to face her. "No, I'm talking about the real thing, the kind of love you develop together, with God at its core. Once you know that love, Monica, you'd never settle for less."

A strange longing welled, along with an ache in her heart. "How is it you know so much? Were you in love before?"

"No."

Relief flooded through Monica. Yet, she had no desire to develop a serious relationship with Greg. Or with God. Did she? She changed the subject. "This trail is steep, yet it's well maintained."

Greg remained silent, probably debating whether to let her change the subject.

Determined to do so, Monica asked, "Is this a state park or part of a recreation area?"

Still Greg didn't respond. She picked up her pace to avoid the thoughts crowding her peace.

To her relief, Greg finally spoke. "We're in a National Forest. The trail was constructed by volunteers."

The trail widened as she came around a bend. Monica paused to observe the view of the canyon below. Greg stepped beside her. His gaze penetrated—deep, assessing.

Uncomfortable, Monica pointed to a side canyon. "Do we climb through that?"

"There's a trail up there, but we continue up and over this pass."

"The other isn't maintained?"

He took the canteen she offered and drank. "Not as well as this one."

"What about the people who worked on this trail?"

"What we're on is part of the Pacific Crest Trail. The goal is to hike this one from the Mexican border to the Canadian."

She refastened the lid of the canteen. "Who volunteers for a project of that scope?"

"Different service organizations take on parts of the trail; Boy Scouts, school clubs, etc. Environmental organizations such as the Sierra Club promote efforts to volunteer. Many of the workers are people who come to the Basin to vacation."

He nodded toward the trail as he spoke, and Monica started

back on the steep climb. From behind her, Greg continued talking.

"The local newspapers publish the hours and locations of the section of the trail that's under construction. The Forest Service provides equipment. Each volunteer shows up with their own water and food and sets to work."

"Doesn't sound like a very exciting vacation."

"Some people don't know how to relax. They see the accomplishment as a form of recreation."

Monica related to that. She wasn't very good at relaxing either.

The trail curved around a cliff face with steep steps carved into the granite. Afraid to look down the sheer drop, Monica walked carefully. "I, for one, am thankful for the volunteers. I don't think I'd like this trail without these steps."

"It'll be easier going once we make it over this rise," he assured her.

"I hope so. I forgot to mention that mountain goat isn't in my family genes."

Greg laughed.

True to his word, the trail leveled out as it wound across an alpine meadow. Wildflowers brightened the grassy field with splashes of yellow, pink, and purple.

"These are California poppies." Greg pointed to the delicate blossom. "They're the California state flower."

She pointed to stalks of purple. "And these?"

"Blue lupines."

He walked a few steps farther and pointed to a yellow flower that looked like a daisy. "Those are mule's ears. They bloom right after the snow melts."

The large green leaves shaped like the ears of a mule had a soft fuzz covering them. Across the meadow, in the shade of the trees, were patches of snow, giving evidence of the recent thaw. A slight movement captured her attention. At the edge of the grass, a deer and her spotted fawn stood frozen and watching.

She turned to quietly point and saw that Greg had already seen them. His expression reflected pure joy. Monica shared the peace and wonder.

The deer sniffed the air for several moments and then moved into the trees. The fawn kicked up its heels in a playful leap before following its mother.

Monica moved close to Greg and spoke in a low voice. "I'm glad you brought me here."

He reached across and brushed a strand of hair behind her ear. "In spite of that steep climb?" he teased.

"It's over. I can be more generous now."

He laughed. "Don't get too settled in. We've only just begun. We haven't arrived at my secret hideaway yet."

"This is a wonderful spot. We don't need to go any further to make me happy."

"But it would make me happy."

She shook her head, his statement reminding her of Stephen. She glanced at the teasing eyes and knew he hadn't meant anything more than what he'd said. She also realized he really wanted to go on. There was an expectancy in him.

She smiled. "This must be a special place. Let's mush on. I'm getting hungry for lunch."

Greg watched her swing around and start across the meadow. Afraid she'd argue and delighted she hadn't, he passed her at the edge of the meadow and led the way along the obscure path that few people knew about. It wound through a stand of ponderosa pine trees and then began another steep ascent across the domed granite prevalent in the Sierra Madre range.

Awareness of Monica's presence behind him quickened his pace. His anticipation involved more than Monica. He'd wanted to come to his special place for over a month now. To have Monica accompany him enhanced his pleasure.

A slight breeze rushed through the trees. The cool air refreshed his exerted body. Birds sang. Squirrels scattered in front of him. Pleasure coursed through Greg as the stirrings of spring transferred from nature to him. He looked around and thanked God again for His wonderful creation, and thanked his forefathers for the wisdom to preserve it.

For the first time in months, peace settled in his heart. At this moment, he could conquer the world. Monica's presence had a lot to do with it. He enjoyed showing her his secret places—a part of himself.

He reached the meadow and took off his pack. Monica helped him spread the straw mat he'd brought, but didn't sit on it. She stood admiring the scenery.

"Greg, this is a lovely spot. So perfect and pristine."

Her pleasure doubled his as he saw the small lake and forest through her eyes. He followed her as she hopped across the granite boulders that formed a mini-peninsula in the water.

"Look how clear the water is. You can see everything below."

More interested in looking at her, he marveled at how the sunshine reflected on her hair. Her eyes danced and her smile widened.

"Are there any fish?" she asked.

"Not this high up. They can't survive because this lake freezes solid most winters." He pointed to a chipmunk that scurried across a log. "The Forest Service stocks some of these high-altitude lakes, but only those with easy access."

"I can see why. It would be a chore transporting them on that trail."

"They fly over and airdrop them."

Monica stepped close to him. "It's so isolated up here."

He draped his arm around her shoulders. "We're all alone, Monica. Very few people know of this place."

It seemed automatic to slip his hands along her trim waist and pull her back against him. She fit perfectly with her head tucked under his chin. With one arm draped across the front of her, he held her close. With his free hand he pointed out the landmarks and named the surrounding mountain peaks.

She tilted her head back and smiled up at him. "From the way you talk, I can tell how much you love this country."

"The mountains have always been a special place."

"The Sierras are different. They're drier and less dense than the Rockies or the woods back East."

"They're high-altitude desert, actually. We have dry weather. The rain in the Rockies gives it the lush greenery we don't have."

"And the mosquitoes and flies."

He laughed. "So you've noticed those, have you? They aren't as bad here because of the dry air."

"I never could figure out why God created those pests." She gestured to the mountains around them. "I can understand this beauty, but *mosquitoes?*"

Greg turned her around and searched her face. "So you do believe in God."

Her cheeks turned pink. "Well, I..." she stammered.

He waited and prayed, wanting her to believe.

"I guess so. I never think about it much. Do you?"

He looked deep into her eyes. "All the time."

Her brow creased in a frown. He smiled. Planting the seed was enough for now.

"When the water warms up, we can go swimming in the lake."

She studied him for long moments and smiled back. "Brrr.

I felt that water. It's going to have to warm up a lot more to interest me."

He took advantage of her shiver and hugged her tight against him. The scent of her perfumed hair caused shivers of another kind.

She tensed and pulled away. He left his hands on her waist and let her see the desire in his eyes. She glanced up, and he saw the answering reaction. Her fingers traced his jaw, their soft touch sending chills along his spine. He turned his face into her hand and kissed the palm.

"I want you, Monica," he whispered before he bent to kiss her forehead, then her cheek, and finally her lips.

Her moan shuddered through him. He wanted more. So did she. He tasted the hunger in her. He wrapped his arms around her and brought her close.

Monica's arms slid up his back and pressed tight as her kiss sweetened. She finally pulled away and rested her head under his chin.

"This is wrong." Her words cut into his euphoria.

What? With a gentle pressure, he tilted her chin and gazed at her face. Her eyes clouded with passion. Relieved, he bent to kiss her again.

For a moment, she tensed and resisted the pressure. Suddenly her lips softened and opened to receive his kiss. Greg sighed with pleasure as he traced his palms along the curves that felt so right.

She pulled away, the movement so sudden he almost lost his balance atop the uneven boulder. Greg could ignore the first show of resistance, but not the second.

Reluctantly, he let her go. "What is it?"

She wouldn't look at him, only shook her head and stared down at the water. Her chest heaved with deep breaths, as did his. She had been as moved by the kiss as he had.

He reached up to touch her hair but paused midway. They needed to talk. Not now. Later, when they could think.

Keeping his voice low and calm, he urged her to come with him. "Let's get at that lunch. The hike gave me more than one appetite."

She turned to face him, and he saw elements of relief along with her smile. Surprised, he studied her. Monica didn't seem like the type to be reticent about passion. He figured she'd have the same zest and emotion for ardor as she did for everything else in her life. In fact, he'd swear she did if that kiss were anything to judge by. Something was holding her back. Or someone.

Greg jumped off the rock and landed on the needle-carpeted ground. Maybe he didn't really want to have that talk.

Monica saw the confusion in Greg's expression as he studied her. She understood. Desire and common sense warred and confused her own thinking. Her senses had skyrocketed when he'd kissed her. His touch caused longings and unmet needs to swirl to the surface.

Why hadn't she seen it coming? Or had she? The moments of intimacy on the sailboat, at restaurants, and with friends. They'd all been clues. The truth was, she had denied them. Or had she encouraged them? She was tired of being alone, tired of a celibate life. Maybe it was time to explore a true relationship. That thought terrified her.

Monica followed Greg to their picnic site and stretched out on the straw mat opposite from him. Silently, he opened the knapsack and began to set out sandwiches, chunks of cheese, and a plastic container of sliced vegetables.

"Greg," Monica stopped him by placing her hand over his.

Their glances locked. What was he thinking?

Greg broke the silence first. "I care about you, Monica. Surely you must know that."

His words touched her heart and plucked at her conscience. "I care about you too, but I'm not sure I'm ready to give you what you need."

"A kiss isn't so much to ask for."

"You want more than a kiss."

He started to protest, but she reached across the space between them and put her fingers to his lips to silence him. "I'm not talking about physical wants. Your ideas of commitment are very different than mine. I don't want you to be misled into believing we could be moving toward a permanent relationship."

"Don't you think it's a little premature to be discussing permanent involvement?"

Her smile broadened at that. "Don't deceive yourself, Greg. There is nothing casual about you or me. When we become involved, it will be intense. Because that is the way both of us are. We should be very sure of what we want before the commitment is set."

"I know what I want." He grabbed her hand and pressed a kiss into her palm.

Monica waited for the wave of desire to recede. When she spoke, her voice barely carried, but the truth was there. "I'm not sure what I want."

His smile broadened. "That's not a problem. I can think of all kinds of enjoyable ways to persuade you to my way of thinking."

Monica's laughter rang across the lake. "I do believe you could do that."

"Will you let me try?"

For several long moments, she considered the possibilities. His passion for life stimulated her. And she was lonely.

"Can't we just keep on going like we have been for a while

longer? I need to get this mess with Jones behind me. I want to finish my father's house—"

He interrupted. "That could take a year."

"I can't give you any more than that. Not now."

"Later?" he pushed.

"Maybe." It was all she could give him.

Silence hovered. Her mind reeled with options.

Monica unwrapped a sandwich and handed it to Greg. The conversation had tempered their appetite, but they managed to make a dent in the meal.

Monica regretted that she'd spoiled the outing for Greg. It saddened her to realize that after this, he may not want to see her anymore.

Not wanting to dwell on it further, she stood and headed for a patch of plants that had leaves with sharp, thorny edges.

"What is this?" she asked, wanting him to return to his earlier amiable mood. "It looks like holly."

Greg seemed just as eager to lighten the atmosphere. "That's squaw carpet. It's quite rare and indigenous to this region."

"Another endangered species?"

He nodded.

What a fortunate choice of plants to pick for conversation. Ecology was a good, safe subject. Greg could talk about that all day.

"In the populated areas of the Basin, much of this has died out. It's very sensitive to foot traffic." He went on to explain about the plant's rare qualities.

Monica listened with half of her attention. Greg's kiss had stirred up emotions she didn't know existed in her. Her gaze followed Greg as he walked her around the small alpine meadow and explained the delicate ecology. Instead of focusing on his words, she studied his hands and remembered the way they felt. Giving herself a shake, she forced the thoughts away and listened closely to the lesson.

"Remind me to show you the Tahoe yellow cress when we get back to my place. It's a great example of how our environmental controls have brought a dying species back to a healthy recovery."

"What does it look like? Maybe I have some on my property."

"I'm sure I saw some. It's very tiny and has downy leaves and branches. It's a member of the mustard family."

Monica frowned, trying to place the plant. Memories of her mother came unbidden to her mind. She'd plant a garden wherever they moved, no matter how long they would live there. Monica had hated the gardens because her mother spent most of her time there—instead of with her and Armand.

Greg led her along a narrow path that wound around the small lake. "I'll show you when we get home. It has an interesting story behind it."

Monica forced herself to listen when he went on to explain how a botanist had discovered the plant recently and had done a study on its precarious existence. "Because of her efforts, it's made a big comeback."

"I understand what you're trying to tell me, Greg. It's wonderful that you care about protecting all of this beauty." She gestured toward the lake and surrounding area. "I guess we don't think enough about our connection to it. Because of that, we don't really care."

"That's because our advanced technology has removed us from the vital association with the earth and nature. But we are connected."

She chuckled. "You sound like my mother. She always thought being close to plants made us close to God."

"I think I'll like your mother."

Monica sobered. "She passed away when I was thirteen."

He grabbed her hand and squeezed. "I'm sorry. That must

have been a rough time for you."

She didn't want to remember. "She was into ecology. Like you."

He picked up on her cue. "She was right. Our survival depends on the planet's survival. We are on a giant life-support system, and we are trashing it up."

Monica had to smile at the earnestness in his voice and expression. "That's what I like about you. When you become involved in something, it's wholehearted."

"That's the way I want it to be with you too, Monica."

His words silenced her.

He stepped close and traced his hand up and down her arm. "I'll give you time. You're as valuable as the rarest flower. And you have my full attention and patience."

CHAPTER 12

ALMOST EVERY TOURIST in the Basin, as well as a big share of the locals, had attended the benefit concert. Even some of the opposition came to see and hear the top-name stars, which made Monica smile.

Of course the same thing would happen later this month when the opposing coalition staged their concert. People were fickle when it came to their own interests. Where the proceeds of the tickets went didn't matter to most of the audience. Their only concern was seeing the famous performers.

It still rankled that the coalition had taken Monica's idea and used it to counter the impact of their concert. Judy, however, pointed out how much more publicity they would attract by having the two performances benefiting opposite positions of the controversial issue.

Judy had been right. Major television networks sent teams of news reporters. They had been interviewing the stars all week. Now the whole nation knew about the environmental issues of the Lake Tahoe Basin.

Greg helped Monica into his car after they left the hotel where the post-concert party was still going full swing. "Are you sure you don't want to stay longer and come back with Rhonda?"

"I hated to leave," Monica admitted. "The party is great, but I'm absolutely exhausted."

Greg shut her door. She could see him chuckling as he walked around the front of the car to his side. When he sat beside her, he shook his head. "I never thought I'd ever hear you say that. You've got more energy than ten people."

"Putting on something this big takes that of a hundred. I'm going to have to admit that I'm done in."

"I'm surprised that Rhonda wanted to stay on. I'd think she would be tired after such a big event."

Monica chuckled this time. "Rhonda will party 'til dawn. Performing hypes her up. Believe me, I know. Why do you think I wanted to come on home?"

The car picked up speed as Greg turned onto the highway. "I'd hoped it was because you wanted to be alone with me."

Monica shifted under her seat belt. "We haven't had much time to spend together. Your days have been busy, and my evenings have been too."

"Now that the concert is over, do you think you'll be able to take a day off?"

Monica glanced at the trees lit by the full moon. Even at this hour traffic filled the highway. The summer tourists had arrived and crowded the Basin since Memorial Day weekend. Time was flying by.

"Rhonda will be here this weekend. I suppose when she returns to Los Angeles, I'll have some time. How about you?"

"For you, Monica, I'll make time. You know that."

Desire flared. Her stomach tightened and her breath caught. Uneasy with the longings, she gripped the console. "Call me Monday after work. We'll make plans."

"I won't see you this weekend?"

"Not unless you change your mind about coming to the barbecue tomorrow. Rhonda's having all of her friends over. It should be a real bash." She wanted him to come.

Greg shook his head. "I've had enough partying this week

to last me for a year. Besides, they aren't really my crowd."

"Too sophisticated for you, mountain man?"

He cast her a mock glare. "Too fast and noisy is more like it. You know I prefer being alone. You've been enjoying these parties, Monica, but I'm only tolerating them so I can be near you."

"How can you say that when they're up here donating time and their fame to promote the cause of environmentalism? That should give you plenty to talk about."

"Oh, I talked to them all right. Most of them had no idea what the real issues are. They can repeat a few 'buzz phrases,' but they could care less about what happens to Lake Tahoe."

She glanced at his profile in the dim light, enjoying the conversation and the intimacy of sitting alone with Greg. "Most of them have places here. Sure they care."

"Some do care, I grant you that, but most have a place here because it's the 'in' thing to do, or because they need to impress each other."

Monica chuckled. "How can you sit there and be so cynical about people who've just raised hundreds of thousands of dollars to save the Ponderosa Inn?"

"And what's that going to do for the ecology of Lake Tahoe?" Greg tightened his hold on the steering wheel, making Monica aware of how much the topic of conversation upset him. "Be honest, Monica. Why are you going to all the trouble? It isn't because you care about the inn or the Basin. You're after revenge."

Her smile disappeared. She gripped the console again. "Getting Mitch Jones out of the Basin would do a lot for this area. You know how much damage he's done with his underhanded schemes."

Greg maneuvered around another curve in the road. "Thwarting him on this project isn't going to get rid of him."

"Yes it is." At last she had something to say that Greg

would want to hear. "We found out that Jones has sunk all his capital into this mall, including the money he made off of me, I might add. If this project goes belly up, so does Jones."

Greg's considering look disconcerted her. "You sound like that prospect brings you pleasure."

She opened her mouth to admit that it did, then closed it when she realized how unattractive that sounded. She frowned. "I suppose you're going to accuse me of being a barracuda like Judy has."

"Does the name fit?"

Monica clamped her jaw shut.

"I've told you revenge is best left to God, Monica."

Rhonda's drive came into view, saving her from responding. Greg pulled up to the house. Before he could get out to help her with the door, Monica had opened it herself.

"You can just let me off. It's late and I know you have a long drive ahead of you."

Greg placed his hand on her arm and turned her toward him. "You could invite me in."

Monica knew it would be rude of her not to. "I don't want to continue this conversation."

"You can't avoid it forever, but I agree about tonight. I don't want us to say goodnight on a sour note."

"Come on in. I'll make you some coffee."

Monica waited for him to help her out of the car, wishing she wasn't so glad he would be with her for a while longer.

He helped her out and held her hand. Walking the uneven ground in high heels could be tricky. Her long evening gown rustled against her legs. Once on the porch, she opened her purse to search for her keys.

Greg halted and pulled her to a stop with him. "Don't bother with the keys," he muttered under his breath.

His tone puzzled her until she followed his gaze to the

open door. Monica clasped her throat. "Someone's here."

"Or has been." He pushed her behind him. "Wait here until I check this out."

"No way. I'm not staying out here alone in the dark."

Greg paused and considered the options. "Okay, but stay close behind me. Your visitor could still be in there."

Greg pushed the door open. "Where's the light switch?" he whispered.

"On the left. Here. Let me." She slipped around him and reached for the panel of buttons.

The outside lights flooded the yard. Inside, rooms lit up as her fingers traveled along the electronic system. No sounds came forth.

"Who's here?" Monica called out.

Silence echoed in the house. She started to enter, but Greg held her back. "Follow me," he ordered.

Monica obeyed, but didn't let him get too far ahead. A chill coursed through her. Something was terribly wrong.

In front of her, Greg froze. Monica collided with his back just as he gasped.

"What is it?" she asked, peering around his shoulder. She nearly collapsed when she saw the broken dishes and crystal littering the floor. Holes gaped in the upholstery. Lamps were overturned, and pictures had been torn off the walls and scattered across the floor. Cold ashes from the fireplace stained the white carpet.

"What does this mean?" Monica could barely speak.

"It's not robbery," Greg commented as he held up a valuable piece of silver. "Vandalism."

"I'll go check the other rooms. They might not have known what was valuable."

"Wait. Let me go with you. They might still be around."

The thought sent shivers down Monica's spine. "You

won't get any arguments from me."

"For once."

She put her fisted hands on her hips and glared at him. "We really don't need humor right now."

He shrugged. "It's laugh or cry."

Picking her way through the mess, she followed him down the hall and looked into the bedrooms, moaning louder in every room. Each torn mattress, each emptied closet and pile of ripped clothes, fueled her temper.

"Jones is responsible for this. I know it."

Greg didn't stop her from rushing ahead. The vandals had left.

"They came during the show. What a lowdown, sneaky stunt to pull," Monica ranted from the bedrooms.

Greg righted the lamp and searched for the telephone. His own anger easily matched hers. The angrier she got, the louder she became. Greg was the opposite; the silence indicated his degree of temper.

What if Monica had been here? He shuddered, thankful they had been gone.

The telephone cord was tangled among some pillows. Grabbing it, he followed the lead until he came up with the phone. Just as he expected: dead. He checked his cell phone. No reception.

"We'll have to drive to the store and call the sheriff."

"You go on ahead," Monica yelled from the back. "I'll stay here and try to pick up this broken glass."

He found her in the bathroom scooping up the remains of the bottles that contained the expensive perfume she'd always enjoyed.

"I'm not going to leave you here alone."

She glanced up, and he saw the same fire he'd seen in her eyes the first time he'd met her. "There's no danger to me," she snapped. "But the poor sucker who would dare to walk in had better watch out. I'd invite him so I could personally strangle his perverted neck."

Greg forced himself not to smile. The situation was anything but funny. It was just that he could picture Monica giving some poor dude all kinds of trouble for this.

"Don't touch another thing." He grasped her arm and tried to coax her to stand. "The sheriff needs to make a report."

She stood up and gazed incredulously around. "I can't just leave this mess. What will Rhonda say?"

"Probably the same thing you're saying now."

He managed to get her out of the bathroom and down the hall. She pulled free and stopped cold. "He's going to pay for this. No one does something like this to me and gets away with it."

"You don't know for sure it was Jones."

Her eyes glittered in the bright light. "Who else would do such a thing? It's not theft. My jewelry has been thrown all over the place, necklaces broken and ripped apart, but nothing was stolen."

He had to admit Jones was at the top of his mental list too. "You can't go making public accusations without evidence. A man like Jones would just as soon sue you for slander."

"Has anything like this ever happened before?" she demanded. "If there's a bunch of kids who routinely get their kicks out of doing this, I'll reconsider. But if this is a first, we both know who's behind it and why."

"I'll concede to a suspicion. Let's call the sheriff. Maybe he can discover evidence in all of this mess."

It took several minutes before Greg could make it to the front door. Monica stopped every two steps to pick up something. He let her rant on. He figured he was doing the sheriff a favor by letting her release some of that steam before he had to face her.

Two hours later, Monica was still carrying on. The sheriff, obviously used to reactions from disasters such as this, tolerated her outrage with remarkable patience. By the time he left, she'd calmed down.

Greg watched her pick objects off the floor on her way back from letting the sheriff out. "Where are you finding the energy to do that?"

She placed an ashtray on the table. "It's adrenaline. I got so mad, I must've pumped it right into my system."

"I wish I had some of it." He could barely keep his eyes open. "Let's call it a night. You can clean this up tomorrow."

"No way. Rhonda will be here by morning. Can you imagine her reaction if she came home and saw this?"

"I don't have to imagine. I saw yours, remember?" He took the bronze statue out of her hand, and guided her to her feet. "Come on. I'm putting you to bed. You're worn out, and so am I."

Concern reflected in her eyes. "You're right. You have a long drive. You go on ahead. I'll manage fine on my own."

"Oh no." He backed away, shaking his head. "I'm not leaving you alone."

For the first time since they'd arrived at the house, she stopped talking. Astonishment crossed her features before she shuttered her eyes and turned from him. "I'll be okay."

"I'll sleep in one of the extra bedrooms or out on the couch.

Whoever came could return. I don't want to take any chances."

Before he could move she turned, flung herself against him, and pressed close. Surprised, he wrapped his arms around her shoulders and held her to him, savoring the feminine feel of her body.

She leaned back. "I didn't realize that I didn't want to be alone until you just now mentioned it. Of course I want you to stay."

"Monica," he whispered, before bringing her close enough to kiss. The vandalism, the concert, and his exhaustion didn't matter anymore. Every sense and every thought focused on the woman in his arms.

The kiss lasted for long moments. Desire flared as inhibitions disappeared when she smoothed her hands across his back.

"I don't want anything to ever happen to you," he whispered, realizing the truth in those words.

She brushed another kiss across his lips. "I'll be fine as long as you're here."

The simple statement sent a protective surge through him. "I want to take care of you, Monica. I'd take care of you forever if you'd let me."

His words hit him like a truck. The longings he'd experienced all spring. The premonition something big was about to happen. The yearnings for more meaning to his life. Monica. Her love would provide so many answers.

She gazed up at him. "Forever is a long time, Greg. You don't know what you're saying."

"Forget about the future. Just think about now." He lowered his head to kiss her again.

"I don't want to think about what happened here," she murmured against his mouth.

"Shh. Be quiet." He kissed her neck and then moved back to her mouth.

Nothing was going to interfere with this moment. He wanted to focus on what he felt for Monica.

Love. The word excited him and sobered him at the same time. He wanted Monica to love him too, but he knew she wasn't ready yet to give it.

"I love you, Monica," he whispered.

"Kiss me."

Desire raged, but he tamped it down. "We're both vulnerable tonight. I don't want to do something we'll regret."

"I'd never regret holding you like this."

Didn't she understand? She was making him crazy. He wanted to make love to her. More than he'd wanted anything before. But doing so went against his values. So he simply held her close.

Monica promised herself she would hug Greg for only a second more. Seconds turned into minutes. Passion raged while she battled with her conscience. She wanted Greg, but she had no right to lead him on with the idea that there could be anything permanent between them. Love was what Greg wanted and deserved. She had no right to disillusion him, because she didn't know if she could ever offer him that.

His strong and powerful arms wrapped around her and melted her resolve. It had been so long since a man had held her like this.

Monica pulled away. "Let me go," she said breathlessly.

"No." He smiled, and she almost gave in. "Did you clear off the sofa?"

Taking a deep breath, she made her voice firm. "Greg. This has to stop."

Reluctantly, he loosened his arms. "It's tough letting you go, but I'm glad you believe in abstinence also."

She backed away to boost her courage. "You're right; I do." She staggered to the nearest chair, cleared off the debris, and plopped down. "But it's more than that. I'm sort of engaged. Maybe."

He stared, swallowing hard. He rubbed his hands across his forehead and down his cheek. Remorse flooded her, fearing that she might have hurt him.

"I'm sorry. I never mentioned it because Stephen and I have been separated for a long time."

His expression brightened. "Then it's over between you?"

"I wish it were as simple as that. I can't explain it to you because I can't even explain it to myself."

"You have to give me more than that."

He was right. She put the cushions and afghan back on the couch. "Sit down here. I'll try and explain.

"Stephen was a partner of my father's. They were very close, like brothers, except that Stephen was about ten years younger than Armand. It was my father's idea for us to marry."

Greg looked incredulous. "You mean an arranged marriage?"

Monica shook her head. "You'd have to know my father to understand. He was very domineering. He was so self-confident that he figured whatever he wanted was for the best, never thinking to ask either one of us." She picked at the loose strands on one of the damaged decorator pillows. "He loved both of us, so I guess he figured we should marry."

"And this Stephen, how does he feel about this arrangement?"

Monica sighed. "He's very much like my father. He assumed I would want to be with him."

"And you don't?"

Monica stood and began to pace in front of the window,

noticing that dawn was about to break. "It's not because I don't love him. He's been a big part of my life. But he's very controlling, like my father. I don't think I can be the wife he wants. I broke off the engagement."

Greg spread his feet out in front of him and leaned back into the couch. "Sounds to me like you are through with each other. So how does he affect a relationship between us?"

"If I can't commit to Stephen, how can I commit to you?" She planted her feet apart and faced him, hands on hips. "I don't know how."

He straightened. "You can learn."

Yearnings welled, threatening to bring tears. Turning her back to him, she pressed against the window. She wanted to be with Greg, but she didn't want to hurt him.

He came up behind her and placed his hands on her shoulders, gently massaging them. "Look, the sun is coming up. We've been talking all night."

Monica spun away from his touch. "Let me make some coffee."

"I won't turn it down."

She smiled. "At least you're still talking to me. I hope we can be friends. I treasure our friendship."

He leaned against the counter and watched her fiddle with the coffeemaker. "No matter what the circumstances, we're more than friends."

She locked gazes with him, unable to hide her joy in his comment. "But that's all we can be."

"For now, I'll concede to that. But it sounds to me like you need to face facts and make a final decision about Stephen."

"Building my father's house was a ploy to put that off. I'll admit to that." She poured in the water and measured the coffee. "Hopefully by the time I finish the house, I'll know what I want."

"You can't make decisions if you don't think about the issues."

The coffee pot gurgled as water began to seep down. The aroma of fresh coffee filled the room. "You're right of course," Monica said. "But I'm too tired to think straight, let alone deal with this."

Greg came from around the counter and draped his arm across her shoulders. "I don't believe now is the time either." He tilted her chin up so that she could look at him. He smiled. "Just tell me you'll make that decision soon."

Her heart raced. "How can I refuse when you give me such a smile?"

His grin widened. "That's my plan."

Her knees buckled. Her breath caught. "I'm too weak to argue."

He tilted his head back and laughed. "Weak is not a word in your vocabulary. How about you're too wise to argue?"

"Hmmmm. You're a dangerous man to be around. I can see that."

Wheels crunching on gravel interrupted their conversation. Greg frowned over the interruption. "Must be Rhonda," he guessed.

Mention of Rhonda sent Monica into action. "Go out and prepare her. I'll try and clear up the living room."

"Give it up. She's going to have to face it."

"Let her at least have one room she can bear. It's all my fault. If I wasn't staying here, Jones—"

Greg interrupted. "Don't say it, Monica. You promised me. Not a word to anyone about your suspicion of Jones."

"All right," she conceded. "But let me at least get it off my chest with you."

"Just me. Promise?"

She nodded. The promise wouldn't be that hard to keep because she intended to have evidence soon. Then the whole

Basin would know about Jones.

Car doors slammed outside. Greg hurried to the foyer while Monica rushed around picking up the last items off the floor.

Rhonda rushed into the living room. "What's this I hear?"

Monica explained, ending with, "The sheriff promised to keep it out of the news. That way the vandal"—casting Greg a glance, she bit her tongue to stop herself from mentioning Jones— "whoever it is, won't get the satisfaction of knowing our reaction."

"That's wise," Rhonda agreed. "I'll call my attorney later on today. He'll know how to handle the details."

It surprised Monica that her friend didn't seem that upset, even after viewing the damages.

Monica followed her around. "I'm so sorry, Rhonda. I'll make it up to you."

"Forget it, darling. These things happen. Thieves broke into my place in Newport. At least nothing was stolen here."

Monica bit her tongue to keep quiet after Greg sent her a meaningful glance.

Rhonda turned toward them. "You two look beat. Why don't you go turn in? I'm about to do the same. That party was something else."

Maybe Rhonda had the right idea after all. Greg started to gather his things.

Monica stopped him. "Stay and sleep here. You're too tired to drive to the South Shore."

It didn't take much to persuade him. Rhonda helped and within a half-hour, they had the mattress in one of the guest bedrooms turned to the un-slit sides and put in shape to sleep on.

After Rhonda went to her room, Greg touched Monica's arm. "I have an idea," he said, following her in to her room.

"I'm too tired to—"

"No. I'm talking about the future."

"Greg, I—"

Again he interrupted her. "I don't want you to make a decision, just hear me out."

Too exhausted to argue, she sat down on the bed.

Greg sat beside her. "Whoever did this is obviously trying to tell you something."

"I won't be intimidated," she insisted.

"That's why I'm going to insist that you stay with me. No strings attached. Just as friends."

Monica's head shot up. "What are you talking about?"

"Rhonda will only be here a few days. When she leaves, I don't want you to be alone."

"No one is going to hurt me. They wouldn't dare." Her bravado was strictly for Greg's benefit. His words actually made her nervous.

"You aren't going to alter your campaign. If vandalism hasn't stopped you, whoever did this may take it a step further."

Monica remained silent. She didn't want to admit to needing Greg, yet what he said made sense—too much sense.

"Thanks for your offer, Greg, but I'm too tired to decide right now. When Rhonda leaves, we'll discuss it."

"Just promise me you'll consider it."

She nodded. "I will."

Greg kissed her forehead before leaving her room.

Monica closed her eyes but couldn't sleep right away. Too much had happened too fast. The concert, the vandalism, and then baring her heart to Greg.

She'd come much too close tonight to seeking love in a physical way. That had never happened before. No one had ever stirred her senses like Greg had. Was it because she was tired and vulnerable? Or could she be falling in love? Her head spun as she tried to sort out her feelings.

Monica moaned and rolled onto her stomach. This was no time to try and figure it out. She'd been going nonstop for a week with very little sleep and none last night.

Come rest awhile, Child.

Yes, Mother. I need to rest. Monica thought of the times she'd laid her head in her mother's lap. She closed her eyes, and peace settled over her.

CHAPTER 13

GREG TURNED into the parking lot of the office building complex and parked the agency Bronco. He glanced at his watch and then at Carl. "It's almost one-thirty. I'm ready for lunch, aren't you?"

"I'm starved. That was a long drive out to that piece of property." Carl peered outside. "There's only one problem with your plan, my friend."

Greg set the parking brake. "What's that?"

"There's no place to eat here."

"Strange you should mention that." He grinned. "There's a pizza place down the road, two blocks from here. They have the best combo on the North Shore, and at this time of day they have them cooked and ready to go."

"Sounds good. So why are we here?"

"I have an appointment. It's personal, so I wanted to make it on my break. Do me a favor and go pick up that pizza. By the time you return, I'll be done and we can take it down to the beach."

Carl raised his brow at the unusual request, but Greg wasn't interested in explaining further, nor did he have the time.

"Look, I've got to go. I'll be here by the time you return." He pointed to the parking lot and then waved.

Carl drove off shaking his head. Greg swung around and headed up the steps toward Mitch Jones's office.

The smart-looking secretary greeted him, then left to announce his arrival to Jones. Greg took advantage of the moment to peruse his surroundings. The office had class. Jones was doing all right for himself.

The secretary returned and ushered him into an office that showed a continuation of good taste. He would have felt comfortable if it had belonged to anyone but Jones.

"Linsey. What can I do for you?" Jones's welcome sounded friendly, but underneath Greg heard the wariness. "I have to admit to being surprised that you called for an appointment. I can't imagine you're in need of my services."

Greg didn't take the proffered hand, but sat down in one of the chairs. "I was in the area and thought I'd pay a social visit."

Jones quirked his brow. "I wasn't aware we had anything to be social about."

"Sure we do, Mitch." Greg hooked his ankle across his knee in feigned casualness. "It is all right if I call you Mitch, isn't it?"

"Actually, no." Jones straightened papers on his desk. "I don't want to waste my time with a call we both know has nothing to do with social amenities."

Greg struggled with the urge to stand up and strangle the man. "Let's get to the point then. My time is valuable too. I'm here to tell you that from now on I'm taking a personal interest in the projects you submit to the agency."

Jones stilled behind his desk. "What's that supposed to mean?"

Greg held up his hands. "It doesn't mean anything, except that you'll get special attention. Isn't that what everyone is after these days?"

Jones jumped up, sending his chair flying behind him. "Don't mess with my submissions, Linsey."

Greg leaned back. "I wouldn't mess with your submissions. That would be unethical."

Jones placed his hands on the desk and leaned toward Greg. "What are you suggesting?"

Greg shrugged. "I don't understand why you're so upset. I thought you'd be relieved to know I'd be handling every one of your projects. Sometimes a personal touch speeds things up."

Jones scowled. "Or slows them down."

"Now why would I do that?" Greg gritted his teeth, forcing himself to sit calmly and keep a phony smile plastered across his face. "I could get fired for even suggesting such a thing."

Jones frowned suspiciously at him. "You're right about that, Linsey. I'll be submitting the proposals for the inn. If I so much as smell a delay, I'll have you in court so fast…"

"Sounds to me like you're the one making threats here. I come in here offering to make things easier, and you thank me with talk about lawsuits." Greg gestured to the room. "I thought you were a smart businessman."

"No one offers without a reason, especially someone in your position. What's in it for you, Linsey?"

"Sit down and we'll talk about it," Greg offered. He could afford to be generous since he now had the upper hand.

"I thought so." Jones brought his chair back and sat down. He pulled a cigar out of an inlaid box on his desk.

He offered one, but Greg shook his head, thankful Jones didn't light the one in his hand.

"What exactly do you want from me in return for this special service?" Jones asked.

"It seems to me that since we all work and live here in the same area, we should strive for a better working relationship. I know you haven't been pleased with some of our decisions, so resentment naturally occurs."

"Naturally." Jones rolled the cigar between his fingers. "So how will your personalized handling help me?"

"I doubt it'll *help* you at all." Greg lowered his foot and stretched his legs out. "I thought it might ease your mind, knowing I'll take a personal interest. That way you'll be sure if there are delays, you won't be lost in bureaucratic paperwork."

Again Jones frowned. "How so?"

Greg smiled. "I have a lot of friends here in the Basin. You know one of them—Monica Scott."

"She's no longer my client."

"I'm aware of that. A shame what happened to her the other night, wasn't it?"

Greg studied Jones closely, but only a flicker of emotion showed in his face. "Am I supposed to know about something happening to her?"

"We did have the sheriff keep it out of the media. But I thought perhaps you knew something about it."

Jones only smiled in answer.

Greg clenched his fists, aching to prove Jones was responsible. "Are you interested in knowing what happened?"

Jones tapped his fingers on top of his desk. "I could care less about Monica Scott."

Greg stood. "Well she does concern me. You see, Jones, I care very much about Monica Scott's welfare. If anything should happen to her, I doubt I'd get much work done from all the worry."

Jones threw his cigar on his desk and stood up. "I think our social visit has come to an end."

"I've made myself clear, then."

"Very clear. Your generosity overwhelms me."

"Here's to good and productive business then." Greg flipped a mock salute and strode out the door.

Carl pulled into the parking lot. Before he came to a complete stop, Greg had yanked the door open.

"Perfect timing," he commented, hopping into the vehicle.

Carl shifted into gear. "What's going on? I saw Jones's sign when I drove in. Don't tell me you were with that shyster?"

Greg nodded. "Man, that pizza smells great. I'm starving."

"You aren't getting a bite until you tell me what you're up to. I can't imagine what you're doing with that—"

"Don't say it," Greg reminded him.

"As long as I'm not around the boss, I can call Jones what he is."

"Using foul language now is what makes it a habit that comes out at work."

"Okay. Forget the descriptive nouns. What'd Jones have to say?" Carl pulled the Bronco into the beachside parking lot and stopped where they could view the lake.

No one else was on the obscure beach. Greg helped himself to a slice of pizza, then described the meeting.

Carl ate in silence as he listened. Finally, he spoke. "I can't believe you said that to Jones. There's no way you can interfere with his proposals."

"You know that and I know that. I'm counting on the fact that Jones doesn't."

"You never came out with a direct threat. How are you so sure Jones would think you meant one?"

Greg bit into another piece of pizza and pulled on the thick strings of cheese. After he'd swallowed, he said, "It's the way Jones operates. In his code of values, a threat would be the standard mode of operation."

"I hope it works. You're going to be in a jam if he calls a supervisor and complains."

"About what? All I said was that I had personal concern for his projects. If he thinks I'm implying interference, that's his problem."

Carl slammed the palm of his hand on the steering wheel and laughed. "I've got to hand it to you, Linsey. You're one clever son of a gun."

Greg lifted his can of soda in a toast. "It better work, because if Jones messes with Monica again, I will do something that could get me in big trouble."

"If he does, call me. I'll join you. We can queue up in the unemployment line together."

Nodding his appreciation for the support, Greg pulled apart another slice of pizza. "I just wish I could influence Monica as easily as I did Jones. She's so blasted stubborn."

"She does like doing things her own way," Carl agreed. "What's she going to do now?"

"I tried to talk her into staying with me at my place, but she's putting off the decision as long as Rhonda's still there."

Carl sipped on his soda between bites of pizza. "Sounds serious between you two. Are you actually going to commit to someone?"

"I would if I could," Greg admitted. "Monica is the first woman I've met whom I'd like to live, sleep, and be with forever. Sometimes I think she feels the same way, but then at other times she seems so far away. It has to do with the fact that she's sort of engaged."

Carl choked on a piece of pepperoni. "She's what?"

"He's in the Middle East. Some job connected with the United Nations. They've been separated for two years, but seems there're still issues between them." Greg explained as much as he could without revealing any of Monica's personal feelings.

"Tough break," Carl said. "Don't get too involved until you're sure it's over between them."

"I'm keeping my cool. Don't worry about that."

"Doesn't sound like it if you're inviting her to move in with you."

"She'd be staying as a friend."

"If you say so." Carl scoffed. "I don't want to see you bite the dust."

Shifting uneasily, Greg shrugged. "It's cool. I'm in control."

Saying so was easy, but in reality Greg knew he was treading on thin ice where Monica was concerned.

Monica sat on Rhonda's deck, folding fliers. She glanced at Rhonda and Judy, stretched out on chaise longues and enjoying the afternoon sun. "You were right, Judy. Those two concerts brought the environmental issue of the Basin into the national news. Letters have been pouring in."

"Checks too, I hope."

When Judy turned over to get her back tanned, Monica said, "You're going to get skin cancer if you stay in this sun."

Judy opened her eyes. "You've been around Greg too long. You're beginning to sound like him."

Rhonda glanced at Monica's smug smile. "How serious is it with the two of you?"

Monica tied the fliers she'd folded into a bundle. "I'm trying to keep my feet on the ground and operate in reality."

Judy nodded. "You're too practical for a wild idea to get a chance."

Monica started on another stack of fliers. "I get responses, don't I?"

"Unfortunately, yes," Rhonda sighed.

Monica stopped folding and looked at her friend. "I'm so sorry, Rhonda. What happened to your house is my fault."

Rhonda sat up. "If you apologize one more time, I'm going to kick you out of here for good. It could have happened with or without you here. In fact, three years ago I had a break-in and all of my stuff was stolen. That's why I was so thrilled to have you staying here. I thought the chances for theft would diminish."

Monica slapped her hand on the pile of papers. "And that didn't happen. If I hadn't been here, your house would be the same. I really should find another place to live."

"You sound like you're looking for an excuse to go stay with Greg," Judy pointed out.

Monica resumed folding the fliers, muttering, "I should never have confided that to you."

"What's this?" Rhonda asked, her eyes sparkling.

Judy braced herself on her elbows. "Greg doesn't want Monica staying alone. He invited her to come live with him."

Rhonda leaned over and placed her hand on Monica's arm. "You don't have to stay here if you don't want to."

Monica dropped a folded flier onto the table. "I'll move out of your place if you want, but only to protect your property. The decision will have nothing to do with my relationship with Greg."

"So there is a relationship?" Rhonda pressed.

Monica stared at her friend, wishing she would drop the subject. "I'm not about to get involved with Greg until I'm positive I don't want to go back to Stephen."

"Personally, I think it's high time you ended your relationship with Stephen for good. The man is a domineering manipulator."

Monica took off her glasses and twirled them around. She agreed, but until meeting Greg, she'd assumed all men were manipulators. She'd decided staying single would work out better. "But I promised my father I would marry him, and Stephen is holding me to that promise."

Rhonda plopped back down on the lounge chair. "He's stupid to want you for a wife if you don't love him."

Inwardly, Monica cringed. She really had to make Stephen understand she didn't want to marry him. Sure, they would always be part of each other's life, but not as man and wife. "So what does my love life have to do with my staying here? Don't tell me you're going to make it a condition for your hospitality."

Rhonda tugged a pillow under her cheek. "Come off it, Monica. You know me better than that. Stop using my words to salve your own guilt."

Monica flared up. "Guilt is not an issue here!"

"Isn't it? What about Greg Linsey? Aren't you using him to avoid dealing with Stephen?"

Hating the fact that Rhonda saw through her, Monica leaned back and shoved her glasses on to hide her eyes. "If you weren't one of my best friends, Rhonda, you'd never get away with saying that."

Rhonda eyed her fingernails. "I'm glad to hear I still have that much status." She glanced at Judy, who had been attentively silent. "What do you think, Judy? Is Monica serious about Greg? Should we convince her to go live with him?"

Judy paused, then leaned toward Monica. "Greg is crazy about you. If you aren't sure of your feelings, don't hurt him. If you are, go for it."

Rhonda laughed. "Now there's an ambiguous answer filled with good advice."

Monica made a face as she finished another stack of fliers. "I'm glad you both have so much confidence in running my personal life. In reality, I don't have time for either Stephen or Greg, so this discussion is theoretical."

Rhonda stretched her toes to the sun. "Now isn't that convenient? A full schedule is always your excuse. What will you use when the Ponderosa Inn issue is settled?"

Monica clenched her fists, but refused to respond.

Rhonda put her finger to her cheek. "I know, it's your father's house. We must finish that now," she said, mimicking Monica's voice.

Monica jumped up, fliers scattering. "Enough, Rhonda. You've made your point."

Rhonda smiled sweetly, which only infuriated Monica until she really looked at her friend. Ridiculous. She laughed. "Blast it, Rhonda. You know how I hate it when you're right."

"You may be able to fool the rest of the world, but you don't fool me, sweetheart. I can read your selfish head like an open book."

"Oh please. Selfish on top of everything else?"

"That's the core, isn't it?"

Judy stood and grabbed a pile of fliers. "I think we better get back to work."

Glad for a change of subject, Monica began stacking the folded fliers in a box. "What we should be discussing is our next plan of action. We now have the public's attention. We need to feed them information while we can."

Rhonda tilted back her sunglasses. "This reminds me. I have to fly to Los Angeles tomorrow. My agent arranged a spot on one of the late night shows."

"You're leaving?"

"Just through the weekend," Rhonda assured her. "Why don't you stay at Judy's while I'm gone?"

"Sure," Judy said. "You're welcome to stay over any time. You know we have the room."

"Why can't I stay here alone like I have been the past few months? I only told you about Greg's offer because I thought maybe you'd prefer I leave. I'm certainly not afraid of being alone."

Relief crossed Judy's features. Monica suspected Jim would have a fit if Judy invited her to stay without asking him first. She turned to Rhonda. "Will you be able to plug our cause on the talk show?"

Rhonda reached for the suntan oil and spread more on her arms. "That's the reason I've been invited. Seems like the producer is interested in the environment issue and wants me to tell the audience about our concert."

Monica held up her fingers in a V, making a sign of victory. "All right."

Judy bent down and gave Rhonda a hug. "That's wonderful. You'll have to tell us which night. Imagine being on live television." She twirled around, unable to contain her excitement. "Wait until Jim hears this. It's his favorite show."

Monica smiled at Rhonda in silent thanks, knowing that what seemed so important to Judy was blasé to a star.

Rhonda smiled back and said, "I need to talk to Greg Linsey and some of the others from your group who can give me technical information. Do you think we can brainstorm statements that'll pack a wallop in the few minutes I'll have on the air?"

This kind of action was more to Monica's liking than soul searching. Within the hour, she had a meeting lined up for that evening. "We'll have it here to expedite matters. You aren't going to have time to travel all over the lakeshore."

"That's right," Rhonda smiled. "We must keep my public image in mind."

Monica curtsied in mock reverence. "The ravishing beauty, Rhonda Remway."

Judy joined in the laughter. "I'm glad you're coming back, Rhonda. Being around the two of you is anything but boring."

Monica raised her brows. "Boring? The word doesn't exist in our vocabulary."

Monica sat beside Greg in one of the chairs they had circled around the deck. After the discussion earlier this afternoon, she felt uncomfortable—guilty. His cologne and woodsy scent

207

wafted around him. She wanted to touch his arm, smooth her fingers in his hair. She breathed deep and shoved all personal feelings aside when Greg took over the meeting.

"The TRPA was originally initiated by a compact ratified by Congress." Greg's low voice commanded everyone's attention, especially Monica's. "It established environmental standards that determine what changes an area can withstand without damaging the environment."

"There were many controversies over its establishment, if my memory serves me," Rhonda prodded as she passed out glasses of iced tea.

Leave it to an entertainer to know how to appeal to the public, Monica thought. Stating the purpose of the agency would make boring dialogue, but dealing with the controversies would grab the audience. Greg understood Rhonda's ploy as well. A look of disgust crossed his features, but he was too tactful to ignore the impact and publicity.

"You're right, Rhonda." He took a glass of tea and sipped on it before continuing his lecture on the TRPA.

Monica passed a tray of cheese and crackers. "A person who buys property here rarely knows what he's in for."

"At least he's supposed to," Judy reminded her. "If they hire a consultant like Jones, they may never know until it's too late."

Monica didn't respond since she'd been one of Jones's victims.

Greg smiled as he set his glass down and began snapping his fingers. "During the litigation they worked out the Individual Parcel Evaluation System or, as we call it, the IPES program, which enables people to find a way to use their property by a point system. They can add points by purchasing them or restoring environmentally sensitive property."

"Similar to what Monica is doing with hers," Rhonda interceded.

Greg slapped his knee. "Exactly. Environmentally sensitive areas are restricted. Monica may still have problems with her lot because of the stream."

Monica resisted the urge to debate her personal interest. Now was not the time, nor would it be wise to confront Greg in front of all these people. Her personal project must be left out of the debates.

"These plans are very innovative," Greg continued talking, evidently concurring with Monica on leaving out specific cases. "No other agency or region that I know of employs such strict regulations to protect the environment."

"What's important to note," one of the committee members added, "is that this project shows the public that commercial interests and environmentalists can come to a workable agreement."

The discussion continued for another hour. Monica thought she'd heard it all from Greg, but found there was even more information she was unaware of. The agency did have some innovative and commendable features, and from all accounts they seemed to be effective.

Rhonda finished taking notes and amazed Monica when she came up with about three comprehensive and qualitative statements. They even impressed Greg.

"You'll be able to accomplish a tremendous amount for environment everywhere if you can get those concepts across on national television," Greg told her.

"I'll try. It's all I can promise." Rhonda shrugged as she guided her other guests to the door. "Thanks for coming. It's been very informative."

After closing the door, Rhonda turned to Greg. "I'm glad, actually, that all of this happened. If the vandals hadn't attacked, I would have left with only a broad idea of this issue."

Greg smiled. "Now the trick will be to see if we can convince the public."

Rhonda stood and took a bow. "We have a good start with the publicity from the concert and the late-night talk show."

"Speaking of talk shows," Greg grabbed Monica's hand and brought her attention to him. "I have a good friend who produces one in San Francisco. Why don't I call him and get you on his program?"

Monica squeezed his fingers and shook her head. "I'm a good organizer, but leave me out of television."

"You'll be great," Greg assured her. "You are now informed enough to know what to say. We'll go down together. I want you to meet my family."

Chapter 14

Many tourists had arrived in the Tahoe Basin for the Fourth of July celebrations. The heat wave on the coast helped drive them to the mountains. Plenty of people were influenced by the publicity for the Ponderosa Inn. Working the PIC booth, Monica glanced across the crowded beach. Whiffs of barbecue and popcorn made her stomach growl.

Red, white, and blue banners flapped in the cooling breeze. Several young men and women played a tough volleyball game that had drawn a crowd of onlookers. Bright fluorescent colors accented all the shades of tan. Umbrellas, towels, and ice coolers full of every drink imaginable covered the sand.

The country-western band at the fair had taken a break. A lull in activity gave Monica a chance for a much-needed rest. Unfortunately, it also gave her time to think and fret.

True to his word, Greg had arranged for an interview with a major network morning show popular in the San Francisco Bay Area. Fortunately, their show wasn't scheduled until the week after the Fourth of July. The date also coincided with Rhonda's return to Los Angeles. Monica had flown to LA with her for the late-night talk show. The trip had done a world of good for Monica's emotions. Getting away from the pressures of PIC and her relationship with Greg had lightened her mood.

When she and Rhonda had returned to Tahoe, preparation for the booth took up most of her time and attention, which gave her no time to worry about her relationship with Greg. Once the holiday was over, her reprieve would be also. Rhonda had to report to the studio to begin filming a new movie. Greg still insisted that she not stay alone. She hadn't written Stephen, and he was due to call.

Monica sighed as she glanced across the crowded beach. To keep from thinking about future decisions, Monica focused on the activities going on around her. In the water, paddleboats, floats, air mattresses, and Jet Skis entertained the swimmers. The warm day made the cold water inviting. Perspiration beaded across her brow and down the V of her neck. Yes, a swim would be a welcome treat. Maybe when Judy arrived she'd go down to the water and have a refreshing dip.

Behind her the band started warming up, and Monica returned her attention to the art fair where PIC had set up their booth. Crowds of people milled around the booths of crafts and art that were set up among the huge ponderosa pines in the beach parking lot.

Judy strolled up just as the band began its first country-western song. "We should be busy again now that they're back." She gestured toward the musicians. The lively dance music did attract people their way.

"Most of the tourists seem supportive," Judy said as she slipped behind the booth to join Monica.

"They have nothing to lose and everything to gain," Monica pointed out. "People who own property are the only ones fighting this, mainly because they're afraid they won't be able to sell their places. If they don't have anything to lose, they'll support saving a historic point of interest."

Judy ignored Monica's comment. "Look who's coming? This ought to brighten your day."

Monica glanced in the direction Judy was pointing to see Greg heading their way. He waved. Monica waved back, his presence indeed lightening her mood.

He thumped a tune on their counter. "How's business? Getting signatures for support?"

Monica flipped the stack of pages filled with names and addresses. "You bet."

Greg snapped his fingers. "If I decide to run for office, I'll sure know who to get to head my campaign."

"Are you planning to run for office?" Monica asked, easily picturing Greg as a legislator.

"It's crossed my mind. I've had plenty of experience with politics since this job has been a political hot potato since its conception."

Monica picked up her glasses, which she'd placed by the cash register, and began twirling them around. "You'd make a good politician. You're diplomatic yet forceful. You were able to convince me to your way of thinking."

He flourished a bow. "I'm flattered. Want the job of running my campaign?"

She definitely liked the action, so the idea appealed, especially since it involved more time with Greg. "Depends on when you plan to run. I'm booked for the next year or two with that house."

Greg placed his hands on the counter and leaned close. "The way I figure it, we have a whole lifetime ahead of us to decide."

His words hung between them, heavy with meaning. Monica's heart fluttered with anticipation. "If you can wait, so can I. Don't forget, I'm getting good at that game. You've been a good instructor in that department too."

Greg groaned, then grinned to let her know he was teasing. "When are you finished with your duty here? I want to take you out to dinner." He glanced over at Judy. "You and Jim are welcome to join us."

She eyed Judy, who shrugged. "I'd love to, but Jim has plans."

Greg nodded and smiled at Monica. "We could invite Carl."

"Trying to prove it's just friendship?" she teased.

He shook his head no, but his eyes said yes. She should refuse, but Rhonda was attending a party tonight. Monica didn't want to be alone. "Sounds like a plan. But let's just go the two of us. I'll close shop after the fireworks start. Come by then."

"Good. We'll watch the show and then head for this place I know of that has the best fried chicken in town."

Monica shoved her glasses on top of her head. "Sounds appropriate for the Fourth of July. I guess I'll stay away from the hot dogs."

Greg shook his head and laughed. "We're off to a party up the road. I promised some of my coworkers we'd stop by."

Monica leaned against the counter, her expression serious. "You sure you want to come all the way back here?"

He reached across the booth and traced his finger down her cheek. "Count on it."

The touch silenced any further protest. She wanted to follow him as he walked toward the parking lot. For days she'd been pushing aside the memories of Greg's embrace. But did she want to explore the sensations further?

Mitch Jones stood at the edge of the art fair and peered down the walkway at the PIC booth. He puffed on his cigar, cursing silently to himself. Wasn't there anything that broad didn't think of?

When Linsey left, he was sorely tempted to go over and give her and the Myers woman some static. As soon as the thought occurred, he dismissed it. The booth didn't need more attention than it already had. Several more curses soothed some of his frustration.

Candy Rogers, a prominent real estate agent along the North Shore, approached. "Jones, I'm surprised to see you here."

Jones turned and smiled. "I'm showing a couple of clients around. They saw the fair and wanted to stop. What are you up to, Candy?"

Candy shrugged, her brow furrowed into a frown. "Not much. Glad to see you're busy."

"This week usually is. Lots of tourists up for the holiday."

"Normally I can make that claim myself, but this year…" She paused and nodded toward the fair. "With all the talk about problems with building and buying up here, my clients are leery and reluctant to commit."

PIC again. Jones clenched his fingers around his cigar. "I've fielded several questions directed at me along those lines, myself. It's taken some fast-talking to overcome the client's fears."

Candy pointed to the redhead that leaned forward from the PIC booth. "And we have her to thank."

"Monica Scott. What did we ever do to deserve the likes of her?" He'd give anything to take back his business dealings with the woman. She'd warned him not to cross her, and he had underestimated her threat.

Candy asked, "When is your deal with the Ponderosa Inn going to be finalized? We'll all be better-off when the publicity over that is over and done."

Jones glared at the real estate agent. His nerves tightened. This group was out for profit. Forget altruistic causes. If his cause prevented business, they wouldn't hesitate to cut loose their ties.

"It won't take much longer," he hedged. Actually, his current client would provide him enough profit to make another payment on the Ponderosa Inn project, which was the only reason he'd consented to sticking around this zoo. A quick glance confirmed the couple was still browsing through the booths.

Candy broke into his introspection. "For all our sakes I hope it's going to be soon. We can't stand this kind of trouble for the whole summer season."

Jones didn't comment but focused his gaze on Monica Scott. It wasn't his business deal that was killing the market. It was her. "The problem will be taken care of. Count on it," he muttered more to himself than to the real estate agent.

When Candy Rogers walked away, Jones went over to the booth operated by the businessmen of the area. They sponsored the food concession every year and used the money to purchase equipment for the local fire department. Jones didn't care about that. He wanted information.

"Hand me a Coke, Joe." He slid some coins across the counter.

The young man who'd attended several coalition meetings nodded a greeting as he filled the order. "Here you go. What's happening?"

Jones took the paper cup. "I was hoping you'd be able to tell me. Has the PIC booth been this busy all day?"

"Busier."

Jones groaned inwardly. "They plan to stay open all evening?"

"I heard that Scott woman say she'd close up shop during the fireworks. That's about when we'll all be shutting down."

Jones didn't chat much longer. His clients were still browsing. With the information he needed, he headed toward his car.

Slipping into the vehicle, he set down the soda and picked up his cell phone. Packard answered immediately, which boosted Jones's confidence.

"What's up? Got another job for me?"

"You bet. Are you free tonight?"

The sunset presented a natural display of color for the national holiday. Bright pinks blended into spectacular reds and oranges on the wispy clouds hovering over the lake. As Monica watched the crowd gathering on the beach for the fireworks show, she realized she hadn't been in the United States for very many of its birthday celebrations. Strong feelings of nationalism amazed her.

Families streamed past her booth, uninterested now in what she had to say. They weren't stopping at the other concessions or booths either. She was tempted to close up early and call it a night.

A quick glance at her watch showed it would be another hour before the fireworks began. She might as well stay open. It would keep her occupied until Greg showed up. Besides, she noticed that after people had established their place to sit, they'd begun strolling around. She could get some more signatures.

A few minutes later, two young men came up to her booth. One laughed unnaturally, his eyes dilated, probably doing drugs. "You must be selling something good from the looks of you."

Monica stepped back. She didn't need that kind of publicity. "I'm about to close up. Why don't the two of you go on down and find yourselves a place at the beach? Spots fill up fast."

"I found my spot here."

"I think she means at the beach." The young man's friend slurred his words.

The first one to speak widened his eyes in mock disbelief. "You mean she's trying to get rid of us?"

Monica began gathering the papers off the counter in pretense of shutting down. The two men did not respond to the hint. Instead, they leaned across the boards, sending pages flying. Annoyed, Monica pushed their elbows off the counter.

"Time to move on, boys." She emphasized the word "boys," hoping they would become insulted and leave.

They became insulted all right, but they had no intention

of leaving. Monica began to pack up in earnest. No one would come to the booth with these two hanging around. She might as well end the whole thing.

The two traded insults and then aimed a few at her. Ignoring them, she piled the papers in the briefcase behind the counter. One of the boys started to climb on the counter. Muscles and nerves tightening, she clenched her fists around the briefcase, ready to slug him with it if he came any closer.

Someone came up from behind the man and yanked him back down to the ground. The county sheriff's deputy stepped between her and the men.

Sighing with relief, Monica let go of the briefcase. "I'm sure glad to see you," she told the officer after he sent the two men on their way. "I thought I had the situation under control until that one guy jumped up here." She patted the counter.

"I had my eye on them," the officer assured her. "When I saw they were getting out of hand, I decided to come pay you a call."

A low "woof" came from outside the booth, and Monica leaned forward to see a beautiful police dog sitting patiently beside his master.

She smiled. "I see you're well-protected."

"You bet. We're out in full force on a night like this." He gestured toward the beach, and Monica saw what he meant. Along the sand and in the parking lot several uniform-clad deputies patrolled in pairs, some others with dogs, like him.

"It's reassuring to know you're here. Thanks for the help."

"Anytime." He smiled and, calling his dog, walked toward the other booths.

Monica had just about decided to close up when a couple stopped by and asked about PIC. Others came after them. Monica lost track of time. She'd rather be busy than waiting the hour out for Greg to return from his gathering.

A welcome free moment arrived. Long shadows fell across the booths from the street lights in the parking area. Suddenly the sky lit up bright orange. A loud explosion followed. Monica dashed outside the booth to see that the display of fireworks had begun.

Applause and whistles echoed along the beach with each loud burst of color. Infected by the festive mood, Monica stood in front of the booth and *ooohed* and *aaahed* with the crowd. It had been years since she'd seen a fireworks show. It brought back memories of her father.

No. She wouldn't think of her father. Not tonight.

This was an evening to celebrate and have fun. Greg would be arriving any minute. That thought motivated her to unlatch the awning that converted into siding for the booth after it came down, making it into a shed that could be locked. She hurried inside and snapped shut the latches to lock and secure the small booth. No light penetrated inside with the walls all closed up. Monica fumbled around for her purse and her briefcase.

Something banged against the wall. Monica paused. "Is that you, Greg? I'm inside getting my stuff. I'll be out in a minute." Excitement coursed through her at the prospect of spending the evening with him. She pictured his smile, heard his laughter. Would he kiss her tonight? Since she'd told him about Stephen, he'd kept his distance.

The door opened, letting in a burst of purple light from another firecracker. Monica chuckled. "I'm coming. I'm coming." She stuffed the last bag in her purse.

Before she could turn, someone stepped behind her. Still hurrying, she swung around to be greeted by an ugly grunt and foul breath.

Panic welled. "Who are—?"

Rough hands wrapped around her throat. Monica clawed, her fingernails scraping the cheek of her assailant. She kicked at his groin. He sidestepped. Her foot landed in his thigh. He tripped.

Thinking it was one of the young men she'd thwarted earlier, she tried to push her weight against him. If he was ripped on drugs, he could easily lose his balance. He stood his ground.

Monica struggled wildly, but the man was too strong. She'd barely get one arm free before he'd grab it. In seconds, he pinned her against the wall. She couldn't kick him.

"Don't move and you won't get hurt." His foul breath made her gag. His words infuriated her. Before she could scream, something cold pressed against her throat. Fiery pain sent a chill of fear. He had a knife, and he intended to use it. Blood trickled down her neck.

"I'm going to take my hand off your mouth. If I hear one peep out of you..." He pressed the knife against her throat. Pain shot through her.

When his hand came off her mouth, she took deep breaths. "I don't have any money. We only signed petitions and handed out fliers."

"I know," he growled.

Monica cocked her head. He didn't sound like one of the men who'd been there earlier.

"It's not money I'm after. It's *you* I want."

That sounded like the druggies who had harassed her before. She fought the urge to struggle. If he was under the influence of drugs, she didn't dare take any chances. Not when he had a knife in his hand. Drugs made people too unpredictable.

"Look, I won't say anything or scream," Monica whispered desperately. "There are sheriff's deputies everywhere. In fact, they said they would be by every few minutes. Why don't you just slip out of here, and you won't get into any trouble."

His laugh sounded low and ugly. "No one's going to bother me. Don't count on being rescued either. As far as the deputies know, you've locked up and gone home."

If he planned rape, surely someone would hear. Monica would scream. If he wanted to kill her... She shuddered. "What do you want?"

"You've been a real pain to us, woman. Ever since you arrived in this area."

Suddenly Monica realized this wasn't one of the boys who'd bothered her earlier. She wished he was.

"Jones," she spat out. "Did he put you up to this?"

"No one puts me up to anything," he said, then called her several foul names. The sharp blade cut deeper into her skin.

She had to think of a way to escape. Even a slight movement could cost her life.

"A murder will only bring Jones more negative publicity," she whispered, trembling with fear.

"No. We don't intend to make a martyr out of you. But I'd be doing this planet you are so concerned about a favor if I made it so you couldn't talk anymore."

The pressure on Monica's throat increased. Terror weakened her knees. Nervous perspiration trickled down her spine. The walls of the booth closed in on her. *Greg. Help me*, she silently begged.

Do not be afraid, Child. Pray.

Mother, I wish I knew how to pray. Monica closed her eyes. *Think. Stall for time.* Greg was due any minute. Maybe a deputy would walk by. A dog might smell her fear.

"Whatever he's paying you, I'll pay you double," she said. "We can walk out of here and forget the whole thing."

"We're going to forget everything all right. You're going to drop out of PIC, but before you do you're going to make sure any future efforts are ineffective."

"How am I supposed to accomplish that?"

"We'll arrange for you to embezzle the funds. Not only

will that discredit you, it'll leave the group powerless."

"You're crazy." The words were out before she could think of the implications of what she'd said. Too late. The knife pressed and again blood trickled. Monica moaned.

Greg. Will I see you again?

"Don't ever call me crazy."

"Okay. I'm sorry. But no one is going to believe I would embezzle."

"Don't give yourself so much credit."

"I don't need the money. It doesn't make sense."

"It doesn't have to. The public loves scandal. Especially when someone gets caught at crimes of greed." His laugh sent chills down her spine.

"What if I refuse?"

"You won't refuse. You like to talk too much." He paused for a moment. "Besides, if you don't agree, we'll make things very unpleasant for your actress friend."

"You can't hurt her."

"I've been in her house once. I can get in again."

"You swine," Monica sputtered, wishing she could see his features in the dark.

"I don't think she'll be very popular with a face cut up and scarred, do you?" The knife pressed deeper.

The icy edge to his voice warned Monica that he would carry out the threat. She took a deep breath, fear paralyzing her. Waves of dizziness clouded her thinking, causing images of Greg to float in front of her. The man's arm was a tight steel band preventing her from reaching out to him. She sobbed when Greg's image faded.

"Greg!"

Suddenly the door of the booth flew open and flashes of green light brightened the interior of the booth. A blood-curdling yell deafened Monica. A force of energy ripped her assailant away from her.

She staggered to the far corner of the booth.

"Don't move."

Greg. He was with her.

A new fear tore through her. "He has a knife," she screamed and tried to see if she could help Greg in any way. What if he were killed!

Someone grunted. Monica screamed, edging her way to the door. "Help! Someone help us! We're being attacked!"

Outside, footsteps came running. *Hurry, hurry.* Monica screamed, hoping help hadn't come too late. The door burst open. Flashlights beamed into the booth. The man straddling Greg had his knife poised to stab him in the chest. Monica kicked his wrist.

With a mighty roar, he jumped upright and tore out of the building, knocking the deputy aside on his way. The dog yelped in pain and scurried into the booth to his master's side.

Greg struggled to his feet. Monica gasped when she saw a damp red blotch spreading across the side of his shirt. She yanked the scarf off her waist and pressed it against the wound.

Greg wrapped his arm around her shoulders and whispered, "I'm all right. Are you?"

Monica looked up and saw his smile lit by another burst of color from the fireworks display. Her heart burst with relief and love.

"I'm fine now, but you took your time getting here," she muttered, just before she passed out.

CHAPTER 15

GREG SHIFTED the Jag convertible into gear as he made the turn onto Lombard Street. He caught the look of surprise on Monica's face and chuckled. "I can't believe you've never been on San Francisco's curviest, steepest street. With all your traveling, you'd think you would have ended up here at one time or another."

Monica braced her hand on the dash of the sporty convertible. Her hair streamed behind her as she laughed. "I told you I've been here several times, but only at the airport, changing planes on connecting flights."

"I'm glad, because it's fun showing you around."

"I hope it isn't all like this."

Their tires squealed as they rounded the sharp corners of the steep grade. The city was in one of its rare and best summer moments. Clear skies, a crisp breeze that wasn't too cold, and flowers blooming everywhere.

"This is only a taste. Wait until we try the hills around Chinatown."

"I've heard about the restaurants there. I'll brave the steep streets with my eyes closed."

"And ruin the fun?" he teased. "It's good to see the smile in your eyes again." The incident on the Fourth had been near tragic and traumatic for both of them.

Monica placed her hand over his. "It's nice to be away. A

change of scenery is doing us both good."

He'd never in his life felt an emotion like the rage that boiled up when he'd seen Monica under attack. He never knew he could want to kill. Harming another person was against his every principle. Yet in the flash of a second, he had been ready to hurt and even kill the attacker. That knowledge unnerved him.

"Are you feeling better?"

She squeezed his hand. "I've traveled the globe and lived in countries where violence was part of the culture, but never have I been as frightened as I was that night."

Greg glanced at her, admiring her outwardly tough and determined look.

She shifted sideways so she faced him. "I think what scared me the most was the fear that he was hurting you."

He reached over and grabbed her hand. "I'm touched that you care, but I'm tougher than you think. I'll be all right."

"I would feel more confident about that if they had arrested the guy."

Greg agreed with her there. The man had disappeared in the crowd, and they hadn't gotten a good look at him.

"Too bad they couldn't connect him with Jones. From what the man said, I know Jones was behind the attack."

"The sheriff is working on it." He tugged on her hand. "Let's forget about the whole thing and concentrate on having fun."

The trip to San Francisco couldn't have happened at a better time. Greg's supervisor hadn't been too pleased with time off during the busiest season, but after he'd explained what had happened, the time had been granted.

Topping another hill, he glanced at Monica. She tried unsuccessfully to gather her hair with her free hand.

She gave up and laughed. "I'm surprised your mother let

you borrow her car knowing you drive like this."

Grinning, Greg geared the Jaguar. "She doesn't know. That's why I can take it whenever I want."

"You have her wrapped around your little finger. I've never seen two men as spoiled as you and your father are."

He thought it wouldn't hurt for Monica to see a woman who was completely satisfied with her role as wife and mother. "It's even better when my brother Ed is there too. It makes her happy to do things for us."

"And I'm sure you enjoy that arrangement." She smiled, her tone ironic.

Greg refused to take the bait. "When a woman pleases a principled man, Monica, he in turn makes every effort to please her. That's called love. It's the way love works. You put someone else before yourself. In appreciation, that person does the same."

"Isn't that idealistic?"

Greg straightened, tightening his hold on the steering wheel. "It's real. I've had a lifetime of watching what genuine love is, Monica. Maybe you didn't see that with your parents. You have such a cynical view of love. I wonder if you'd really like to know what love is."

"We all want to experience love. Unfortunately, I find it ends up being a rather selfish bargain. One side gives her all and the other side takes, takes, takes."

His heart ached for the loneliness and pain in her voice. "Is that your experience?"

"That's the way it was for my parents. My mother gave and my father took." She glanced sadly at him, her eyes full of confusion. "You are a rare and fortunate person to have the family love that you do."

"It is rare. I've been around the families of enough friends and relatives to understand the reality of that." He headed the car toward the marina, where sailboats dotted the bay. "But just because it's rare doesn't mean it's unattainable. Anyone can experience that kind of love."

"You make it sound so easy, but if it was so simple, more people would have it."

"Ah, but you see, it's just like the issue with the environment."

"What?" Monica exclaimed, slapping her hand on the dash. "Love has nothing to do with the environment."

"No, but people's attitudes affect both. The problem with most people is that they won't commit to love because they are more interested in themselves."

When Monica remained speechless, he wondered what thoughts were spinning around in her head. "Can't you see the similarity? The interest in self versus the interest in the environment. Or interest in self versus interest in the family? Or the interest in self versus interest in God."

"How can you accuse me of being selfish?"

"Am I?"

"I'm doing a lot toward saving the environment. It's why I drove down here with you, to tape that interview for television."

"You were selfish before your views on the environment changed, Monica. You used to care only about your piece of property. Now the whole Basin concerns you."

Greg stopped at a red light and turned toward her. "You can change your attitude about love also," he said softly. "And about God."

Monica stared at Greg until the green light forced him to refocus on his driving. "You can't begin to compare the two," she protested. "The issues have nothing to do with each other."

Did they?

Monica settled into the seat as the breeze teased her hair. She closed her eyes. Was it possible she could love Greg and still maintain her independence? Could she trust him to allow that?

Your father loved me, Child.

Yes, but he controlled you, Mother.

God loves you, Child.

And can I trust Him? He wants total submission also. In spite of her reasoning, yearnings tugged. She looked at Greg and wondered if he could fill the emptiness clawing at her heart.

Greg pulled into the parking lot adjacent to a large grassy park. "This is the Marina District. The yacht club is over there and ahead, across the bay, is Sausalito."

Her brain spinning in turmoil, Monica readily accepted the change of subject.

"Isn't that Alcatraz, the infamous prison?"

Greg nodded as he stepped out of the sports car and walked to her side. He offered his hand. "Come, let's walk along the marina, and I'll tell you some points of history."

Monica grabbed his hand and didn't let go when they started walking. He tucked her arm under his, and she leaned into him, absorbing his strength and confidence. The breeze tugged at her hair and clothes. She breathed in the salty air of the sea.

For an hour they toured the area. Most of the time they sat on the grass and watched the sailboats or the array of kites.

"Does it make you wish you had your boat?" Monica pointed to the white sails.

"This is where I learned to sail."

"Your family means so much to you, and from the way you talk about the city in such a fond manner, so does San Francisco. Why did you leave?"

His brow furrowed as he thought about it. "My father wanted me to join the law firm. I guess I wanted to get away from that pressure in order to pursue my true interests. It was tough to do that because I know my decision disappointed my father."

"Yet you made it."

"I wanted to establish my independence."

"Which is exactly what I'm doing now. Stephen made demands I didn't want to meet and, rather than disappoint him, I left."

Greg turned and grasped Monica by the shoulders. "We are not talking about the same thing at all. A son branches off on his own to establish his life. But a man and a woman make a special commitment when they marry."

She thought about what he said for a moment. "But I've seen what that kind of commitment did to my mother. She had no life of her own."

"Come get to know my parents. See how they strive to please each other. You have this strange idea that committing means being treated like a doormat. The love my parents share empowers them. There is no subjugation, but sacrifice—loving sacrifice."

"Why are you so eager for me to see this? Are you suggesting I should honor my commitment to Stephen?"

His expression appeared as stricken as if she'd slapped him. "No, certainly not. I want you to resolve your negative feelings about a relationship with him and then let them go. Maybe then you can have a positive relationship with me." He let go of her shoulders. "I want you to see how much love can add to your life, because I yearn for that kind of love in mine. Monica, you're the only woman with whom I've ever wanted that kind of relationship."

A longing welled up, threatening to stop her heart. She wanted to love Greg. "What if I never resolve my attitude about love and commitment?"

"I'm willing to take that risk, Monica. You have nothing to lose."

Tears welled, and she blinked to keep them from falling. "I want to try, Greg. But I'm afraid. And I don't want to hurt you."

A tear slipped out, and Greg traced it down her cheek with the tip of his finger. "You can find happiness by believing. Trust Him, Monica. And trust me."

Monica remained silent. She had no right to corrupt his faith. Who knew? Maybe if he believed strongly enough, God could make it possible for her to love and trust.

Greg grasped her hand and swung it between them. "Enough serious conversation. Let's do some more touring. We'll go to Golden Gate Park. If we're lucky, we can watch a game of polo, and then I'll take you to the Japanese Tea Garden for some jasmine tea."

Monica smiled her relief. "After that we'll have to start discussing my interview. I want to be sure I have all the points we want to cover."

"We'll do that this afternoon with my mother. Danielle has a very sophisticated presence when it comes to the press."

"Is there anything your mother can't do?" she teased.

Greg took her seriously. "Nothing I can think of. She's a remarkable woman."

Monica had to admit that Danielle Linsey had her act together. After watching a polo game, touring the de Young Museum, the Steinhart Aquarium, and the Botanical Garden, Monica was exhausted. But Danielle, who'd had a full day also, appeared full of energy.

Monica sat on the couch next to Greg while he described their activities and listened to his parents discuss their day. He tucked Monica's hand in the crook of his arm and looked at his father. "How was the court case today?"

David settled into the chair opposite and accepted a cup of tea from Danielle. "Slow. The district attorney asked for an extension of time." He went on to explain what that would do to his case.

Monica watched as Danielle asked questions and participated in the conversation as if she knew every detail.

David finished his tea and turned to Danielle. "What were you up to today? Did your committee at church take care of their projects?"

Danielle stood and poured more tea, then returned to her chair next to David's. "We also ran into snags today. The store that was going to donate clothing backed out on us."

David made several suggestions of alternative donors. Danielle jotted them down in a notebook she kept on the coffee table.

Greg finished his tea and took her empty cup, as well, setting them on the sideboard. "Didn't you have an art class today?" he asked his mother.

She smiled and settled into her chair. "Yes, I'm working on a sculpture of your father." She turned to David. "I need you to come in sometime next week and sit for me. To fine-tune your facial features."

Amazed, Monica listened to the give and take of the family. They were all interested in what each other was doing. A loneliness crept in. She and Armand would talk, but it was always business. Her father never asked her about her personal life, and she couldn't ever remember discussions with Armand and her mother.

David stood and stretched. "Greg, you wanted to check some resources on the Internet. Come on into my study and we'll see what we can find." He reached for the empty teapot and smiled at Danielle. "We'll drop these off in the kitchen for you."

Greg followed his father.

Monica turned to Danielle. "How do you manage to accomplish so much? I'll certainly understand if you're too tired to bother with our interview."

"Nonsense. What interests my son, interests me. Since he made us aware of the environment, we've become loyal supporters."

"I'm only just beginning to realize what loyalty entails. It seems you make a lot of sacrifices for your husband and your sons."

Danielle strolled to the picture window and stared at the view of the bay, dotted with sailboats. "When you love your family, there's never enough you can do for them."

Monica sighed. "I've never experienced that kind of love."

Danielle turned from the picture window and sat next to Monica on the couch. "Love is an awesome power. You'll find it will give you amazing strength and potential."

Monica turned to face Danielle. "I've always thought it did the opposite. But watching you and David, I can see what you're saying."

"I'm so fortunate, aren't I? I can do that because of the partnership David and I formed. By providing for his needs, he's made the effort to provide for mine."

Monica leaned forward. "But how can you guarantee that will happen? Some men will selfishly take, take, take and never give." She thought of her father and Stephen. "How does love change all of that?" Monica wanted to know.

Danielle lifted her hand. "It's the little things that make it happen. Having his favorite dinner ready after a tough day; packing his favorite photos of us for a business trip; wearing his favorite dress to a dinner party. Little things like that."

Her mother had done those things. It sounded so simple. Yet Monica had always seen it as subservient.

Danielle leaned back, clapping her hands. "When David would become so pleased, I wanted to do more. It made me feel special that I could make him happy with such little acts of caring."

Monica had to admit Armand adored her mother. He would become excited over the silliest things, like a flower by his dinner plate or a love note on his pillow.

Danielle reached over and patted her knee. "He was so appreciative of the things I did for him that he wanted to please me."

"I don't understand," Monica had to admit. This all seemed too unreal, too ideal.

"That's the power of love. Generosity reaps generosity. Tolerance reaps tolerance. Patience and compassion reap patience and compassion."

"Are you implying the converse is true?"

"Of course. Impatience produces impatience in everyone around you. Anger makes everyone angry."

"That I can believe, but I don't see how the other works." Monica slid off her glasses and started twirling them around.

Danielle didn't let Monica's skepticism ruffle her conviction. "Try it sometime. I found out by accident, and I try to tell every woman I meet. Unfortunately, there are many like you who don't want to believe."

"Couldn't that be a sign that you're an exception and most of us couldn't find that kind of peace and happiness?"

"No, it means you are being hardheaded and closing your mind to the possibility. You lack faith in others and yourself if you don't believe you can affect them with love."

Monica would have taken offense at those words, except they were delivered with such sincerity. She reached her other hand over and patted the one of Danielle's that still covered her knee. "I hear you, Danielle, and you are not the first to try and explain this to me. Yet, I can't see how it works."

"You won't be able to reason it out. If we could, it would be easier to explain and believe. It's much like believing in God. It's like faith that can't be explained or reasoned. I guess what you need to do is take an act of faith. Say you believe it and then step out and act on it. See what happens. You have nothing to lose, because not gaining the results leaves you where you already are."

"Loving someone doesn't sound like such a hard thing to do." She thought of Greg. "I guess I need to try it."

"When you do, you'll see results. And when that happens, you'll believe."

Monica laughed, more to relieve tension than for humor. "I guess it reverses the old adage of 'see it and believe it.'"

"Exactly. You have to believe it and then see it." Danielle stood and stretched. "Speaking of seeing, I do see that it's close to dinnertime. I'd better get busy."

Monica stood as well. "Can I help? I'm not much in the kitchen, but I can make a decent salad."

Danielle led the way to the kitchen. "That would be marvelous. I'll show you my secret recipe for Parmesan toast. It's wonderful, especially made with San Francisco French bread."

Monica shook her head in wonder as she followed Danielle. Maybe what the woman said was true. Monica had never been known to offer to help in the kitchen before.

Greg meandered along the floor-to-ceiling bookcases that lined his father's study. He loved being around the books. They had an aged smell about them that brought back pleasant memories of long talks he'd had in this room with his father and brother. Sometimes being here in this study eased the hints of envy he felt toward his brother's success. His father acted as if Greg were just as important. His attitude helped.

"How's Ed doing?" he asked, thinking about his older sibling.

"The same. He and Shari are having a tough time." His father tapped his finger along the armrest of his chair, letting Greg know how that upset him. "Reminds me of your mother and me when we started out. Seems a shame they have to go through that."

"You mean, instead of listening to your words of wisdom and experience."

David Linsey laughed, the sound deep and throaty—a sound Greg enjoyed hearing and hadn't realized he'd missed so much.

He paused to study his father. "And you, Dad, are you feeling good? Taking care of yourself?"

His father straightened. "Couldn't be better, my boy. Glad to have you home. It does me and your mother good to see you looking so fine."

"I'm happy."

"And this Monica? Is she more than a friend?"

"I wish." Briefly, he explained to his father some of the complications.

"Don't count on making a person change, Son. You can bring her here and show her our happiness, but everyone has to decide for themselves what path they wish to walk."

Greg nodded, very aware of the truth of his father's words. "What I was hoping, Dad, along with getting Monica here to meet you, was to ask for advice on this issue with the Ponderosa Inn."

Again, his father listened patiently while Greg explained the situation. He began pacing to focus his mind. "We're gaining public interest in the issue, but Jones still has the legal right to develop his property and, to some extent, we're going to have to approve it."

"Because of the existing establishment?" his father asked, again tapping his fingers on the chair.

"Right. Generally, the agency approves improvements to existing establishments. If a piece of land is already used commercially, it can continue to be used in that way."

"So what exactly is the issue other than the fact he is dishonest?"

Greg had to squirm slightly over that question. He'd confronted Monica enough with it. "The project he proposes would increase traffic in the area by developing a mall with shops, a video-game arcade, and several fast-food concessions—the same as any mall in any city in the US."

"The point being to leave the city in the city," David said, smiling over Greg's heated fervor for the subject.

Greg snapped his fingers. "It irks me that tourists don't come and simply enjoy the mountains."

"Maybe they don't know how. Many people have never learned to relax or entertain themselves without a lot of manmade distractions and noise. I often think they are afraid to be alone with their thoughts because they don't want to have to face that still, small voice of God."

Greg sat in the chair opposite his father. "It's tough to hear that voice when you first have to face yourself."

David chuckled. "Isn't that the truth."

Greg groaned and raked fingers through his hair. "We need something concrete to use to stop Jones from developing the inn."

His father sat silently for a few moments and rubbed his jaw. "What inn are you talking about? I'm trying to place which one it is. We never traveled to the North Shore that much. Once we arrived at our place, I'd settle in for the stay."

"It's that old, old building just after you cross the state line. Remember, we used to joke about it being an inn the pioneers built?"

"Of course, but, Son, that place *was* built by the pioneers."

Greg jumped up as the idea struck him at the same time as it did his father. "That's it. We'll get it listed in the National Register. Jones won't be able to proceed with his modernizing plans if it qualifies."

CHAPTER 16

THE LIGHTS BURNED bright in the television studio. Good thing Monica had bothered with the extra layer of makeup. At first it had seemed like too much, but the assistant had advised her to use it. The producer showed her where to sit and which direction to face.

Greg came up beside her. "Wow, I'd steal a kiss, but..."

"Don't you dare mess this up," she admonished. "It took forever to put this on."

He leaned close and whispered, "Bet I could get it off faster."

Color crept up her neck, but she doubted anyone could see it. At least there was one advantage to the makeup. She shifted nervously in her chair. "I'm petrified."

Greg patted her hand. "I'm teasing. You look great. You'll be fine."

The host came onstage, and Greg shook his hand. "Good to see you, Jeff."

Jeffrey Siefer sat down, and Greg moved over to the sidelines. "We're about ready, Ms. Scott. Watch the producer for your cue."

Monica nodded at the host and wondered at the butterflies in her stomach. "Am I supposed to be this nervous?"

"Good grief, don't mention the word," Jeff said with all sincerity, positioning himself in the chair opposite Monica.

"I could make some crack about the hour. This is a horrible time to get up."

Jeff smiled. "I do it every day. You get used to it."

From behind the glare, a voice warned them of the countdown.

"Remember to stay calm. If you get stuck, just smile and I'll take over."

"You're good at this, I understand."

He quirked his brow and nodded his head toward Greg. "We're friends, so his opinion is naturally biased."

Monica liked the unpretentious attitude of the talk-show host. Although nervous, she had no qualms about her appearance. Her overwhelming jitters were forestalled somewhat by thinking of Greg's idea to get the Ponderosa Inn listed on the National Register. What amazed her was that no one had thought of making the Ponderosa Inn a historical monument earlier.

Jeff interrupted her thoughts by saying, "We're on the air."

Monica smiled through the introductions, but her insides jumbled crazily. Somewhere behind the lights, Greg stood, sending out prayers and mental messages of moral support, which helped a little to calm the jangling nerves.

"Ms. Scott, can you give us a brief background of the issue that has raised such a clamor in our famous mountain resort?"

Monica briefly explained what Jones planned to do with the inn once he took over.

Jeff said, "Some people would call that progress, and since we as a country pride ourselves with that characteristic, how do you expect to rally support?"

"Unfortunately, much of the *progress* in our nation has involved damaging the land. We were a country with so many resources and relatively little population, it didn't seem like we could do that much harm." She tied that fact by giving the statistics of growth in the Tahoe area. "You've seen the increase of population here in the Bay Area and all of California due to immigration."

"We certainly have," the host agreed heartily. "And you're

saying that increase has affected the area's resorts, Lake Tahoe being one of them. According to my sources," he unconsciously nodded toward where Greg stood. "The Tahoe area has a bi-state agency that has been quite revolutionary in their attempts to do that."

Monica obliged by filling in a brief history and description of the TRPA, thanks to Greg and his promptings last night. "The problem the TRPA is having," she continued to explain, "is the planning that developers continue to pursue in spite of the area's overload of such projects."

"The Ponderosa Inn being a case in point."

Monica agreed and explained most of the problems PIC faced.

"Sounds like a Catch-22 situation." The host smiled and then announced a station break.

"You're doing fine." He reached over to pat her hand. "I received a couple of briefs from a coalition that I believe is your opposition."

Monica tensed. How had they found out about her interview? She and Greg had kept it quiet, with only a few close friends aware of their plan.

As if to answer her question, the host handed her a copy and explained. "We always announce future agendas. Someone must've heard, because these came by e-mail."

"Are you going to use this?" She tapped her paper.

"I'd like to. It gives what you have to say more credibility. Conflict will also arouse public interest."

Clever, Monica admitted. He was going to get genuine reaction.

"Go ahead, but I can't guarantee that you'll approve of my response."

"We bleep out the obscenities." Jeff straightened his tie and jacket, as the show was about to commence.

Monica braced herself, thankful he'd given her some warning.

"Ms. Scott, you raise the issue that the Tahoe Basin is over-built, yet isn't it true that you have plans submitted to build a house?"

Behind the lights, Greg gasped, but Monica signaled as best she could that she had everything under control. Tense and gripping the paper, she replied, "In fact, I have plans to build on property that is environmentally sensitive because of a stream running through my land."

"How do you justify your plans and at the same time protest those of others? Doesn't that appear self-serving?"

It did, and Monica hadn't truly made peace with herself about the issue, though she couldn't very well admit that. Taking a deep breath, she said, "The fact the agency could stop or alter my plans was a powerful blow. I'll admit that in the beginning, I fought hard to resist their authority." She smiled to reassure her host and Greg that she was in control. "Because of that battle, I've researched and educated myself to the problem. Now I'm trying to bring public awareness to the large-scale issue."

Strangely enough, as she said them, Monica realized that her words were true.

Then Jeff hit her with the next question. "Wasn't your involvement with PIC a matter of personal revenge toward the man who is behind the Ponderosa Inn project?"

With that question, Greg protested backstage. The producer switched over to a commercial.

Greg shouted at his friend. "What kind of nonsense are you dishing out? Where'd you come up with all that?"

Jeff held the papers toward Monica. "She gave me the go-ahead."

"But not for slanderous remarks," Monica said, feeling slightly hypocritical about her indignation since it was the truth. "Sit down, Greg. I should have known that question would pop up. You've asked about it yourself."

The host's eyebrows lifted, and Monica leveled a confident stare at him. "I'll respond. You can resume your show."

A big sigh of relief came from the producer and the stagehands as well. Monica smiled. Conflict indeed aroused interest.

Once the cameras were rolling, she said, "I've been accused of that very thing by friends as well as foe. And to be honest, my intentions were self-serving when I began my campaign against Mr. Jones. However, as I mentioned earlier, researching the issue has brought to my attention the severity of the problems that we face. Not just in the Tahoe Basin, but nationwide." She paused for effect.

"What I have learned is that we as individuals—and collectively as a nation and as part of a world population—we need to set aside greed, revenge, self-interests and start thinking about the ultimate effects of what we're doing. Our goal should be preservation of our planet."

"While what you say is certainly commendable, the fact is it's still a large planet, and the damage doesn't seem to affect us yet, whereas action that hits home—such as moratoriums on building and strict regulations—does."

"It hits where it hurts," Monica added. "In the pocketbook."

"Not everyone can afford to simply be generous and say, 'Sure take my land and make it a park.'"

"Many haven't thought of that as an option." Monica shifted position, realizing that she was one of those individuals. "The California Tahoe Conservancy has been authorized by California voters to purchase parcels of land that cannot be built upon or that would benefit the area to preserve."

"Their funds are limited compared to the need," the host pointed out.

"And there are still some flaws in the agency's program. However, we must look at the fact that this area has dared to take a step."

"Which brings us to our closing few minutes. Can you tell us what you plan to do concerning the Ponderosa Inn?"

She smiled toward Greg. "We have a new strategy. Given

the age of the inn and the famous people who once stayed in it, we believe it qualifies for the National Register. It may even be a historical landmark."

Her host interceded with information of where the audience could write in their support of the plan. The talk-show host returned his attention to Monica.

"Thank you, Ms. Scott. You've been very informative on a subject that should concern us all."

As soon as Monica stood, she realized she had been more nervous than she thought. It had been those last questions sent in by the coalition. Her knees shook slightly as she walked toward Greg.

He wrapped his arms around her, giving her the support she needed.

"Did my nerves show that badly?" she asked.

He half-laughed. "Those last questions were such winners that I need your support as well." He leaned against her. "I wish I could get my hands on those jokers."

"And do what?"

He feigned chagrin. "Don't ruin my macho image. You did a great job with them. I'm proud of you."

Jeff finished his wrap with the producer and joined Greg and Monica. "Sorry about throwing you curves like that. You handled it well."

"She's a pro at public appearances," Greg agreed. "But I can't say I appreciate your tactics."

Monica held up her hand. "The questions heightened the interest level, I'm sure."

Jeff nodded. "You're right about that. It was your ultimate purpose to attract public attention, wasn't it?" he asked, lifting a brow at Greg.

Monica grabbed Greg's hand, giving him a reassuring squeeze. "Their ploy backfired by adding publicity. Our gain, their loss."

Relief flooded through Monica when Jeff smoothed over Greg's annoyance with the direction the questions had taken.

Jeff ushered them toward the door and asked, "Where are you off to now?"

Greg tugged on Monica's waist. "We're going to do some more sightseeing before heading back to the mountains. I have to be back to work on Wednesday."

"It was great seeing you again."

"Thanks for featuring Monica. It should help out a lot."

Jeff gave her an appreciative glance. "I'm sure the benefits were mutual. A woman as attractive and poised as you helps my ratings."

Monica smiled, pleased and relieved about the morning. When she and Greg left the studio, he asked her what she wanted to see first.

"Breakfast," she announced. "Tension makes me hungry and, as it is, I feel like it should be lunchtime already."

"It's only nine, but not to worry. I'll take you to the Cliff House Restaurant, famous for its breakfast and view of the Pacific Ocean."

Monica had no argument with that decision. Nor did she protest the rest of the places Greg took her. As long as she kept busy, she wouldn't have to think about what she and Danielle discussed, nor what she'd learned about herself this weekend. There would be time enough for that when she returned to Tahoe. Rhonda would be back in Los Angeles, and she would be alone.

Mitch Jones clicked off the television set in his San Francisco hotel suite. "That broad screwed me again."

Jones paced in front of the window, several curses directed at Monica Scott filling the room. He should sue her for slander and defamation of character, but that would only provide her with even more publicity. Bringing in the dirt had only heightened interest, and it certainly hadn't done him any good.

He cursed again and turned to Packard. "What was she talking about? What's the National Register got to do with this?" He pointed to the television set. "I've got news for you, you interfering broad. It's too late for any tricks. I made the last payment, and I'm on my way now to sign the final papers."

Packard ate a cookie from a package on the table. "She can't stop you, can she, boss?"

"No."

"You want me to make sure?" Packard asked, eagerness in his tone.

"Like your efforts have been effective to date," Jones sneered. "I didn't notice she was quaking with fear."

"I was lucky to have gotten outta that booth. Man, those deputies were quick. I could've nailed both her and Linsey if they hadn't shown up. Next time, they won't be so lucky."

"Stay away from them. They might recognize you, and I don't want that coming back to me."

"They won't recognize me. It was pitch-dark. I could barely see who was after me."

"Stay here in the city for a week or two. Once word gets out that these papers are signed, the protests will die out."

"The sellers didn't give you no hassle about what you planned to do with the inn?"

"Naw. They need the money too badly to care. All they want are bucks."

Jones had barely been able to come up with the money. His last two clients had tried his nerves with their indecisions, but in the end they'd come through. Now he could taste victory.

"We're going to make a fortune off this deal. Once we get these papers signed, we can start selling concessions. Once they're sold out and the money rolls in, we can duck out and begin a new project with a nice fat profit."

Packard ate another cookie. "Sounds fine to me. I guess I can entertain myself down here in the city for a while."

Jones straightened his tie and turned to Packard. "Stay away from the games. I'm not wasting my profit on your gambling debts."

"Yeah, yeah." Packard waved him off. "Go do your big business thing and leave me alone."

After the papers were signed, Jones came out of the downtown office whistling between puffs on his cigar. For once in his life, he was going to make it big. Maybe he could even quit the scams and work legitimately. Maybe in Florida or Arizona where they had the warm climate he yearned for. Work with the mainstream businesses. He could easily picture himself as a respected entrepreneur. Visions of money filling his vaults quickened his steps.

Then he wondered if Monica Scott may be onto something after all. It might be advisable to say he was leaving part of the original inn intact. He could always use that as an advertising gimmick to attract the concessionaires. Miss Do-Good had just provided him with plenty of free publicity. All he had to do was make it appear that he had the environmental issue at heart. He'd even look the part of the hero.

Jones grinned at the thought. He could see it now. A carefully laid out nature trail in between the concessions with a printed leaflet describing the natural fauna and historic events, with a blurb on all the things he'd personally done to preserve the natural ecology and local history.

Jones puffed harder on his cigar as his mind raced with ideas. If it was history and the environment the public wanted, that's what they would get. Only it would be on his terms, not Monica Scott's.

Besides touring the city, Greg took Monica by the California State Historical Society to find out the procedure to list the Ponderosa Inn on the National Register. Monica studied the forms and groaned. "This is daunting as well as time-consuming."

"Don't be discouraged about the time element," Greg advised. "Just qualifying puts a hold on any future construction or renovation. They have to determine authenticity and then approve any changes or repairs."

"That'll put a crimp in Jones's plans. He may not be able to afford the wait."

"That's the idea," Greg agreed.

That night Greg took his family out to dinner to celebrate the successful interview and promising prospects.

Again, Danielle impressed Monica with her subtle charm that gave her the appearance of humble meekness when, in fact, she exerted overwhelming power. The men practically fell over each other trying to wait on her. Amused, Monica shook her head while again wondering how Danielle managed.

Ed and Shari joined them this evening. Meeting the brother she'd heard so much about delighted Monica.

Shari picked at the cracked crab on her plate. "I hope you like the fresh seafood. I would have taken you to the new Japanese place. That's the 'in' place to go."

"This is wonderful," Monica assured the family.

"Besides," Ed said in defense of Greg's decision, "you can't say you've been to San Francisco unless you eat at Fisherman's Wharf."

"Just so he doesn't start in on the plight of the dolphins or whales," Shari said, groaning.

"What do you care about an animal anyway?" Ed asked her. "As long as you have your perfume and cosmetics and your way, you're happy."

Shari smiled. "Oh, all this talk about the environment is nonsense. If you cared so much you wouldn't sit here and eat crab. Just think," she said, picking up a leg with her fingers "this poor thing was crawling around on the ocean floor yesterday."

"And aren't we thankful there are still some left to crawl so we can enjoy such a meal?" David piped up. "We take the ocean for granted, when in fact its existence is linked to our own."

"Please," Shari muttered as she buttered a slice of French bread. "The next thing you know, you'll be telling me that you're heading for the rally next weekend to save the whales."

"It's going to be quite an affair," Danielle explained. "Several performers from the area are going to donate time, similar to the concert you had at Tahoe." Danielle glanced at Monica. "We're hoping to increase public awareness."

"What celebrities are going to be there?" Shari asked, then listened, enthralled, as Danielle named off the list.

"Can you get Ed and I tickets for the concert this weekend?"

"Sure," Danielle replied. She turned to Monica. "There are a few front-row tickets left. Do you want to go? You and Greg may certainly join us."

Greg straightened. "We'd love to, but I was lucky to get these two days off. I'll pass the word about the concert when I get home." He turned to Monica. "You're welcome to stay."

Monica smiled, "I need to get back also."

"I'm surprised you're going, Dad."

David smiled at his wife. "She told me I didn't have to go."

Danielle reached over and patted his hand. "He knows how badly I want to, and it was thoughtful of you, dear, to get the best seats."

Monica had to admire Danielle's technique. What she'd said earlier did in fact seem to apply. Without even trying on her part, David was making the effort to please her and yet allowing her to fulfill her own interests.

Shari turned to Ed, and for the first time, consulted him. "Can't we go, darling? It sounds like this could be a real winner."

"I have that soccer game on Saturday. We'd have to leave early."

"Who cares about a dumb soccer game you can play any weekend?"

Ed forced a smile to the group. "It's the championship playoffs with the East Bay."

Greg came to his brother's rescue and wanted to know all about the team.

With a slight sense of shame, Monica watched Shari pout. Greg did all the things Danielle talked about: getting Monica whatever she wished, taking her to her favorite places, thinking of ways to please her. Only his efforts hadn't produced the results Danielle received. Her David had responded in kind to the love. Monica had withdrawn from it, afraid of its power.

What you reap is what you sow, Child. Give love, and you receive love a thousand-fold.

Her mother's words echoed in her head as she watched Danielle and David. She looked at Greg, remembering all of the little things he did for her. Then she glanced at Shari, realizing how getting your own way didn't necessarily mean love was involved.

By the time the meal ended, the conversation had ranged in topics from the environment to politics to the social issues in the city. Monica enjoyed the interaction, but she noticed toward the end of the evening that Greg seemed to tire.

She leaned close and whispered "Is all this social life wearing you out, Mr. Linsey?"

He chuckled, straightening in an attempt to appear alert.

"We've been up since four, and we do have a long drive tomorrow. Maybe we should call it a night."

He turned a hopeful expression her way. "Are you tired and ready to go?"

She wasn't. Monica could have stayed up until the wee small hours. She'd done so often enough with Armand. Maybe a little of the concern for others was rubbing off from her association with Danielle. She feigned a yawn.

"I am bushed," she said so everyone could hear. "Would it be a problem for anyone if Greg took me back to the house?"

Ed and David agreed readily. Shari looked puzzled. Danielle gave Monica an understanding and pleased wink. Monica sent the younger woman a smile of patience, and to the older she sent a smile of respect. The warmth swelling inside of her was surprising as well as rewarding. Danielle did know what she was talking about.

Fog rolled and swirled in the streets, enshrouding them in a misty blanket of silence. Greg escorted her to his own car this time and helped her inside. When they arrived at his parents' house, he guided her to the kitchen nook. With fog billowing against the windows, Monica shivered, glad to be inside.

"Would you like some hot chocolate?" he offered. "I know you probably aren't as tired as you said you are. Thanks for letting me off the hook."

"You could barely keep your eyes open," she teased. "And besides, I know that social gatherings aren't your favorite thing, even when it is family."

"I miss my parents when I'm gone," Greg admitted. "But I don't fit into their lifestyle. My mother understands, but I don't think Dad and Ed do. Sometimes I get the feeling they think I deserted them."

"Because you left the city?"

He put water in the electric kettle to boil. "Because I didn't go into practice with them." He paused, holding the kettle in midair. "Sometimes, especially days when I don't feel like we accomplish anything at the agency, I think I made a mistake by not sticking it out down here."

"So you think lawyers accomplish more?"

"Ed can look back on cases he's won. He's received public acclaim."

Monica peeled the foil off the top of the can of chocolate. "And that's so important?"

Greg shrugged. "To a guy, I guess it is."

"You're successful, Greg. You just don't deal with defined cases like an attorney does. What you do is very important."

He laughed as he plugged in the kettle. "I tell myself every day that what I do matters. I need to, because many days it doesn't seem that way. Besides that, if I'd stayed here I'd have to be involved in too many evenings such as this. Once in a while is great, but not on a regular basis."

Chuckling, she spooned instant chocolate into the mugs he'd set out. "You want to be in the mountains climbing a solitary peak or sailing the quiet waters of the lake."

"You're getting to know me so well." His smile teased. "And speaking of that, how would you like to get to know me even better?" He took the spoon and can of chocolate from her and wrapped his arms around her waist to pull her close.

"Don't tell me you feigned exhaustion so you could get me alone?"

He gave her a look of mock innocence. "Would I do such a thing?"

She studied his expression. "No. That's why I'm confused."

He drew her close for a kiss. "Don't try to reason this one out, Monica. Just feel my love for you."

251

The kiss seemed right, but inside she knew it was wrong. Not yet. Not until she'd decided commitment to Greg would be right. With effort, she pulled away.

"Greg, we can't do this."

He brushed his lips against her forehead. "I know. I just couldn't resist. You looked beautiful tonight."

"Thank you."

He placed his finger below her chin and tilted it upward so she could look into his eyes. "You still have to make a decision by tomorrow. I don't want you staying at Rhonda's alone after we get back to Tahoe."

"I can't come live with you. That last kiss proves it. I'm too attracted to you, Greg. I want very much to make love with you."

His expression clouded with desire. "You don't know how great that makes me feel," he said. "You could stay in San Francisco and continue the battle from here."

Struggling with her own passion, Monica pulled away from the warmth of his body. "No, I have to go back to Tahoe."

"Then come stay with me. I promise I won't let things get out of hand."

CHAPTER 17

DURING THE DRIVE HOME, Greg didn't say another word about Monica staying with him. Evidently he didn't plan to pressure her. Or maybe he was hoping she would decide on her own. She wished she could make that decision.

Normally there would be no doubt in her mind about staying on at Rhonda's. However, the incident on the beach had unnerved her more than she cared to admit. Her reluctance to stay alone in the house stemmed from fear, and that emotion was new to Monica. She had no idea how to handle it.

Trust in the Lord, Child.

Her mother trusted wholly in the Lord. *Did that trust really bring you peace, Mother, or was it Armand?*

Monica glanced at Greg. He trusted in God. Could she? No, but she could trust Greg. He had offered to take away the fear, but would it be fair to ask him?

The hours slipped by with conversation kept to generalities, which suited Monica fine. She didn't like the periods of silence. They gave her too much time to think. She endured them, however, because she knew that Greg needed them.

She glanced at Greg as he kept the car steady on the road. Had she changed? She never used to consider how anyone would need moments of silence. In fact, she usually insisted on a continual conversation or, at the very least, she'd turn on the music while in the car. Now that she thought about it, she and Armand always had the stereo or television blaring.

She hated to be alone with her thoughts. They never gave her peace. Yet, whenever Greg or her mother and even Danielle spent that quiet time, they would come out of it relaxed and refreshed. What did they have to think so much about?

Come rest with me, Child.

Monica shivered, wishing she could once again talk to her mom like she had with Danielle. Her mother always had answers to all of her questions.

When they arrived on the North Shore and pulled into Rhonda's driveway, Monica panicked. To avoid the inevitable conversation about her present residence, Monica discussed the events of their trip. "The committee is going to be thrilled when I report the data we collected from the Historic Preservation officer."

Greg rolled his eyes. "It's not a guaranteed solution. You realize the qualifications must be met before Jones applies for permits? Our agency can't interfere."

"I knew there was a reason we were collecting names and addresses of supporters. We can send out a massive campaign to Washington DC."

Greg parked his car in front of Rhonda's house and shut off the engine, then turned to Monica. "You've avoided the real issue between us for as long as you can. Have you made a decision about coming to my place?"

She looked at the large house set in the pines—in appearance, an ideal place to live. But she couldn't shake the sense of fear she now associated with it. Not after the threats made by her assailant.

"I'm staying here." She tried to sound brave and knew she'd failed miserably when she saw Greg's grin.

"Okay, have it your way," he said. "But I'll be staying here with you."

"No. You don't—"

He put up his hand to forestall her argument. "I can't stay here permanently. It's too far to commute to work. We'll try tonight. If you feel confident about staying, then that's what the decision will be."

Another reprieve. "You've got a deal. Come on in, and we'll make sure there's a room ready."

Monica opened the door and walked inside, turning on lights in the living room. "Looks like Rhonda had the maid service set us up. Food's in the refrigerator. Beds are made. She must've known I was going to stay."

Greg set their suitcases in the foyer. "She knows how stubborn you are. I don't know why it's so hard for me to accept that fact."

Monica took one of the cases from him. "I am trying, Greg. Your way of doing things is foreign to me. I can't reprogram myself to act differently than I've been doing for over thirty years."

"Habits do take time and patience to break," Greg agreed. "I have patience, but time seems to be the problem now."

Monica took his hand and led him into the living room. He sat on the couch and she settled beside him, stretching her legs to relieve the kinks from sitting in the car. "I have the time but lack the patience. Meeting your mother gave me a better understanding of what you think a relationship is all about."

"Relationships can be a bond that strengthens and frees you." Greg trailed his fingers along a loose strand of her hair and slid his arm around her shoulder.

"I always thought loving someone would restrict me. Make me less of a person."

Smiling, Greg hugged her close. "I'm glad you're beginning to realize how love frees you, Monica. Now multiply that with the immensity of God's love, and you'll truly be empowered and free."

She curled against his shoulder, tucking her head under his chin. His breath fanned her cheek. "I have a lot to think about."

He traced his thumb along her cheek. "I can't live like this much longer. I want to commit my love and life to you. I want children with you."

Strangely, his words didn't frighten her. She snuggled close and whispered, "You want all or nothing?"

"That's right. All or nothing."

"I can't make any commitments yet, but I can promise you that I'm not running away. I'm going to face my fears and doubts."

With his arm still around her, Greg reached with his free hand for hers and splayed her fingers between his. "Doesn't a promise like that give you a sense of peace?"

Monica thought for a moment. "Most of the time I'm restless and uneasy. When I let go and stop rationalizing, I do feel peaceful. But once I make that commitment, there will be no turning back."

"That's true. But once you do commit Monica, you'll realize the rewards. Then you'll never want to turn away from God's love—or mine. That is *my* promise."

The week passed slowly for Greg in spite of the backlog of work that had accumulated on his desk. Not only did time drag, but he couldn't keep his mind on the projects piled in front of him. He knew after his visit to San Francisco that he was better off in Tahoe than in his father's law firm. But he still had to deal with a sense of a lack of purpose in his life.

Thoughts of Monica kept interrupting his concentration. She'd decided to stay on at Rhonda's; so he'd agreed on the condition that she phone every evening. The calls had been the highlight of each day.

He turned when a noise from the hall distracted him. Carl walked into the office and held up his hands in mock surprise. Imitating the ribbing he'd received plenty of times from Greg, he said, "Hey man, don't tell me you're actually working?"

"Don't give me any grief," Greg begged. "I'm having a hard enough time concentrating as it is."

Carl chuckled. "I just got back from inspecting some property, and there's not enough time to get into a case. Let's go to lunch early."

Greg glanced at his watch and, wanting a diversion, agreed. "Sure. I'm game. Where are we headed?"

"There's a new place just off the strip I want to try."

Signaling their intentions to their supervisor, Greg followed Carl and hurried down the ramp to the parking lot.

"You must be hungry," Carl teased. "You're heading out of here like a bat."

Greg explained his frustrations as they drove toward the South Shore. "I can't understand why this guy keeps submitting the same plans. He knows we can't approve that much ground coverage."

Carl laughed. "He's probably hoping some new planner will get a hold of them and not know any better."

Greg rubbed the ache in his forehead. "Or maybe he's hoping persistence will win out. Do they think we're made of stone? Don't they know it's no fun for us to keep denying the projects?"

A worried frown framed Carl's glance. "Whoa. You are down today. In fact, you've been out of it all week. What's eating you?"

"Taking a few days off got me out of the swing of it," Greg hedged.

"Vacations are supposed to boost you up, not bring you down."

When Greg didn't respond, Carl asked, "What's happening with the Ponderosa Inn Concern? Have they agreed to apply for the National Register?"

Greg sighed. "They're submitting the forms next week."

"Won't that fix Jones's wagon?" Carl chortled.

"I'm beginning to feel sorry for the guy."

Carl slapped the dash. "What? After what he's done to Monica? Not to mention the hassles he's caused us in the past."

"I know, and when I think of Monica, I feel like he's getting his due. But isn't it pathetic for a man to have his whole life wrapped up in lies?"

Carl shook his head. "You're in more trouble than I thought. Maybe you should take more time off."

The idea tempted. "I could easily picture myself holed up on the shore of a mountain lake high in the Sierras."

"Maybe you should plan on doing that this weekend. Pack up your gear and head out." Carl sat for a moment, then turned a questioning glance toward Greg. "Come to think of it, you were doing that about every weekend last summer. I don't think you've been out once this season."

"I took Monica up one day."

Carl shook his head as Greg parked the car. "You actually shared your secret spot with someone else? Man, you've never taken me."

Inside the restaurant, they read the menu and ordered their food. After the waiter left them alone, Carl leaned forward and lowered his voice to say, "Your whole problem stems from one thing, buddy, and it isn't Jones or work."

Greg ignored Carl and gestured at the Gold Rush décor of the restaurant. The owners had taken an existing building and remodeled. Greg had been the one to approve the plans. It had turned out well. "Remember how this used to have that ugly turquoise stucco, advertising dancing girls with a neon sign?

This looks more like the mountains."

Carl gave a cursory glance at the antique wood paneling and the gold mining artifacts displayed along the walls and rafters. Then he said, "You've got to do something about the relationship between you and Monica. It's tearing you apart."

"There is no relationship between us. We're just friends."

"That's what I mean," Carl tapped the tabletop. "A *friendship* with a woman like Monica is not normal."

Greg stifled his annoyance. "And what's that supposed to mean? You're friends with her, aren't you?"

"Yes, but I don't spend every free minute at her house. I mean, admit it, aren't you going to spend this weekend with her?"

Greg glanced away from Carl's penetrating stare. "I just need some time off alone."

"Then take it," Carl insisted.

Before he could pursue his argument, the waiter brought huge sandwiches made with at least three inches of turkey and pastrami on top of large Kaiser rolls. Greg wondered if he could eat half of it, let alone the whole thing. Maybe Carl had a point. Normally a sandwich like that would give him great pleasure.

When the waiter left, the sandwiches sat untouched as Carl demanded, "What about your phone calls? I bet your phone bill this month outdoes mine for the year."

"Not so," Greg said, defending himself. "You call Michelle in San Francisco every week."

"My point exactly. I don't consider her *just a friend*."

Greg held up his hands in defeat. "All right. So I worry about Monica. You weren't there when that joker attacked her. I call her every night to make sure she's safe."

He didn't mention that he'd convinced the sheriff to have deputies drive by on a regular basis. Nor did he mention how much it annoyed him when her line was busy.

"Look at us," Carl interrupted his thoughts. "We have these awesome sandwiches in front of us, and all you can think about is Monica. Admit it. You're thinking of her, aren't you?"

Greg refused to rise to Carl's baiting. Picking up the sandwich, he took a huge bite.

Carl ignored his sandwich. "I'd advise most guys to go for it. But not you, Greg. You have a value system ingrained in you that's telling you this is all wrong. *That* is where your problem lies."

Slowly, Greg set his food back on the plate. "You're right, you know. I get so disgusted. I keep trying to convince myself that my intentions are altruistic, but they're not. I want her."

"What's stopping you? She's been separated from this dude for over two years. It's not like she's living with the guy and you have to sneak around or something."

"If that were the case, there'd be no problem. It's the fact he isn't around which tempts me."

Carl picked up his sandwich. "So?"

Greg paused to consider the passion and fire in the kisses he'd shared with Monica. She wouldn't have given in to passion unless she had feelings for him. "I think she does care. That's part of my frustration. It's why I keep going back for more."

Carl talked around a bite of food. "The answer is simple, then. Give her an ultimatum."

"I've thought of that," Greg admitted. "But I don't want to force her like that. She has to want me of her own free will."

Mitch Jones slammed down the papers delivered to him that afternoon and swore. "They can't do this to me," he bellowed. "Why me? All I wanted was to make a profit. Isn't that the all-

American way?"

The leaders of the coalition that he'd called together looked from one to the other. No one ventured to speak.

"Answer me. What's wrong with this country? Don't they want businesses to profit anymore? Or have we become a bunch of socialists?"

Candy Rogers leaned forward. "You're upset, Mitch. And you have a right to be. But there is no government plot here—simply a band of activists who must be stopped."

The others began talking at once.

"What if we're next on their hit list?"

"Once they have this victory, nothing will stop them."

"It's a shame what they've done."

Jones slammed his fist on the table, sending papers flying. "You all sound like they've won here. The battle isn't over, ladies and gentlemen. It's only just begun."

He had their attention now. Some of his lost confidence began to return. "You said it yourselves. If they ace me out, who'll be next? It's in your best interest to help me out here."

Candy scowled at him. "No. It's *your* problem. We never had this much hassle before, even with all the controversy over the TRPA. I think we'd be better off cutting any association with you."

Several voices agreed with Candy's statement; others protested. Beads of sweat formed along Jones's spine and forehead. Anger burned. Somebody was going to pay for putting him in this position, and that would be Monica Scott. He held up his hand for silence.

"We can't let our emotions take control here. We have to present a united front. For *everyone's* benefit," he emphasized as he looked each person in the eye. "If the Ponderosa Inn qualifies for the National Register, I've lost my investment. I need your help in fighting this."

Candy interrupted to say, "It's only under consideration."

But that would be his loss as well. Payments on the loan would be due. He needed to sell the concessions fast, and the kind he stood to profit from wouldn't fit in with the historical parts of the place. Of course, he couldn't discuss this part of his problem. The coalition wouldn't appreciate his plan.

"What we need is a full-scale protest against this outrage. It blocks progress and smacks of a plot," Jones said, playing the crowd in a desperate attempt to salvage his investment.

"What did you have in mind?" one of the leaders asked.

"What about a letter-writing campaign to the legislators? Scott's got her group doing it. We need to counter that twofold."

"Who are we going to ask to write?"

"Those who've supported us. What about everyone who came to our concert? We had a sellout crowd."

"Most of the audience came to hear the rock group," Candy pointed out. "Besides, we have no idea who attended."

Rage welled up in Jones. "Why didn't you collect names? PIC has names of supporters from all over the state."

Jones could see some of the coalition members squirming uneasily and forced himself to calm down. He wouldn't elicit their support by threats. Although he could easily strangle their cowardly necks.

"Okay. Let's think this out. We have friends. We can buy time from the media and ask people to write in their protests."

"That would deplete our funds. It's too much for only one member."

Jones couldn't stop himself from flaring up, "Why have I spent all my time and energy to work with you, if, when the chips are down, you're going to cut out on me?"

Several shifted in their seats, but Jones couldn't back down. He was fighting for his life. "What about you, Mrs. Rogers? If your realty business was under attack, I'd want to do all I could to protect you."

In her place, he'd let the broad drown in her own self-righteousness, but no one needed to know that.

He turned to the developer of a condominium complex. "Didn't we stick together when they tried to cheat you out of your building rights?"

The man nodded.

Jones sighed with relief as he saw the tide of sympathy swayed back toward him. "We need to stick together, folks. If I go under, who'll be next?"

"I say we do as Jones suggested and mount a campaign."

Everyone approved. Jones collapsed into his chair. "We need a contact in Washington. Anyone here know of someone?"

"I have contacts," one of the influential attorneys announced. "I'm sure he could put in a word for us."

Jones smiled. "Good. We're set then."

CHAPTER 18

GREG BRAKED his car behind another tourist and forced himself to be patient. This slow stretch of highway had never bothered him before, but today he was anxious to get to Monica's. The TRPA permit papers lay beside him on the passenger seat. Monica would be thrilled to finally get her report.

The out-of-state car pulled off into a vista turnout so its occupants could enjoy the view of the lake. Greg stomped on the gas pedal and sped around corners. Then he had to slow down for another tourist.

"Relax," he muttered to himself, then realized that was something he still hadn't done despite hassles from Carl. "The permit means Monica's going to be sticking around for a while."

Worried about talking to himself anymore, he pulled one of Monica's tricks. He turned the radio on loud. The music kept him from thinking until he arrived at Monica's house. Nerves stretched taut, he left the papers and hurried to her door. When she opened it, he lifted her into his arms and swung her around. He snuck in a quick kiss, savoring the taste of her. "Guess what?"

Her grin widened. "It must be good news. Have you heard about the National Register?"

"No. This is better." He set her down and ran back to his

car to retrieve the papers.

In shorts and barefoot, Monica followed him partway. He stopped to admire her long legs before joining her again. At the door she held out her hand, but he hid the permits behind his back.

She tapped him on the shoulder. "I give up. What surprise do you have for me?"

"Isn't my visit enough, or must I come bearing gifts?"

When she frowned, he lifted her chin with his finger. "I was teasing."

Laughing, she grabbed his hand and tugged. "I'm glad you came to see me. You know I always enjoy your visits. But so help me, Greg Linsey, you have something exciting, and you're playing games with me. You know I'm not going to let this go on."

Greg laughed and slipped past her into the house. He headed for the deck out front and sat in one of the chaise longues.

Monica followed and stood beside him with her hand out-stretched.

He smiled and held out the papers. "Okay. Here it is. Delivered in person from the Tahoe Regional Planning Agency."

Her hand dropped. With a semi-stunned look she sat down on the other chaise. Greg swung his legs down to the deck. "I thought you'd be ecstatic to receive this permit. Your father's house. It's been approved. The board gave the extra points for restoring the Langford property and accepted your proposal."

"I don't know what to say."

He leaned forward and placed his hand upon her forehead in a mock checkup. "Is there something wrong? Are you running a fever? Maybe this isn't the real Monica Scott."

She smiled, but it was forced. "You mean I can build along

the northeast corner?"

"Yes, with minimal changes to your father's plans." He studied her for a few moments. "Aren't you excited about this? Have you changed your mind about the project?"

"No." Her answer was almost too quick. "It's just that I've had it on the back burner for so long. With all the work for PIC, the time has flown. I just assumed there would still be something to shove aside."

"You don't have to restore the Langford place to get those points, you know. It's a lot of extra work. You can buy the points outright." He knew the money wasn't the issue, but maybe time was.

Monica shook her head. "No, now that I have the Langford property, I'd rather go through with that project." She smiled at him. "You made at least that much progress with me, Greg Linsey. I realize how badly the area needs the restoration."

He should have been thrilled with the victory, but her wan smile held him in check. "What are you going to do?"

"I have to readjust my thinking and prioritize my activities."

"Don't put any of the building projects off. You could still get a lot done before the first snowfall."

"The problem is, I've let off the contractors."

Greg stared. "You're kidding. They'll be impossible to rebook this summer."

"I think I'd rather wait until next spring. Then I can have everything lined up and ready to go at my own pace, rather than rushing to get jobs done."

He studied her. "It looks like you've finally taken my advice about easing up on your fast pace of living. Or is there more involved?"

Shrugging, she lay the papers on the table. "I'm committed to PIC. We may need to stage demonstrations and protests if the Ponderosa Inn doesn't qualify for the National Register."

"And you're the main organizer in that crowd."

It surprised him that she didn't acknowledge that point of praise. Her old self would have accepted that statement as her due. Greg studied her closely, appreciating her relaxed and poised manner.

"What about the down payments you made this spring? I can't believe they'll refund it to you."

"The cement company needed a date. When I couldn't come up with one, we decided to revise the plan."

"Revise?" He tensed. "What have you done, gone ahead and poured the foundation without the permit?"

She groaned. "Whatever you think I am, Greg, I'm not a fool. Of course I didn't go ahead and pour the foundation. When would I have had time for that?"

He had to admit he was surprised she'd even had time to talk to the contractors, let alone revise plans. "Okay, I give. I promise not to jump to any more conclusions."

She sat beside him and placed her hand on his. "If it'll give you peace, we arranged to have the concrete I'd paid for poured at the local church. They needed a new parking pad, and my down payment made a nice discount in their expense."

Feeling sheepish, Greg squeezed her hand, and for the first time saw her blush. "This new image of yours is wonderful. I hope it portends a change in our relationship as well."

She frowned, letting him know she hadn't resolved that issue yet. At least she'd left her hand in his.

Greg smiled and changed the subject. "Want to go hiking this weekend?"

"Friday we have a meeting with PIC leaders. The rest of the weekend is free. I'd love to get away from the pressures and the phone."

Greg laughed. "Monica Scott, you're going to end up being a local yokel if you keep going native on us." He tugged on her hand. "Why, I remember as if it were yesterday when you were insisting all cars should have a phone installed as standard equipment."

She laughed. "I admit I've become accustomed to your quiet days and getting away from the demands of others."

"Didn't I promise you that you would appreciate all of this someday?"

"You and your promises."

Saturday dawned bright and clear. Monica retied her hiking boots and slid out of her Jeep. She lifted the lightweight pack Greg had bought for her and looked at the daunting mountains. "I can't believe I let you talk me into this," she groaned.

Greg laughed. "You loved the last hike we went on. You're going to like this one even more."

"At least there's a lodge at the end of the trail?"

Greg slammed the doors shut and locked them. "Food too. Aspen Glen Springs is famous for both."

Waiting for Greg to sign their back-country passes, Monica read the sign board that described the oldest resort in the Basin.

Greg slipped the passes in the wooden box and stood beside her. "We were lucky to get these reservations. They're booked for the whole summer by early spring."

"How did we get them?"

"My boss was signed up for this weekend. His wife got sick, so they couldn't go."

"I'm sorry to hear she's sick, but at least you won't have me sleeping in a tent."

He laughed. "Someday, but I'll go easy on you for now."

Monica eyed the steep trail before falling into step beside Greg. "Easy? That looks like quite a hike. If this restaurant is so famous, you'd think they'd figure some way to get there besides hiking to it."

"It's off the beaten path. Part of its charm."

Monica rolled her eyes, then laughed. "You're enjoying this too much."

He caught hold of her hand. "I need to get out. And so do you."

True, the cool morning air was refreshing. Birds flitted in the brush, singing sharp trills. Insects hummed. Squirrels chased each other up and down the pine trees.

After hiking for about a mile, Greg stopped near a waterfall. He helped Monica take off her pack. The cool breeze against her damp T-shirt felt like heaven.

"You'd think I'd be used to this altitude by now," she puffed.

Greg handed her a water bottle. "Don't forget, we're climbing over a thousand feet. You're doing great."

"We'll see how great I'm doing after we get there."

After another hour of hiking, they reached the springs. "This is quite charming," she said as she lowered her pack. "I was expecting the place to be pretty rustic." She glanced around at the visitor center, where a ranger described the history of the resort.

Greg led her past the dining room nestled among the trees to their cabin. "Let's get changed and go into the hot springs."

The floorboards of the ancient wooden porch creaked as they stepped into the cabin. Monica eyed the lone double bed in the center of the room.

Greg set their packs in the corner. "Don't worry. I brought my tent. I'll sleep outside, but I'll change in here if you don't mind."

Monica bit her tongue. "I'll go put my suit on in the bathroom. You can change out here."

It didn't take long to take off her shorts and T-shirt and put on her two-piece bathing suit. She came out of the bathroom to find Greg sitting on the edge of the bed, in his swimsuit and bare-chested. Her heart raced and her breath caught in her throat.

He stood and moved in front of her, sliding his arms around her waist. Bare skin touched bare skin, charging the air with electricity. "I love being with you, Monica."

"You're so caring." She stroked her palm along his cheek. "You could have insisted on roughing it, yet you provided me this comfortable place to stay."

He turned his face and kissed her palm. "That's because you're special."

Do you know how special you are, Child?

The words tugged at her heart. She tightened her arms around Greg's shoulders. "It's been a long time since someone treated me like this."

He pulled her close. "It's about time someone did."

Monica sighed and laid her head on his chest, hearing his heart thump beneath her ear.

His breath caught. "Does this mean you've made a decision about your ex?"

She lifted her head and smiled. "I did that already. I called him and told him about you."

Greg's arms tightened around Monica, and he lifted her against him. "And you're just now getting around to telling me this?" He spun her in circles. "I love you so. Can we get married?"

Monica laughed and pushed herself back to the floor. "You're going too fast for me. I still don't understand commitment the way you see it. I'm getting there, Greg, but I need time."

He let her go, his eyes lit up with caring. "We'd better go for that swim then. I only have so much patience, let alone control."

Her heart still racing from his touch, Monica grabbed her towel and followed him out the door. She shook her head, marveling at his consideration and tender caring. Peace filled her heart.

The weeks passed, punctuated by weekends spent with Greg. Monica barely noticed the days as another month went by.

Work at PIC slowed down, as they had done about everything possible to prevent the development at the Ponderosa Inn. Evidently, Jones had left town, as no one had seen him lately. Some said he'd gone to Washington DC to lobby against the application for the Ponderosa Inn. Others said he was in New York rounding up investors for his project.

Whatever the reason, Monica was glad he was out of the area. She rested better at night. The creaky sounds around the house didn't unsettle her like they had before.

When the news for PIC came, Monica was spending a lazy, hot Wednesday afternoon watering plants on her deck. Judy came running over with the mail. The expression on her face reminded Monica of the time Greg had brought her permit. She hoped this news wouldn't be so anticlimactic.

Judy hit the deck taking two steps at a time. "We've done it," she yelled. "The Ponderosa Inn qualifies for the National Register. Restrictions for renovations require it remain true to the period and environment."

Monica dropped the watering can. At last—the news she'd been waiting for. Now that it had arrived, she felt numb, as if it were a big joke.

Judy stepped around the petunias and gave Monica a hug. "It's true."

Monica returned the hug. "How did they decide so quickly?"

"It appears we have influential friends in Washington who have taken an interest in our area."

The inn could still be restored. Hopefully the restrictions placed on historical buildings would hamper Jones enough to put him out of business. "So our efforts paid off."

"Yep. We've won."

Monica studied her friend's sober face. "Why so serious? You should be overjoyed."

"I am, but now what? I loved working on that project, Monica. It gave me a sense of purpose."

At least Judy had a reason for her lack of enthusiasm. Monica should feel victorious, but the news left her hollow and empty inside. It seemed like everything she tried to do ended up with a success that felt more like failure. She tried to muster up some enthusiasm. "The group doesn't have to fold. There are plenty of other causes you can fight for. What about the new ski area they want to develop?"

Judy's expression brightened. "Or the new casino? Monica, that's it. We can keep on fighting."

Monica held up her hand. "Not me. You keep going. I'm out of it now."

Judy looked as if she'd been struck. "You can't leave our group. You're the one who always knows what to do."

"Nonsense. You have enough experience now to lead the organization."

Judy looked dubious, but she didn't argue the point. "If you aren't going to be working with us, what will you be doing?"

Monica picked up the watering can and resumed her watering. In truth, Monica couldn't discuss her plans. She didn't know what they would be yet. "I don't know. There are several things I have to consider."

"You going to change your mind and start on the house after all?"

"I might look into that possibility," Monica hedged, giving her pansies a drink. The house wasn't one of her options, but letting Judy think it was would silence her. "I'm not sure what I can do at this point."

"If you don't work on the house, what will you do?" Judy insisted.

In desperation, Monica made up a half-lie, saying, "Maybe I'll take a trip. Go on a cruise. After all, I deserve a vacation."

Judy twirled around in circles across the deck. "Wow! That sounds like fun. Can I join you? We could sail to Tahiti or Bora Bora. Far enough away to forget all this nonsense. Right?"

Monica laughed and shoved her glasses on top of her head. "What are we talking about the future for? Let's celebrate the good news."

Judy stopped twirling and clapped her hands. "Okay, let's plan a big celebration bash for the weekend."

Monica finished the watering and motioned toward the door. "Come inside and we'll call a quick meeting of our key leaders."

"That's a super idea. We'll have it at my place. Let's make it an all-day affair beginning at noon and going 'til midnight. That way everyone who has been involved will get an opportunity to come by."

Monica put the decorative can on its shelf, fully aware that employers and employees in a resort community didn't have much free time on a weekend. Many of their committee members worked at night in restaurants and at the clubs. "Let's call our contacts in San Francisco. We can use some of our leftover cash to announce the party on the news. Some of our supporters might want to come up for the weekend and help us celebrate."

Monica welcomed the busy afternoon of planning. Another reprieve from thinking about her future.

Mitch Jones picked up the message from Candy Rogers when he returned to his hotel in Phoenix. He'd been out hustling in the Arizona heat, and he almost didn't return the call. Hundred-degree temperatures had sounded good in the dead of a Tahoe winter, but right now snow sounded inviting. Maybe he'd try Las Vegas. He hadn't found much in the Valley of the Sun that looked promising.

After a cold drink and a shower, he stretched out on the bed and gave Candy a call. When she told him the news about the Ponderosa Inn listed in the National Register, he wished he hadn't bothered to pick up the phone.

"I'm sorry," she apologized. "I thought you knew."

He knew all right, but he wasn't about to inform the coalition. His desk was piled with messages from creditors. Now he'd be able to duck out of sight and leave them hanging. It'd be foolish to warn everyone of his plans. He still had some things in his office he wanted to keep. If the creditors knew he wasn't returning, they'd confiscate it all.

"Are you going to comply with the restrictions or abandon the project?" Candy wanted to know.

The vulture, he thought. She wanted to pick over his bones like everyone else.

"I'll have to consult with my backers," he lied. "I'll be back next week. We can meet and discuss plans then."

"Too bad you couldn't be here this weekend. PIC is throwing a celebration party."

"Sunday?" he asked hopefully. There was no way he could get there sooner.

"Saturday at the Myerses' place. I hate seeing them publicly gloat."

Jones swore. He wouldn't be able to stop the bash, but he could put a damper on their festive mood. The score he had to settle with Monica Scott would be his last task at Tahoe. He'd do that on Sunday.

"Sorry," he said into the phone. "I have business appointments scheduled through Tuesday. How about if I fly up Wednesday? We can meet in the afternoon."

He could hear Candy writing down the dates, then she said, "I'll call everyone and set up a meeting."

Jones smiled. If he arrived on Sunday, no one would know he was in town until after he'd done his work and left.

Jones hung up the phone and placed a call to San Francisco. "Packard, my man. Mitch Jones here. How would you like a trip to Tahoe? Meet me at my office at noon on Sunday. We'll plan from there." Jones lowered his voice to a threatening tone. "There better not be any mistakes this time."

He hung up and rubbed his hands together before reaching for his cigar. His plans for Monica Scott put him in a much better frame of mind than he'd been in a long time. Monica Scott was going to be sorry she'd ever heard of Mitch Jones or the Ponderosa Inn.

Greg had promised Monica he'd be at the party early, but as it turned out, it was almost six before he arrived at Judy's house. "Sorry I'm late."

Although her brow was furrowed with concern, she smiled her pleasure at seeing him. "Where have you been?"

He smiled back and snapped his fingers. "Forgive me. A thousand pardons. I'll do whatever you tell me."

"You're not accountable to me," she teased, but then grew serious. "I was worried about you."

"I tried to call, but the line was busy."

Monica pressed her forehead with the palm of her hand. "Everyone has been calling friends and advising them to get over here. I'm telling you, it's been packed all afternoon." She cast him a teasing glare. "That wasn't your plan by any chance, was it? To avoid the crowds?"

He held up his hands. "Come on, Monica. Give me a break. I do have a legitimate excuse."

She grabbed his hand and led him through the house. "No excuses. Follow me."

"You bet." If she'd only let him, he would follow her for the rest of his life.

In every room, people milled about. The deck was more crowded. Monica led Greg to the buffet table and asked him what he wanted. "You must be starved."

Greg relaxed, enjoying the special attention. "I am. My last meal was at eight this morning."

She took a plate and started pointing to the items arrayed to tempt and delight. He nodded at some, declined others. With each nod, she placed portions on his plate. When she picked up a couple of olives, he couldn't resist. Grasping her wrist, he brought her fingers to his mouth and let her pop the olives in.

Her laughter rang out. When she glanced into his eyes, her expression sobered, and she turned back to the task of filling his plate with food.

What was that all about? His gut tightened whenever she'd get that faraway look in her eyes. It had been happening more and more this past month.

He shoved the doubts to the back of his mind and concentrated on enjoying himself. With the large crowd, he wasn't exactly in his element. Monica's nearness mattered to him, so he'd do his best to block out the noise and chatter.

They reached the end of the table. "We'd better save the desserts for another trip," she advised.

He took the heaping plate of food. "I don't know how I'm going to manage all this. Let's stop and get something to drink."

She picked up a couple of bottles from a tub of ice. "How about some iced tea?"

He nodded. "Any chance we can sneak off somewhere and eat this alone?"

She looked around and shrugged. "I doubt if there's room for the squirrels around here today. I see an empty spot to sit at the other end of the deck."

He raised and lowered his brows suggestively. "How about your place?" he said, knowing she'd never leave the party.

She looked around as if she wanted to avoid the issue. "I can't leave now with all these people here, but later I'd like us to go over there. We need to talk."

Her answer surprised him more than her behavior. He studied her features, searching for a clue to the reason, but she kept her expression bland. "Am I going to want to hear this talk?" he asked.

She shifted and half-smiled. "What do you mean?"

"I don't know." But he did know. "I get the feeling I'm not going to like this conversation."

"Probably not." Avoiding his eyes, she stood and waved. "There's Sophie. I have to give her a message." She turned to smile. "I'll be right back."

Greg watched the sway of her hips and her wavy hair blowing in the light breeze. A yearning welled up in him. He wanted Monica Scott. He didn't want to lose her. He closed his eyes and prayed that wasn't what she wanted to talk about.

Another idea occurred to him, which had his eyes open in

a flash. With the work at PIC virtually over, she could devote time to him now. Maybe she was ready to move to the South Shore and live at his place.

Finishing his dinner, Greg turned at a familiar voice and smiled as Judy approached. "Congratulations," he said. "You've done a great job with the party."

Judy smiled, pleased with the praise. "It wasn't just me. Everyone did their share."

"But it takes a core group of dedicated leaders to pull it off."

She sat next to him where Monica had been. "Do you really believe I'm a leader? Monica thinks I should keep the organization intact for future projects."

"What are you two cooking up now?"

She shrugged. "There're other issues. Our organization could do a lot for your agency and special interests throughout the Basin."

Greg smiled at her enthusiasm. "We could keep you informed of projects around the lake. Your committee could select from the list."

"So you would continue to help us?"

Putting his plate aside, Greg got up and paced, snapping his fingers. "Why wouldn't I?"

Judy shrugged. "You know. With Monica not being involved, I sort of thought your interest might dwindle."

"Monica's not going to be involved?" He couldn't picture her outside the hub of the activity. "How do you know?"

Judy stood and fell in step beside him. "She told me she had other plans. I tried to talk her into staying on the committee."

Greg eyed her curiously. "What other plans does she have? Did she mention anything specific to you?"

"No." Judy's expression saddened. "But I think she's leaving. She's been bringing boxes inside and packing some of her stuff from the front room."

Greg stopped short. *Don't panic. She's planning to move in with me.*

Excusing himself from Judy, he searched out Monica. There would be no more evasion. He had to know the truth. He found her inside, talking to several men and women. "Come with me," he murmured close to her ear. "We're going to talk now."

Before she could utter a word, he grasped her elbow and guided her outside.

At the edge of the forest, she pulled her arm free. "Couldn't this wait until later?"

"No."

She studied his determined expression for a moment, then said, "We'd better go to my place then."

Moonlight glistened in a silvery path across the lake and cast shadows in the trees as they walked through the forest. Greg wanted to suspend time to this moment, alone in the silence with Monica.

Inside her house, she sat on her sofa and patted the cushion beside her. "Sit down please, Greg. I need you close to me."

His hopes soared. Her admittance of needing him surely meant she wanted to move in. But when he walked toward her, he noticed the brass sculpture, the address book by the phone, and the picture of her father were missing.

He gestured around the room. "Let's make this easy on both of us, Monica, and get to the point. I notice you've packed up several personal things."

Monica lowered her gaze and then lifted her eyes to look directly into his. "I'm leaving Rhonda's house."

"To my place, right?"

She leaned toward him and smoothed her palm along his cheek. "That's just it, my darling Greg. I want to move in with you. I want to make love to you. I want all these things, yet I don't have the right."

"It doesn't—"

She placed her fingers against his lips. "Hear me out. I'm going to my parents' estate in Spain. I've put off taking care of their personal belongings, maybe selling the place. I need to do that."

"I can take a leave of absence and go with you. Help you pack things you want to keep, get rid of things you don't."

She clasped his hand. "I need to be alone. To sort things out in my head and to decide if I can handle commitment or not."

She was leaving him. He was going to lose her. "We're fine the way we are."

She shook her head. "You're the one who keeps saying you need a commitment. I can't give you that now."

He wanted to yell at her and order her not to go. "How long will you be gone?"

"A month or two at the most. You must understand I have to do this."

He reached for her hands and held them in his lap. "I do understand, but I don't want to."

"I have to decide between your world and this crazy conception of mine. I can no longer live with one foot in each. It's pulling me apart."

"You can't decide that here?"

She shook her head. "I'll be gone early Sunday morning. But I promise you, Greg, I'll be back."

"I'll hold you to your promise." Greg watched a tear streak its way down her cheek. He wanted to cry too.

CHAPTER 19

SUNLIGHT STREAMED through the rotunda window, warming the cushions of the alcove where Monica sat. She stared out the window at the gardens on the patio, facing the roll of waves in the Mediterranean. Her mother's gardens. She wiped at the tear sliding down her cheek and reread the letter in her lap.

My dear husband, it is with much joy that I write how much I love you. Do you know how I appreciate all the little things you do for me? Do you know how I treasure the time you give me to work in the garden and commune with the Lord who has blessed us so? Always believe that, my dear Armand.

All these years, Monica had believed that her mother was downtrodden, relegated to gardening because Armand didn't think her capable of anything else, including raising her daughter. And now she knew. Armand had sacrificed much to allow his dear wife to pursue her dreams, her true calling.

Monica fingered the piles of letters strewn around the cushions of the window seat and on the floor at her feet. She had found them in her father's closet. She picked up another and read: *My darling, this design is quite unique. If you would set it against the cliff like so*—Monica studied the sketch her mother had drawn—*the house would meld into the surroundings. Plant some trees in front and it will become part of the cliff.*

Monica set that letter in a growing pile and looked at another.

Dear Armand, this lot has much potential. If you build here, you could allow the stream to flow through the living room and bring God's beauty into the house. Don't cut the trees, but place large windows all around and you will feel like you are sitting in the forest.

Monica placed that letter in the same pile as the last. She stood and paced the room, a room that brought the outdoors inside as if she were seated on the beach.

Mother, you were part of Armand's designs. You are the one who taught him to blend architecture with nature. You stood behind his fame, yet no one ever knew.

Monica combed her fingers through her hair. Images of Greg floated in and out of her mind. *This is the kind of love you were talking about, isn't it?*

Pouring herself another cup of hot chocolate, Monica picked up another letter. *My dear one, please don't be angry at God for what is happening to me. It is part of His plan. I will be with Him soon. I know you will be fine. I will pray for you and our darling daughter. Thank you for not telling her I am so sick. She is so much like you, my dear one. Love her with all your heart as I love both of you.*

No wonder Armand had kept her away from her mother. She was ill and dying. Why hadn't he told her? Why hadn't her mother explained? All these years she had believed her mother didn't want the responsibility of raising her daughter. But Armand, in his love for his wife, had followed her wishes.

Monica sipped on her chocolate. She had told Greg she didn't have a good role model of love, and now she was discovering her mother's love was self-sacrificing and caring. The kind Greg talked about. The kind she'd seen with Danielle and David.

Monica set down her chocolate and started gathering the letters and placing them back in the wooden box where she'd found them. There was the pile of letters that were her mother's contribution to Armand's designs. There was the pile telling of her love for Armand and Monica. And there was the pile telling about her love for the Lord. These letters were Monica's treasure. Messages of love and promises. From her mother. And from God.

Monica had promised Greg she would return in one or two months. It had been almost four. As she drove her rented car through the snow-covered mountains, she marveled at how different the countryside looked in its blanket of white.

Her new inner peace came into play as she neared Tahoe City. She'd come from the Reno airport via Truckee instead of going directly to the South Shore where Greg was working. Being Friday, a weekday, she didn't want their reunion to be in his office, surrounded by people. Knowing she'd be pacing in her hotel until Greg got off work, she decided to visit Judy.

Judy would be expecting her anytime now. Monica had called and said she'd be there in forty minutes. Judy advised her to take an extra half-hour because of the snow. Monica smiled as she glanced at her watch. Judy had timed it to the minute.

Judy stood at her door waving as Monica pulled up. "I can't believe it's actually you. You look great. All tan and rested."

Monica returned the hug she received as she stepped up onto the porch. "It's good to see you too. Even though you've lost your tan, you look great," she teased.

Judy hurried them into the warm house and helped Monica take off her wool coat. "I'm so glad you stopped by. I know good and well that once you're down at Greg's, we won't see you."

Monica laughed, pleased with Judy's new assertiveness.

"Why do you think I came by here first? You didn't tell anyone I was coming, did you?"

"Of course not. You asked me to keep quiet."

"Good. I want to surprise Greg." Actually, she wanted to be sure she was sitting face to face with him. The questions he would ask were not the kind she wanted to discuss over the telephone.

"I promise to get you out of here by four so you can make it to his house."

Anxious to hear all the news, she followed Judy into the kitchen and helped herself to a cup of coffee from the pot Judy always kept brewing.

Judy poured herself a cup as well. "A new member of our group is coming by. You haven't met her. She needs to drop off some fliers and asked if she could do it this afternoon. She barely knows anyone, so don't worry about her spilling the beans about your being here."

"I can always go hide out when she comes," Monica assured her. "Don't let my visit inconvenience you any."

"Nonsense. In fact, I'll put you to work while we talk." Judy brought a box from her side porch and set it on the dining room table.

Monica followed with both cups of coffee. "I see you've picked up some of my bad habits. Working nonstop these days."

"I can't tell you how productive we've been. You really got the ball rolling, Monica. We've polled all the contractors and consultants and have a list compiled of those who actively comply to environmental and ecological considerations in their plans."

"There are enough for a list?" Monica asked, impressed.

Judy sat down at the table and started folding fliers. "You won't believe how important being on the list has become. Thanks to our campaigns in the Bay Area, Reno, the Sacramento Valley, and here, buyers and builders ask to see our list before selecting contractors and consultants."

Monica set down her cup and started to work.

"The realty business is picking up again. Once it became clear that our organization would not harass legitimate projects, investors gained confidence. In fact, we've helped to promote sales because people have the assurance of knowing what they buy or build is not going to damage the Basin."

Monica stopped folding and looked at her friend. "I'm impressed, Judy. See, I told you that you could carry on."

Judy looked pleased for a moment, until a shadow crossed her features. "I just wish Jim was as thrilled. My personal life has been zooming, but my marriage is falling flat."

Monica frowned as she sipped on her coffee. "He doesn't approve of your involvement?"

"He says he doesn't mind. He even brags to his friends about how active I am with the local issues."

"But?" Monica prompted.

Judy shrugged. "He's not happy. He complains because I don't bake anymore. He gets all bent out of shape when I have a meeting to go to the same night he entertains friends."

Monica sighed. For how many years had she had this same problem? Thanks to her mother's letters, she'd finally seen the light. "Is your work with the committee more important than Jim?" she asked.

Judy looked taken aback. "Of course not. You know I love Jim."

"But does he know that? I've discovered that misunderstandings are the cause of most problems." Monica shook her head, wondering how she could come off sounding so wise when she'd wasted so many years on her own self-interests.

"I'm speaking from experience, Judy. You don't want to have to quit your work on the committee, so coordinate it so your work doesn't conflict with Jim's schedule. And make sure he knows you love him."

Judy pondered Monica's words. "I think I see what you mean. I can give it a try."

"There's no guarantee, but I bet you'll see a difference."

"What about you?" Judy asked after pausing to sip on her coffee. "Tell me what's happened in your life these past four months."

Monica folded another flier, more careful than she needed to be. "A lot has happened and, yet, I can't give you specifics other than I went through my parents' things and learned more about them."

Judy exclaimed her delight and sat listening, forgetting all about the fliers as Monica sketched out her activities.

"Judy, I finally realized what they've said about love is true."

Judy held up her hands. "Whoa. You lost me there."

Fortunately, the doorbell rang, giving Monica a chance to regroup her thoughts. She wasn't ready to talk about her new revelations yet. Not to Judy. She needed to talk to Greg. She looked at her watch, wishing the time to speed up.

Judy forgot her intentions to keep Monica's presence a secret and ushered the new recruit into the kitchen and introduced her.

"Carol Sikes, I'd like you to meet Monica Scott."

"*The* Monica Scott." Carol surprised both women with her enthusiastic response. "I've heard so much about you. You're my idol, you know. I watched you on television in San Francisco and have wanted to meet you ever since."

Flattered, Monica shook her hand. "There's nothing that I know about organizing action to protect the environment that Judy doesn't know. You'll learn just as much from her."

"You taught me everything," Judy acknowledged.

Carol frowned. "Won't you be working with us? I mean,

286

now that you're back."

"I have some personal business to take care of."

When Carol left, Judy poured more coffee and brought it to the table. "She's a great worker. Asked all kinds of questions about our campaign against Jones. Seems like she's anxious to learn the ropes."

"Have you heard what happened to Jones?" Monica asked, more out of concern than malice. Her mother's letters about forgiveness had helped her overcome her feelings of anger and revenge.

"He went bankrupt. Title of the Ponderosa Inn went back to the original owners. With all the publicity, they decided to keep the place and use the down-payment money Jones had put up to make the place a museum."

Monica chewed her lip. "You didn't hear what happened to Jones? Where he went?"

"He disappeared. Left a big pile of debts too."

"I'm sorry to hear that," Monica said with all sincerity.

Judy looked at her with a strange expression. "I thought you'd be thrilled."

"Not anymore," Monica murmured. Her mother had taught her that hateful emotions only drained one's energy. Those who were dishonest generally ended up caught in their own trap. They didn't need her help in getting there.

The conversation turned to generalities and remained there for the rest of her visit. Jim came home from work early in honor of Monica's visit, and the three friends enjoyed a relaxing afternoon in front of a cheery fire.

"You going to do any skiing while you're here?" Jim asked.

"I thought I might ski Heavenly since I'll be on the South Shore. I'll be staying at a nearby hotel, and they feature shuttle service to the ski area."

"Be sure and take the tram," Judy told her. "Remember I

talked about it all summer?"

Monica chuckled. "I remember."

As it turned out, her option to ski occurred sooner than she thought. After driving to Greg's, she discovered he wasn't home. She waited around for an hour and then decided he'd gone out for the evening. She thought about leaving a note on the door, but she'd rather surprise him in person. Tired from her trip, she went ahead to the hotel and checked in. She asked for an early wake-up call and went to bed, dreaming of Greg.

The next morning she discovered Greg wasn't home again. At first, she panicked, thinking he might have left for the weekend. After calming down, she noticed several things around that Greg wouldn't have left out for a weekend. She peeked into his porch and noticed the skis she'd seen there last summer were gone. She'd look for him on the slopes.

In case she missed him, she wrote a note with the name of the hotel she was staying at. She also included a description of her fluorescent pink, black, and white ski outfit in case he came home for lunch. He had told her last summer that he would do so before returning to ski in the afternoon. Forget the surprise; she'd cover all bases.

After leaving Greg's, she drove to her hotel. In an hour, she was on her way to the ski slopes. Hopefully she would find Greg. The majestic Sierras would be a fitting place to tell him her news.

Mitch Jones flew into the airport in Reno early Saturday morning. After a call to Packard, he changed his plans from driving to the North Shore and headed his rented car to South Lake Tahoe. So the broad had finally returned. He'd missed her that Sunday four months ago. He wouldn't this time.

Jones turned up the heater, glad now that he'd settled in Vegas where the climate was considerably warmer.

Packard had been keeping watch on Linsey's place. Jones figured if she returned, it would be to him. Just in case, though, he'd planted a contact in the organization that had caused him so much grief. It had been a good move. Carol Sikes had called him last night with the news that Monica was back in the Tahoe Basin. Now all he had to do was find her.

At the state border, Jones pulled into a small casino where he met Packard.

"Good to see you, boss."

"Likewise," Jones muttered, although after he'd dealt with Monica Scott, he would have no more use for the man. He'd found other more resourceful contacts in Vegas.

"Where is she?"

Packard ordered a drink from the cocktail waitress. "She stopped at Linsey's place. I read the note she left."

Jones struggled to remain patient. "Note? Isn't she there?"

"Linsey's off skiing. She checked into a hotel and went out on the slopes, probably to join him."

"What? Why didn't you stop her? How am I supposed to find her in the middle of a ski resort?"

Packard shrank back from Jones's wrath. "You said not to touch her. That you wanted her all to yourself."

"Right, right." Jones managed to calm down. He had to think.

"She described her outfit. It shouldn't be too hard to find her: fluorescent pink, white, and black." Packard sat forward in his enthusiasm. "Actually, boss, the slopes are a good place to get her. It'll look like an accident."

Jones considered Packard's suggestion. Maybe the man had some brains after all.

Packard spoke again. "If you can't ski, I'll go get her. I'm great with the sport."

Jones lit his cigar and puffed. "No, she's mine. *I'll* find Monica Scott and *I'll* take care of her. You stay away from her."

Jones had been waiting too long for this. Monica Scott had been the cause of all his troubles for entirely too long. It was time she learned she couldn't meddle in his affairs without paying a price.

After settling with Packard, Jones drove by the hotel to make sure Monica hadn't returned. The receptionist gave him a better description of Monica's ski outfit after he explained he was a good friend. Just in case he couldn't find her, he asked the receptionist to keep his request a secret.

"I want to surprise her," he said as he checked into a room near Monica's.

It didn't take long to unpack and change into the ski outfit he'd brought. The sport would help him wear off some of the adrenaline thrill of killing Monica.

Renting skis took over an hour because of the long lines. He should've brought a pair, but he hadn't wanted to bother with them at the airport. Now the problem would be to find Monica, providing she was still here. "Too bad about the perfect snow conditions," he muttered. This kind of weather brought hundreds of tourists from the cities.

He headed for the lift and waited in another long line. If Monica was here, she hadn't been able to make enough runs to tire her out. He searched the lines, thinking he might be able to see her.

While Jones waited for the lift, he ignored the spectacular view of snow-covered peaks and trees. He didn't care about seeing the lake. His glare remained focused on the slopes while he relived the events that had made Monica his enemy.

He had worked hard to build up the deal with the Ponderosa

Inn. It had been one of the most productive schemes he'd come up with until Scott had come in to ruin it all. Now he was back at the bottom, scraping and dealing to set up another gig.

It shouldn't be that way. He should be on easy street, chalking up interest and kicking back. But no, he was out hustling again, thanks to Monica Scott.

"Not for long," he muttered into his scarf. "Soon we'll be even."

He searched the slopes again. Florescent colors flashed everywhere as the latest styles in ski apparel reflected the fads. Sunglasses matched the outfits in bright greens, yellows, and pinks. Several times Mitch thought he saw Monica, but it turned out to be someone else. As he neared his turn at the lift, he cast one more glance up the slopes.

A lone skier tore down the hill toward the lodge. Red hair flew from under the pink knit cap. It had to be Monica.

When she reached the lodge, Jones gave up his spot in the line. He edged toward Monica until he noticed she was searching the area as he had been earlier. Quickly he wrapped his wool scarf around his face so she wouldn't recognize him. In all likelihood she was looking for Linsey and wouldn't take note of his shorter stature. Still, it would be best not to take any chances. Jones kept to the edge of the crowd as he stayed within fifty feet of Monica, prepared to follow wherever she went. Occasionally he'd glance around for Linsey, but fortunately the planner didn't show up.

Finally, Monica headed for the lift line. Good. She was taking a lift to the higher elevations. If she was looking for Linsey, he'd be skiing the expert runs. Probably Mott Canyon. Less people skied in that area. That'd be perfect.

Jones waited impatiently until about twenty skiers were lined up behind Monica. He couldn't chance getting closer. He swished his skis into position and rubbed his hands together in eager anticipation.

In his inside pocket, his pistol weighed heavily against his side. He hoped he wouldn't have to use it. If Monica was headed for Mott Canyon, he probably wouldn't. There were plenty of steep precipices and slippery slopes where a fatal accident could occur.

Greg twisted his body into perfect Christies down the slope in spite of the horde of tourists brought by the new layer of powder snow.

Sunlight reflected off the icy crystals as he made another turn, tearing straight down what he and his buddies had termed "the Devil's armpit." Wind whistled past his ears as he sped along. Days like this helped him to forget Monica. Last night he'd dreamt about her again. The dream had seemed so real, he'd felt as if he could reach out and touch her.

It didn't take long to ski through most of Mott Canyon. After skiing down Vertigo, he headed for the lift. The lines were getting longer. Thankfully, he'd arrived early and had already made several runs. Maybe he'd go for lunch and then come back to battle the crowds. Before he could make a decision, he heard someone shouting his name. He turned and searched the lift line, where the voice had come from. Someone near the front of the line was waving at him and signaling.

Greg didn't hesitate, but skied over to find Carl waving his arms in excitement. "Have you seen her? Did she find you?"

Greg twisted his skis so he could glide alongside Carl. "Who are you talking about? Did I see who?"

"Monica Scott. She's here."

Greg froze. His heart pounded against his chest. "Monica's

here? How do you know?"

"I stopped by your house this morning to pick up my ski poles. Remember, I left them on your porch."

Greg impatiently stomped the snow off his skis. "Yes, yes. Go on."

"There's a note in full view, so I read it. You know me. I'm nosy. I'll admit it."

Greg ground out between clenched teeth, "Get on with it. What did the note say?"

Carl finally relayed the message and described Monica's outfit. "I think I saw her. That's why I came up this way. You know I don't usually go down Vertigo or Hang 'Em High."

"I talked about Mott Canyon several times last summer. If she's looking for me, she'll think I'm up here."

"The clothes matched the description, and the woman I saw had long red hair."

Anticipation raced through Greg. He had to find her. "How long ago did you see her?"

"She was getting on the lift when I got in line. She's almost a half-hour ahead of me."

Greg had had a strong feeling he should hang around the top, but he'd ignored it. Now he'd missed her. "Let me have your place in line. I might be able to catch up to her."

Carl switched places with him and winked. "I think I'll go down from here. It's more my speed. More snow bunnies too."

Fortunately, Carl had been near the front of the line. Greg had only two turns to wait.

The lift climbed rapidly up the steep slope. Lake Tahoe sat like a crystal blue gem in a setting of silvery white mountaintops.

The skier sitting on the lift next to him gestured toward the view. "It's beautiful, isn't it?"

He agreed as he glanced below. From this height, the skiers looked small. Would he miss her? His mind filled with images of Monica. How did she look? Was she here to stay? Would she be in his arms again?

At the top, Greg asked the attendant if he'd noticed what direction Monica had gone. After giving him her description, the attendant smiled and inquired, "Who is she anyway? You're the second person to ask which way she went."

"Which way did she go?"

"She acted like she was looking for someone too."

"Probably me. My name's Greg Linsey. If you see her again, tell her to wait here, okay?"

The attendant grinned. "Sure enough. Won't be a problem at all." He pointed in the direction Monica had taken. "I'm sure she headed toward Mott Canyon. That other short dude took off after her, too."

When the attendant mentioned the word "short," Mitch Jones came to mind. Impossible. No one had heard from Jones in months. Nevertheless, Greg took off after Monica with a panicked sense of urgency.

He'd skied for about ten minutes when he saw movement up ahead. His nerves tightened. A flash of pink, white, and black convinced him it was indeed Monica. She was perilously close to the cliffs. She didn't know this area and wouldn't realize she was in danger. Greg yelled, but his voice didn't carry through the trees.

His heart leaped when he saw the figure in black directly behind her. "Monica," he shouted. Greg dashed through the trees as fast as he could go.

Too late. The man reached Monica.

She screamed as he shoved her over the edge of the cliff.

"Monica!" Greg yelled in horror.

CHAPTER 20

MONICA HEARD a shout before someone plowed into her. Arms flailing, she flew through empty space. "Help!"

Her body hit a snow bank and rolled. Frantically, she grasped with her hands. Her body thudded into something solid. She thumped to a stop.

Lightheaded, she breathed deep to calm the panic raging through her. The cool snow against her cheek revived her. Slowly, she opened her eyes, seeing only white.

She brushed snow off her face and glasses. Looking around, she froze. Fear stabbed her heart. Empty space yawned for several hundred feet. Sharp, craggy rocks projected out of the snow below her. All that held her back from certain death was a spindly pine tree.

For an instant, she thought she was already dead and was watching the whole event from outside her body. Nothing seemed real. Everything blurred, then would come into focus before blurring again. Nothing made sense. Why was she hanging on the edge of a precipice? What was she doing here? Without moving, she tried to remember. She was looking for someone. Yes, that was it. Greg. She'd been nervous about the steep drop, but she knew if she wanted to find Greg, she'd have to search the area.

"God, please help me," she murmured, closing her eyes.

Monica looked up when she heard a strange noise twenty feet above her, like fighting. Two men struggled perilously close to the edge. She screamed a warning, but no sound escaped her lips.

Loud swearing came from the edge, but she couldn't see the men anymore. The voices sounded familiar.

Monica tried to think. She'd heard a shout before being bumped. Had a skier been out of control and tried to warn her? No. The shout had come from the trees and it had sounded like...

Greg!

Monica opened her eyes. Was Greg on the cliff above her? But why was he struggling with the man?

Shouts sounded again. Monica listened carefully. Yes, one of the men was Greg. The other sounded familiar also. A chilling fear that didn't have anything to do with the drop below took hold of her.

"Greg!" she screamed with all the strength she could muster.

Jones heard the shout, but so did Linsey. Jones braced himself against the taller man and took advantage of his distraction.

"She's down there, Linsey. Probably hanging by her nails on some rock."

"For God's sake, man. Let me help her."

Jones took pleasure from the look of desperation in Linsey's eyes. This man's warning had cheated him out of torturing Monica Scott. Now it looked as if he'd be able to prolong her agony. And in the meantime, Linsey would suffer also.

"How you doing, Monica?" Jones shouted over the edge, watching Linsey warily. "It's me. Your ol' business partner, Mitch

Jones."

"You snake," Greg hissed between his teeth. "When I get my hands on you…" He lunged and caught Jones by the waist.

Jones struggled to free himself and yelled. "Can you hear us, Monica? Have you fallen?"

Linsey paused to hear a reply. Jones kicked free and landed his fist in Linsey's face. Greg leaned and returned several blows. Jones staggered. Greg bent to tackle him, but Jones swung the butt of the pistol and caught Greg on the side of the head. He lay stunned. Jones had no qualms about kicking him in the head to make sure he'd be no problem.

"I'll push you over later, you piece of scum."

Carefully he peered over the edge. What he saw delighted him immensely. "Soooo," he called, drawing out his greeting. "We meet again, and under such pleasant circumstances."

"What have you done to Greg?" she demanded.

"You sound brave for someone who's hanging on the edge of a cliff."

She glared at him.

"This must be my lucky day. I had only planned to finish you off, Monica, but now I've gotten Linsey, too."

She closed her eyes. "Is he dead?"

"No, but he will be, and I won't even have to use this." He waved his pistol so she could see it. "Now it'll look like the two of you had an accident."

"Don't do it, Mitch. I'm praying for you," she called, something like pity in her voice.

"Pray for yourself," he screamed furiously. "You want Linsey so bad—here, let me drop him down to you. The weight of his body'll break that pitiful tree you're clinging so hard to."

"Help us both, Mitch, and save your soul," she said with a calmness that unnerved him.

Jones glared down at her. "I'm considering bringing you up

just so I can wrap my fingers around your throat and strangle you."

She closed her eyes, but he saw her lips moving. Let her pray. She was going to need it once he tossed Linsey down on top of her.

Greg struggled to clear his head. A threatening voice penetrated the fog. Mitch Jones. Monica's voice reached him, clearing away the last traces of dizziness.

She was still alive.

He opened his eyes and slowly lifted his head. A dark figure leaned over the edge of the cliff. Jones was talking to Monica. She wasn't dead. By some miracle she must have caught hold of something.

He clenched his fists and remained still. Monica's voice came from directly below. If he shoved Jones from behind, Jones's body could knock her down the cliff.

When Jones turned, Greg closed his eyes and pretended he was still unconscious. When he felt Jones's breath on his face, he grasped the man around the neck. Squeezing his fingers tight, he rolled them both over until he straddled the smaller man.

Jones's face turned purple. Although tempted to press until the man was dead, he relaxed his fingers. Jones took deep gulps of air. He glared hatred at Greg. "You should have killed me when you had the chance," he snarled.

Greg kept his fingers around Jones's neck. "You aren't worth what it would do to my peace of mind."

"You won't ever have any peace as long as I'm alive."

"You aren't exactly in a position to threaten."

"Just wait. I'll get my—"

Greg increased the pressure. "Shut up, Jones."

He searched the area, trying to think of a way to put Jones out of commission so that he could help Monica. Taking deep breaths to restore his strength, Greg looked around, hoping to see another skier. No one came into view.

"Monica," he shouted. "Are you all right?"

"Greg. Are you?" Relief sounded in her voice. "I'm fine as long as I don't move," she yelled back. "I need help getting out of here. I'm trapped."

"I've got Jones under control. Can you hold on a little longer?" It tempted him to just kill Jones off so he could go to her. If she needed him, he would. "Don't move. Stay there, and I'll figure a way to get help."

"Don't count on it, sugar," Jones yelled before Greg could shut him up. "Linsey can't sit on me forever, and there's no one around."

"Greg, he's got a gun."

Just as Monica's warning reached Greg, he felt something hard pressed into his side.

"I'll use it," Jones snarled. "I have no qualms about my conscience."

Greg didn't move. Emotions tore through him. He could press the life out of Jones, but the man would still get his shot. Someone needed to stay alive to help Monica. Mott Canyon didn't usually have many skiers because of the difficult runs, but with all the tourists this weekend, someone was bound to show up.

"You may not have a conscience, but you won't get away with this."

Jones's grin reflected his intentions. "You can't stop me. Now get up and walk to the edge of the cliff."

"You expect me to willingly walk to my death?" Greg stalled.

Jones jabbed the gun against Greg's side. "Face it, Linsey. You're going to die, either now or over there. I'd be a fool to let you live."

The truth of those words hit Greg. Very slowly, he shifted his weight off of Jones.

Monica's voice came from below. "What's happening, Greg? Are you all right?"

Jones's grin turned from menace to pleasure. "He's fine, sweetheart. He'll be joining you shortly."

A man had to be riddled with hatred or sick to enjoy this kind of torture. Greg felt sorry for Jones until he turned around to see a cold steel barrel pointed at his chest. Jones lowered the gun. "Maybe I'll just shoot you in the knees. That way you'll still be able to feel the fall over the cliff."

"Bullet wounds will give you away, Jones. You won't be able to claim this was an accident."

Before Jones could respond, two skiers came out of the trees. They halted when they saw the gun trained at Greg. Greg lowered his eyes, afraid he'd clue Jones into their presence. Would those two be able to handle the situation?

"Don't shoot," Greg pretended to plead. "I'll do anything you say." He started to back up slowly, keeping Jones's attention on him.

"It's going to be a pleasure killing you, Linsey."

The men signaled to Greg to keep Jones talking while they approached. One of them took off his skis and crept toward Jones. The other sidled around to attack from another angle. If Jones did hear them, Greg realized, he'd have to decide which to go for first. When he did, the other two would nail him. Hopefully Jones would surrender before shooting anyone.

Greg took another step back to distract Jones. "Go ahead and kill me, but spare Monica."

Jones laughed and moved a step toward Greg. "No chance,

Linsey. I wouldn't say you were in a position to bargain."

One of the skiers sunk into deep snow with a rustle of ice crystals against his nylon jacket. Jones swung around, his pistol raised to shoot. Before he could, the man near the trees swished toward him. "Mister," he yelled. "You can only take one of us."

Jones backed away. When he saw he couldn't face all three men at once, he waved the gun at Greg. "Stay out of this!" he screamed. "It's him I want."

"We're Green Berets. You'll be dead before he is."

Jones snapped his head around to see the man push off and start his descent. Greg dove for Jones's arm, knocking the gun up. It went off, the bullet going wild.

"Greg!" Monica shouted.

"I'm all right," he quickly reassured her. "We've got help."

The other skier swooshed up to Greg and Jones. He stomped his ski on Jones's wrist. His companion ran over and yanked the gun from Jones's hand.

"Looks like we got here just in time," one of the men stated coolly as he eyed Jones and then Greg.

"What's going on?" the other asked.

"Watch him," Greg yelled. He hurried to the edge of the cliff.

Monica peered up at him with a relieved smile. "You're all right," she exclaimed. "You're safe."

There was only one thin tree trunk between her and death. "It's almost over," he said, struggling to sound confident. "I'm going to get you out of there, I promise."

"I'm okay." she assured him.

Terrified, he wondered how she could be so calm. "Just stay still and don't move."

One of the skiers came closer. Greg turned to the man. "Get back. If this snow bank collapses, she'll go down with it."

Aware of the danger, the man quickly slid back and described the situation to his friend.

Greg crawled back also. "Jones pushed her over."

The skier twisted Jones's arm behind his back. "Attempted murder." He glanced at Greg. "I'm Mike." He pointed to the other man. "That's Larry. And who are you?"

"Greg Linsey. We need to get some help up here. I don't know how long that tree will hold."

Larry, who'd seen Monica, confirmed Greg's claim. "He's right. We have to get her outta there."

Mike thought for a minute. "Let's tie this one up." He motioned to Jones. "Over there in those trees."

Larry yanked the cords out of his parka and tied Jones's wrists behind a narrow tree trunk. From the look of the knots and the efficiency with which he worked, Greg believed his earlier claim of being a Green Beret.

Larry motioned for Greg to wait next to Jones. "You stay there while my friend goes for help."

Greg protested. "Let me talk to Monica. She needs me. I'm not going anywhere without her, believe me."

"Okay, I'll get the Ski Patrol." Mike snapped into his skis.

"Tell them to bring a rescue team," Greg ordered. He crawled to the edge and peered down at Monica. "You hanging in there?"

Relieved to see he was safe, Monica smiled wryly. "This isn't the best time for puns."

"Better that than tearing my hair out with worry."

"Come on, Greg. You're always the confident one."

"Yeah. When we're sailing or walking or sitting on the couch. Your situation calls for a new strategy."

Monica sobered. "You are going to get me out of here, aren't you?"

"You bet. A rescue team is on the way."

"What about Jones?"

Greg briefly explained what had happened.

"Thank you," Monica yelled up to the man that had helped Greg. Then she whispered her personal thanks. God had sent help.

"What were you doing here?" Greg asked.

"I'm sorry, Greg. I was anxious to see you. I had no intention of getting us into this mess."

"Never mind that. What were you so anxious about?"

Monica closed her eyes, trying to ignore the pain in her ribs. Did she want to tell him now, like this, in front of strangers? What if they couldn't get her out of here? What if she died? She had to. "I love you, Greg."

Silence. Had he heard her?

"Greg?"

"I'm here. I love you too," he said, his voice catching.

Monica closed her eyes. She didn't want to die now, when she had so much to live for. "Dear God, please help us both," she whispered.

"Monica, talk to me."

"It's hard to talk. There's something pressing against my chest."

"Lay still then, but open your eyes now and then. You scare me to death when you close them."

"Don't go away," she begged when his head disappeared.

He came back into view. "I wish I had a rope. I could get it to you and get you out of there."

The tree creaked. Monica held her breath. What if she blacked out? She'd fall. "Keep talking to me."

For the next hour he told her what he had been doing

since she'd left. She heard about hiking trips, his family in the Bay Area, his work. Underlying the dialogue, she heard the loneliness. It saddened her to know she'd caused him so much pain.

"The rescue team has arrived," Greg finally announced.

A man looked over the edge of the cliff. "Do exactly as we tell you."

Monica had no intention of trying anything on her own. She'd learned the value of putting her trust in a higher authority.

They dangled a rope and body harness down for Monica to slip under her arms.

Panic built. "I can't get it around me. My arms are numb."

"Rub them if you can. You've got to secure yourself. If we lower one of our team, he could start a slide that would knock you loose."

Fear flooded her body with adrenaline. She inched her hands around her arms and started to rub, refusing to look down as snow tumbled below her. Over and over again, she repeated the word her mother had taught her in the letters. "Jesus." The word calmed and reassured her.

Greg's voice cut into her chant. "Slip the harness around your waist."

Pain shot through her arms as feeling started to return. She grasped the rope, but couldn't get it under her.

"Tie yourself to the limb."

Her heart pounding, she draped the rope around the limb. It took painful minutes to tie a knot. When she'd accomplished that, she tugged on the rope and let them know she was ready.

As they predicted, when the man dropped over the side, snow tumbled around her. Monica's heart thumped as she feared she would be dislodged and plummet down. The pressure of the rope helped. So did the word *Jesus*.

"Believe it and you will make it," she repeated over and over.

A voice spoke nearby. "You *have* made it."

Monica looked through her snow-covered glasses to see a man dressed in red hanging beside her. With a cry of relief she wrapped her arms around his neck. He quickly untied her from the limb so the team could hoist both of them to safety.

Seconds later, Monica found herself in Greg's arms. "Thank God you're alive," he said, tears streaking down his cheeks.

"Thank God we both are."

It took hours before Monica was released from emergency. When they were sure that she had not sustained any major injuries, they finally let her go. Following that procedure, she had to go through with her statement to the authorities.

At least the two skiers had given their statements already. It made Monica's and Greg's easier to file. The eyewitness accounts ensured that Mitch Jones would be put out of harm's way for a long time.

Greg didn't give Monica the chance to feel remorse. As soon as they were free from their civic obligations, she knew the time had come for a serious talk.

"Let's go to my place," Greg offered. "There're too many reminders of Jones at your hotel."

Greg didn't push for conversation until after he'd made sure they were both comfortable in front of a roaring fire.

Greg spoke first. "You were gone so many months. I thought you were never coming back."

"It took longer to sort through my parents' things than I thought it would. I still have more to do." She reached for his hand. "But I wanted to come back and tell you how much I love you."

He took hold of her hand. "Are you sure?"

It was her turn to look away from him and into the flames. "Yes, now I am. I used to be afraid of that love, but you taught me how wonderful and caring love could be. I never understood that before."

His jaw clenched, and she didn't blame him. Her indecision had caused him pain. "I'm sorry that it took so long."

He grasped her hand and looked deep into her eyes. "You're here now."

She stroked his cheek, hearing the rasp of his day-old stubble. "I found letters from my mother. She wrote so many things about love."

Greg reached around her shoulder and pulled her close. "Thank God for that. I want you to believe, Monica. It'll strengthen our love."

She took a deep breath and pulled away to sit on the edge of the couch. She needed to tell him everything before his kiss made her forget. "I found the letters in my father's closet. They opened my eyes to their relationship. I harbored so many misconceptions."

The words of love and commitment swirled in her mind. "I always thought that my mother gave up everything to love my father. She didn't have much of a life—at least that's the way I saw it."

Greg stood to put another log on the fire. "I don't understand."

"I always compared her life to Armand's. He was gregarious, active, almost hyper. Mother always stayed in the background, tending her gardens or reading."

The couch sank as Greg sat next to her. "And you perceived that as weakness?"

"No, it wasn't weakness. It was her way." Monica shifted uncomfortably as she faced the truth. "My father loved her so much that he allowed her the freedom of her privacy. He loved her so much that he honored her desire for contemplative prayer. He kept me at his side to give her that time alone. I thought my father was putting her down, making her into a doormat, not allowing her to be herself." She shrugged. "And in reality he was promising to allow her to fulfill her full potential, allow her to be what she wanted."

Greg brushed back a strand of her hair. "And you thought she was rejecting you?"

Monica leaned into his touch. How could she explain? Restless, she stood and began to pace in front of the fire.

"And you figured this out from her letters?"

Monica nodded and returned to the couch to sit beside Greg. She grasped his hand. "Ever since my father died, I've been hearing this voice. It was Mother's." Monica paused, wondering if he would think she was crazy. "It was all the words she used to tell me as a child—words about love and about God."

Greg pulled her into his arms and kissed her forehead.

"I do love you, Greg. You and your family helped me to see what true love is."

"Will you marry me, Monica? I promise to show you the whole gamut of love."

She stroked his cheek, adoring the rough feel. "Before we marry, I need to take care of one thing."

"Your father's house?"

She nodded.

He reached over and grasped her hand. "I'll help you."

Yes, she knew he would, not because she couldn't do it herself, but because he loved her and he had promised he would.

EPILOGUE

Spring 1987

THE FIRST WILDFLOWERS were beginning to bloom. Greg saw several yellow blossoms as he drove up the steep road to Monica's property. When he arrived at the creek—the site she'd originally planned to build on—he parked the agency's Bronco.

Monica gathered the box of papers that sat between them. "I can't believe the crowd that has shown up."

Greg maneuvered out of the cab. "Your father was a famous man. His plans are going to be worth a lot."

Monica worked her way around to the front of the vehicle and met Greg so they could walk together toward the crowd. He tugged on her arm and paused. "You're sure about this now?"

She nodded, "I want all proceeds from the auction of Armand's plans to go to the Tahoe Conservancy."

Greg gestured around them. "You've already given them the Langford place and this property."

Monica smiled.

Greg nodded. It wasn't the money that mattered. It was

something he'd finally figured out this winter. Just as wealth wasn't necessarily a measure of success, neither were grandiose accomplishments. The fact that he continued to plug away at the environmental issues day by day, bit by bit were enough. His efforts didn't always appear effective, but the long-term results would prove their impact. He had to have faith and act on it. Simple yet true.

He looked around at the picnic tables and hiking trails that Monica had donated for the new park. The day-use park for visitors to enjoy would be named the Armand Scott Preserve.

"This park turned out great. I'm sure it will be a popular place," he commented.

Conversation ended as they joined the crowd. Monica headed toward the podium. Greg recognized several people. Jim and Judy Myers were with their crowd of friends. Rhonda Remway had arrived with friends also. Greg wouldn't be surprised if she bid on the plans.

The majority of the crowd were strangers to Greg. Members of the press were on hand. This sale had attracted an impressive group of the rich and famous. He hoped Monica was pleased with the way things had worked out. He searched the podium area and saw her auburn hair shining in the sun as she talked to the people heading the auction. He stayed back and watched, enjoying her animated enthusiasm.

After a few minutes, Greg delivered the papers to Monica. "This project is almost over. Are you ready?"

She nodded. "And wondering what will be next."

"I'm sure we'll find something to keep you occupied."

"Said like a politician. Maybe you'll be running for office." She placed her hand in his. "Or starting your own consulting firm."

Greg smiled. Maybe he would. He gave her a quick kiss and returned to the outskirts of the crowd.

He watched the proceedings, remembering the first time he'd met Monica here on the property. She'd been such a fireball of nervous energy and protest, testing his every concept about his work. But he'd relied on his faith, and his belief had been rewarded. If Monica could change, then so could others. She had instilled that hope in him.

When the auction ended, Monica joined him. "That went well."

"You've done a beautiful thing here, Mrs. Linsey."

Monica smiled. "As you've said, Mr. Linsey, the world's in trouble. Man can take care of it if he just stops to realize there is a need."

Greg wrapped his arms around Monica and held her close. "Don't forget about God. We can always call on Him for help. He promised."

DISCUSSION QUESTIONS

1. Monica promised herself that she would build her father's last house as a memorial gesture. What were the underlying reasons for making this promise? How does Monica resolve these issues?

2. When we meet Greg, he is feeling restless and unsettled. What are the underlying causes of his restlessness? How does he resolve these feelings?

3. What are the reasons Monica gives for not wanting to marry Stephen? What do you think are the *real* reasons?

4. Why does Monica hire Mitch Jones instead of the consultant recommended by her friend and confidant? How does Monica resolve her mistake?

5. What misconceptions does Monica harbor about true love and marriage? How does she overcome these misconceptions?

6. What is Greg's role in changing Monica's views on love and marriage? How does he show her true love?

7. How does Greg's faith carry him through times of discouragement? What advice would you give Greg?

8. How does Monica's faith evolve?

Author's Note & Acknowledgements

My husband and I purchased a house at Lake Tahoe back in the eighties. It was a "fixer-upper," but when we started the process of fixing it up, we ran into the Tahoe Regional Planning Agency (TRPA). My husband was a Biology major, and we both have always loved nature and have been interested in the preservation of the environment. In spite of the fact that the policies of the TRPA made it difficult at times to make improvements, we were fascinated with the project and the impact of the agency.

My interest led to research, which eventually led to the writing of this book. Many employees of the TRPA gave me wonderful information and assistance. Since the research was conducted in the eighties, I set the story in 1985 so the policies that were presented to me would still be applicable to the characters.

Extensive interviews with Mike Dill, former Associate Planner of the TRPA and consultant in the Tahoe Basin, provided much of the basis for the environmental conflict contained within this story. The story is fictional, but with Mike's expertise, it portrays the conflicts and function of the TRPA. Mike read the manuscript for technical accuracy.

The manuscript was also reviewed for technical accuracy by Pamela Drum, Environmental Education Coordinator for the TRPA. Every attempt was made by the author to follow her recommendations and establish an authentic portrayal of the TRPA.

The TRPA states in their promotional video that "a Regional Plan now exists to guide us through the next twenty years. We've reached the point that few communities in the world have.

We've described a state of the environment we wish to have at Tahoe, and we've fashioned a plan to accomplish that goal. Now we have the means to move into the future confident that Tahoe will remain an outstanding part of the world." (TRPA 1987)

The TRPA was created by action of the states of California and Nevada and ratified by the US Congress. The primary purpose of the TRPA is to ensure an equilibrium between the Tahoe region's natural endowment and its manmade environment. This is to be done by the establishment of Environmental Threshold Carrying Capacities (referred to as Thresholds) and implementation of a Regional Plan designed to maintain those Thresholds. In pursuit of its goal, TRPA may approve such projects as are determined to be consistent with its adopted Thresholds.

Any activity which has the potential for causing significant environmental impact on the Tahoe Basin is defined as a "project" requiring Agency approval. In order to approve any "project," the TRPA must make specific findings to ensure that the project will not result in degradation of the environment or cause violation of adopted Thresholds. (Tahoe Regional Planning Agency Governing Board, First Annual Report, Year ending December 31, 1988, page 2)

Further thanks to the following people for their input and information:

~ Robert C. Reiss, Senior Building Inspector, Placer County Community Development Department, Tahoe City, California

~ Doug Sherman, Contractor, Sherman Homes, Tahoe City, California

Please be advised that the characters and most of the businesses, restaurants, clubs, and inns in the story are fictional. They are a figment of my imagination created to give the story depth and meaning.

About the Author

Sandra Leesmith loves to travel in her RV and explore all of nature's beauty, discover America's history, and fellowship with the wonderful people she meets while on the road. She enjoys reading, writing, hiking, swimming, and pickleball. Learn more about Sandra and her books at www.sandraleesmith.com.

You can connect with Sandra on Facebook, Twitter, and Goodreads. You can also find her and her talented writing buddies at the Seekerville blog.

If you enjoyed this book, please consider leaving a review online.

Thank you!

Books by Sandra Leesmith

Love's Promises
(Amber Press, 2014)

Love's Refuge
(Amber Press, 2013)

Love's Miracles
(Amber Press, 2013)

Current of Love
(Montlake Romance, 2012)

The Price of Victory
(Montlake Romance, 2011)

LOVE'S REFUGE
(Amber Press, 2013)

"A haunting story of a girl trapped by the trauma of her past. The refuge she's found has become a prison and when love finds her she must face her deepest fears in order to claim that love."
~Mary Connealy, bestselling author of
the TROUBLE IN TEXAS series

Skye loves her peaceful life on Leeza Island in Puget Sound—especially the safety from big-city dangers. Danny doesn't realize how desperately he needs a rest until he meets Skye, but his work and home in Seattle keep Skye at bay. An isolated island girl with painful memories. A dedicated city boy with a wild past. What will it cost for them both to find a refuge from their storms?

Available in paperback, Kindle e-book, and audiobook formats

LOVE'S MIRACLES

(Amber Press—Second Edition, 2013)

"From heart-wrenching to heart-soaring, Ms. Leesmith's
LOVE'S MIRACLES *will not only steal your heart and your sleep,*
but your thoughts for literally weeks after."
~Julie Lessman, award-winning author of the
DAUGHTERS OF BOSTON and WINDS OF CHANGE series

Only by reliving her own wounded past and helping Dominic
Zanelli confront a terrible memory from the Vietnam War could
Dr. Margo Devaull set them both free—and save their last
chance for love.

Available in paperback, Kindle e-book, and audiobook formats

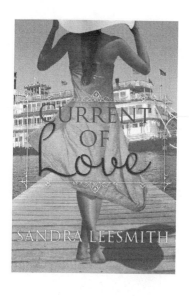

CURRENT OF LOVE
(Montlake Romance, 2012)

While on a steamboat cruise up the Mississippi, Janelle Edwards and Everett Jamison III must make a decision: continue running from their emotions—or let the current of love sweep them away.

Available in paperback and Kindle e-book formats

THE PRICE OF VICTORY
(Montlake Romance, 2011)

Can Sterling Wade help Debra Valenzuela follow her dream and in the process discover new purpose for his own life? Will they accept the price of victory?

Available in paperback and Kindle e-book formats